W9-BSA-888

This must be real....

He leaned forward, his gaze intent upon hers, his hand on the arm of her chair as if confining her to its bounds. She could feel the warmth of his closeness and smell the hint of a spicy scent on his skin. His knee bumped hers, and she felt an awareness of his presence tingle over her body. She lost herself in the deep hazel of his eyes, where the flame of the candle flickered.

As if moved by a force beyond herself, Caitlyn lifted her hand and reached toward his face. A spark of surprise touched his eyes, but he didn't move away as she lightly touched his cheek.

His skin was soft as velvet. Her lips parted on a breath, and she stroked his cheek, feeling the sharp prickle of whiskers roughening his jaw. The sensation on her fingertips was sharp and real, and it stirred awake a sleeping part of her mind.

I'm dreaming. She blinked in surprise, her hand freezing in place. *He's not real. This isn't real.*

OTHER BOOKS YOU MAY ENJOY

Wake Unto Me

LISA CACH

speak

An Imprint of Penguin Group (USA) Inc.

SPEAK

Published by the Penguin Group

Penguin Group (USA) Inc., 345 Hudson Street, New York, New York 10014, U.S.A.
Penguin Group (Canada), 90 Eglinton Avenue East, Suite 700, Toronto, Ontario, Canada
M4P 2Y3 (a division of Pearson Penguin Canada Inc.)
Penguin Books Ltd, 80 Strand, London WC2R 0RL, England
Penguin Ireland, 25 St Stephen's Green, Dublin 2, Ireland (a division of Penguin Books Ltd)
Penguin Group (Australia), 250 Camberwell Road, Camberwell,
Victoria 3124, Australia (a division of Pearson Australia Group Pty Ltd)
Penguin Books India Pvt Ltd, 11 Community Centre,
Panchsheel Park, New Delhi - 110 017, India
Penguin Group (NZ), 67 Apollo Drive, Rosedale, North Shore 0632,
New Zealand (a division of Pearson New Zealand Ltd.)
Penguin Books (South Africa) (Pty) Ltd, 24 Sturdee Avenue,
Rosebank, Johannesburg 2196, South Africa

Registered Offices: Penguin Books Ltd, 80 Strand, London WC2R 0RL, England

Published by Speak, an imprint of Penguin Group (USA) Inc., 2011

1 3 5 7 9 10 8 6 4 2

LIBRARY OF CONGRESS CATALOGING-IN-PUBLICATION DATA
Cach, Lisa.
Wake unto me / by Lisa Cach.
p. cm.
Summary: When fifteen-year-old Oregonian Caitlyn Monahan earns a scholarship to an
exclusive French boarding school, she hopes to escape the terrifying dreams that haunt her, but
instead she encounters centuries-old mysteries at the Chateau de la Fortune, where she has a
princess for a roommate and she falls in love with a seductive ghost that visits her at night.

ISBN 978-0-14-241436-1 (pbk.)

[1. Supernatural—Fiction. 2. Nightmares—Fiction. 3. Boarding schools—
Fiction. 4. Schools—Fiction. 5. France—Fiction.] I. Title.

PZ7.C1137Wak 2011

[Fic]—dc22

2010021027

Speak ISBN 978-0-14-241436-1

Printed in the United States of America

To my niece, Elizabeth

Between two worlds life hovers like a star,
'Twixt night and morn, upon the horizon's verge.
How little do we know that which we are!
How less what we may be!
—Byron, *Don Juan*

Prologue

CHÂTEAU DE LA FORTUNE, FRANCE

"Is she the one?"

Eugenia Snowe felt an unsettling mix of distaste and compassion as she picked up the photo that she and the other women of the Sisterhood had been staring at. In it, Caitlyn Monahan, a fifteen-year-old American girl with long black hair and a pale face, held a notebook to her chest, her shoulders hunched, her hair half concealing her features.

"Maybe," Eugenia replied. Caitlyn wore her insecurity like a coat, on the outside for all to see. Eugenia loathed weakness in women.

On the other hand, this girl had likely grown up suffering severe feelings of alienation from the mundane people around her, so it was little wonder that she should be a miserable creature. According to what the private investigator had uncovered, Caitlyn had no one in her life who could possibly understand what she truly was.

What she *might* be, Eugenia corrected herself. They didn't know yet if Caitlyn was one of them.

"We can't be certain that Caitlyn is one of our lost sisters," Eugenia said aloud. "Genealogy can take us only so far. Her family tree on her mother's side is spotted with uncertainties; we have had to make calculated guesses about her heritage, based on what records we can find. She may be nothing more than an average teenage girl."

"But your great-grandmother's prophecy of the Dark One," Greta Klenk said, her plump, kindly face filled with anxious hope, "it seems to fit her." She recited the verse they all knew by heart:

> *"From the New World's western shore*
> *Comes a Dark One, young and poor,*
> *Black of hair and pale of face,*
> *Without bidding she will chase*
> *The source of Sisters' power real*
> *In the heart of Fortune's wheel.*
> *Only when this Dark One's found*
> *Can our powers be unbound.*

"It speaks of someone with dark hair, from the western shores of the New World, just like this Caitlyn Monahan," Greta said.

"Yes, but that is no guarantee that Caitlyn *is* the Dark One, or even that Caitlyn is one of us. We cannot make her the girl of the prophecy simply by wishing it," Eugenia said. She tightened her jaw, tamping down her impatience. She had spent her whole life trying to decode her English great-grandmother's short, prophetic verse, and to find the heart of Fortune's wheel herself, and with it the original source of the Sisterhood's psychic powers.

She hadn't found it; she hadn't even figured out exactly what Fortune's wheel was supposed to be, other than a figurative idea about the goddess Fortuna, or possibly a reference to the legend of a Templar treasure buried beneath the castle. Her failure to solve the puzzle had forced her to practice both humility and patience, neither of which suited her temperament. She had, at last, turned her efforts to finding the Dark One. Caitlyn was her best hope of being that long-sought girl.

"She looks like nothing," Marguerite Pelletier sneered, her hands on her slender, hard hips. The riding instructor had a sharp-featured face and black slashes of eyebrows that scowled her disapproval. "She does not look like anything special. I don't think she's the Dark One, nor do I think we should take a chance on her. This is our first time trying to bring a lost sister to the Fortune School, and she seems a very bad bet. We should only bring girls who have culture and sophistication, who will fit in well with the regular, 'ordinary' paying students."

"But the prophecy says she'll be poor," Greta said. "Caitlyn is poor."

The group of eight women looked to Eugenia for guidance. At thirty-five years old she was the youngest of them, but she was also the strongest. She was their leader.

A DNA test could tell the Sisterhood for certain whether Caitlyn was related to them, but it would not answer the most crucial questions: *Had* Caitlyn inherited any psychic gifts? If so, were they of a strength worth developing? And most important of all, was Caitlyn the Dark One of the prophecy?

There was no way to know, at least not yet. They had to bring Caitlyn to Château de la Fortune and let the girl prove her worth. If Caitlyn was the Dark One, she would lead them to the heart of Fortune's wheel.

"I have goals for the Sisterhood that will never be met by playing it safe," Eugenia said at last. "We will bring Caitlyn here, to Château de la Fortune, where we can discover firsthand whether or not she is the one we seek."

"And if Caitlyn is not the Dark One?" Marguerite demanded. "Or if she is not a true member of the Sisterhood? What do we do with her then?"

Eugenia shrugged one elegant shoulder, dismissing the issue and the girl. "We get rid of her. If she's not the Dark One, she doesn't matter, does she?"

Marguerite grunted her approval.

Eugenia's lips twitched in amusement. Marguerite: so quick to anger, and yet so easily manipulated. Eugenia hadn't even had to reach into Marguerite's mind to make her behave. It had only taken words.

Too bad. She enjoyed practicing her gift for mind control and welcomed every chance to hone her skills. She couldn't yet achieve total control over another person, unfortunately. But she *could* nudge, and implant an impulse. Coupling this with old-fashioned verbal persuasion and Eugenia's extensive training in psychology, there were few who could resist bending to her will.

When Eugenia at last found the heart of Fortune's wheel and the Sisterhood's source of power was unbound, though, she was certain that her powers would be doubled. Trebled, even. With greater power, no one would even think to obstruct her, and she could begin in earnest her work to bring the Sisterhood to eminence. The Sisterhood would become a force to be reckoned with. There were no limits to what they might achieve, or to the influence they might wield. With Eugenia as its leader, the Sisterhood could alter the course of the world itself.

"No one matters," Eugenia said again, her voice as cold as steel. "No one, except the Dark One."

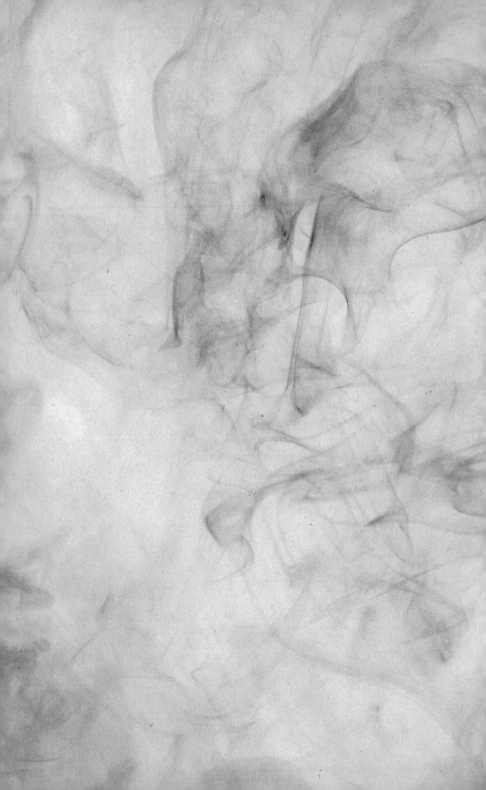

CHAPTER
One

Caitlyn's pencil moved over the paper in harsh, rapid dashes. A picture began to emerge: flames, smoke. A face in agony. A stake of wood.

Caitlyn's breath came in short gasps as her pencil brought the image from last night's eerie dream to life. She felt the heat of the flames against her own skin, the smoke choking her, her lungs searing as she gasped in great gulps of burning air. Panic flooded her body as she fought against the ropes that bound her to the stake. She was desperate for escape, desperate for someone in the jeering crowd beyond the flames to scream out against the wrong that was being done to her.

"Hey," a panting male voice said, the sound impinging on the edges of Caitlyn's awareness. She ignored it and kept drawing.

Caitlyn could feel the thoughts of the woman being burned at the stake. *It was no use. She was not one of them. Always an outsider, she had suffered their fear and their hatred for her her*

1

whole life. And now they had finally found a way to be rid of her forever: *Witch*, they called her.

"Whatcha drawing?" the same male voice asked.

With that one word, they were free to destroy her. Thou shalt not suffer a witch to live . . .

"Yo!" A large pale hand appeared between her face and her art journal, waving back and forth. "You in there?"

The crackling flames of the medieval pyre faded into the squeaking of tennis shoes on the gym floor. Annoyed, Caitlyn Monahan looked up from the journal in her lap, blinking herself back to present reality. Pete Fipps, strands of his dark hair plastered to his temples with sweat, was breathing at her. What did *he* want? Probably to make fun of her, as usual.

"You really like to draw, huh?"

"Yes." Caitlyn slipped her bookmark—a tarot card of the Wheel of Fortune—into the journal, closed the cover, and pulled it up against her chest. Without her noticing, practice had started for the boys' varsity basketball team. Caitlyn's perch at the end of the fifth row of the bleachers was no longer a quiet, private place to wait for her friends Sarah and Jacqui.

"What were you drawing?"

She felt the intrusion of his gaze and was vaguely threatened by his looming closeness. She wished he'd go away. "Nothing."

"Nothing, huh?"

Caitlyn remained silent, entranced by a big zit on the side of his neck, the red spot brilliant against his pale skin.

"You must have been drawing *something*."

Caitlyn held the journal more tightly to her chest, her shoulders hunching. "Just . . . someone I saw in a dream last night." What gave Pete the right to torment her? Since the start of school a month

2

ago, he'd been sniggering with his friends whenever she walked by. She'd dealt with the jokes for years and didn't understand why it was suddenly getting worse. Did entering tenth grade automatically up the jerk factor in people?

"Were you drawing a *guy?*" Pete asked, voice leering.

"No, not a guy!" she said, a little loudly. Why was he still talking to her? Some of his friends had stopped tossing balls around and were standing, watching them with grins on their faces, as if waiting for the payoff to a joke. "I was drawing a wise woman, if you have to know."

"That like a wise guy?" Pete put on a bad New Jersey accent. "You lookin' at me? You lookin' at *me?*"

Caitlyn rolled her eyes. "A wise woman was a healer, or midwife. But some people thought they were witches."

"They burn 'em?"

For a moment, Caitlyn felt herself thrown back into the dream. *Ignorance, all around her, destroying that which it could not understand.* She felt the searing smoke in her throat, squeezing off her air. "Yes," she coughed.

He snorted. "Guess they should have rethought their choice of careers. Witches! You gotta know the fire's coming for you, one way or another."

Anger and loathing welled up inside her, hatred burning in her soul. It had been faces like Pete's that had laughed from beyond the circle of flames; ignorant minds like his that had destroyed her.

Caitlyn blinked and shook off the thoughts. Where had *that* come from?

"Fipps!" Doug Hansen called from midcourt.

Pete turned just in time to catch a basketball thrown at his head.

"Leave Moan-n-Groan alone and get your butt back on the court!" Doug shouted, making his friends laugh.

Caitlyn winced at the nickname, a play on her last name, Monahan, the taunt a familiar stab to her heart. It'd begun in seventh grade, when she'd started wearing black goth-inspired clothes and had shown her misery on her face. She'd gotten better at hiding her feelings in the three years since then, and had moved on to more colorful vintage clothing from the thrift store, but the nickname had stuck. Only now, boys said it with a raunchy, knowing lilt to their voices.

She looked toward the girls' locker room door, willing Sarah and Jacqui to appear and rescue her.

Pete gave his friend the finger.

Caitlyn slid the journal into her backpack and started to get up.

Pete grabbed her arm. "Wait!"

She jerked free. "Why?" she asked, cautious.

"I'm having a party tomorrow night; my parents are going out of town. My brother is getting a keg. Wanna come?"

She stared at him, too stunned to think. He was inviting her to a party? That's why he'd been talking to her?

Pete's face colored under her surprised gaze, and his hands flew in wild gestures as if to avert a misunderstanding. "With Sarah and Jacqui, I mean! If you guys want to. I'm inviting half the school. I wasn't inviting *you* in particular."

The fragile butterfly of flattery that had begun to flutter in her chest was smashed beneath the rubber soles of his shoes. "Of course you didn't mean me," she said flatly, embarrassed to have misunderstood. She knew better than to let down her guard with guys like Pete; she *knew* better! All they ever wanted was to make fun of her. "Why would you invite Moan-n-Groan anywhere? You wouldn't be caught dead with me."

4

Pete's pink cheeks turned scarlet, the red seeping up his forehead. "Caitlyn, I—"

"Gotta go," Caitlyn said, grabbing her backpack and heading to the end of the bleacher row. "I wouldn't want to hang around and let people get the wrong impression!" She jumped off the end of the bleachers just as Sarah and Jacqui came out of the locker room, and jogged over to meet them. Caitlyn looped her arm in Sarah's and dragged her out of the gym, Jacqui trotting to keep up. Wolf whistles and laughter followed them.

"What was that all about?" Sarah asked as they came out into the autumn sunlight and the gym doors clunked shut behind them. Her brown hair fell in thick layers to her shoulders, as glossy and effortlessly stylish as if she'd just stepped out of a shampoo commercial. Her dark brown eyes were wide with questions.

Caitlyn rolled her own pale, sea-green eyes and told them what had happened.

When she finished, Jacqui grabbed her arm, squeezing a little too hard. Her round, freckled face was mottled with excitement. "Pete totally likes you!"

Embarrassed, Caitlyn shook her head. "He doesn't. He made *that* clear."

"Oh my gosh, of course he does!" Sarah said, and shook her head. "You are so dense."

"Am I?" she asked uncertainly, getting her first inkling that she might have just made an ass of herself.

Sarah lightly slapped her on the side of the head. "He asked you to a party. How you managed to read an insult into that, I don't know."

"She's too defensive," Jacqui said.

Caitlyn's shoulders sagged. She felt like a fool. Maybe Pete *had* been trying to be nice to her, and she'd gone all wacko on him. "Well, even if he does like me, so what?" she asked, seeking some small measure of dignity. "I don't like *him*."

"Pete's a nice guy," Jacqui said. "You should give him a chance."

"I don't have to like a guy just because he likes me," Caitlyn said.

"But why don't you like him?" Jacqui asked. "His family's rich. They own a chain of furniture stores."

Caitlyn turned a puzzled gaze on her friend. "Furniture is supposed to make me like him?"

"Hey, I'd be happy to marry a guy who owned a chain of furniture stores," Jacqui said.

"We're in tenth grade! Who's thinking about marriage?" Caitlyn cried.

"No one with any brains," Sarah said dryly. Sarah's parents had separated early in the summer, sending shock waves through Sarah's life.

Jacqui shrugged. "So forget marriage. But you want a boyfriend, don't you, Caitlyn? Everyone *normal* does. Why not Pete?"

"He's not my type."

Jacqui laughed. "You don't *have* a type. I can't remember the last time you talked about someone you thought was cute. You don't like *any* guys. You don't think anyone's good enough for you."

"That's not true," Caitlyn said. "I just don't like any of the guys *here*."

Sarah blew out an exasperated breath. "They're all the same, wherever you go. You're an idiot if you think otherwise."

They walked a bit in silence, and Caitlyn felt her own confusion about why Pete Fipps and guys like him were so lacking in her eyes. Why couldn't she like him?

"It's not that I think the guys in Spring Creek are *bad*," Caitlyn mused aloud. "It's just that I keep feeling that out there, somewhere,

6

there's someone better. Someone who will understand me. Someone who *gets* me."

"You think you're so special that no one here can understand you?" Jacqui asked, one eyebrow raised.

"Not special. 'Freakish' is more like it," Caitlyn said glumly.

"You're not a freak," Sarah insisted, but her words carried no conviction.

"Yes, I am," Caitlyn mumbled. "You two both know it."

Jacqui grinned and held up her thumb and forefinger, pinching a half inch of space. "Well, maybe you're a *leettle* freaky. But we put up with you anyway."

"Great. Thanks." Caitlyn subsided into silence. They weren't going to understand.

She barely understood, herself. For as long as she could remember, she had felt certain that her future boyfriend was far from rural Oregon and her present life, thousands of miles away, living a life completely different from her humdrum one here. This unknown guy was her soul mate, and someday, when she least expected it, they'd find each other. It would be love at first sight, because they would have been seeking each other for all their lives.

Foolishly romantic, yeah, sure, maybe; but she'd rather have dreams of Prince Charming than the reality of Mr. Wrong.

The three of them walked home to their neighborhood, Caitlyn listening with half an ear as her two friends started gossiping about other members of the drill team. It was juicy stuff and should have been interesting: two members of the drill team had been caught smoking and were now in danger of being dropped from the team. Meetings were being held, the principal was involved, parents were in an uproar. Everyone was talking about it. Everyone cared.

Except Caitlyn. High school dating, drill team, school spirit—it all seemed silly to her. Why did it feel like high school was crushing her soul? She had nothing concrete she could point to. All she knew was that she didn't belong here.

She preferred old, used clothes to new ones; her iPod was full of classical music; and photos of castles and reproductions of old European art covered her bedroom walls, including a Renaissance painting of a young girl in white, named Bia. It should have been pop singers on her wall, or movie stars.

She spent all her free time either drawing the strange things she saw in her dreams, or with her nose inside historical novels. The world held in the pages of history felt like the real world, and the present day an illusion she had to suffer through until she could escape back into the pages of a book.

Or escape into the rich dreams of sleep. She always woke with reluctance, feeling that she was being torn from a more vivid world. She rarely remembered more than snippets of her dreams, but when she did, the images and sensations were so lifelike that they were indistinguishable from reality, and sometimes she couldn't remember whether she'd dreamed something, or lived it.

Other times, though, sleep brought her nightmares that carried her far beyond terror, waking her and the entire house with her screams. Those were the Screecher dreams. In the midst of sleep, she was sometimes attacked by howling, ghostlike apparitions. She didn't know what they were or where they came from, whether they were real or figments of her imagination, spirits or delusions, and for lack of any better name she called the apparitions the Screechers.

Both the extremely vivid good dreams and the distressing Screecher nightmares had started at puberty. She didn't know if it was a blessing or a curse, to have both types. Her father and stepmother, she knew, feared that the Screecher nightmares might hint at mental instability; that she might be a little crazy, like her long-dead mother, who had thought she could predict the future.

Overall, books and art were a safer escape from reality than sleep.

The weird dreams couldn't entirely explain her sense of alienation from her classmates, though. It was something deeper than that, something that made her think that she didn't belong there.

She needed to escape her life entirely. College had always been her light at the end of the long, dark adolescent tunnel. Lately, though, college felt a thousand years away. Three years might as well be three decades. Her inability to change her present life had left her teetering on the edge of a vast pit of despair. She needed something to change soon, or she'd fall in.

Right now, she had one small hope for how she might escape the pit.

In July, she'd received a random e-mail from the Fortune School, in France. She'd never heard of it, but assumed they'd gotten her e-mail address from a pen-pal service she'd signed up for the year before, through her French class (unhappily, her French pen pal had given up the effort of friendship after a single illiterate e-mail from Caitlyn; French, alas, did not come naturally to her).

The girls' boarding school invited her to visit their Web site and apply for both admission and a scholarship. She'd snorted in disbelief at the scholarship part; these people obviously hadn't seen her grades.

Still, it seemed harmless enough to look at the Web site.

The moment the school's home page came up, and she saw the photo of the castle that housed the school, Château de la Fortune, she felt her soul being called to the Fortune School. She hadn't known that what she yearned for was to go to a French girls' boarding school, but the photo of Château de la Fortune, perched on a cliff overlooking the Dordogne River in southwestern France, convinced her that attending that school was the only thing that could possibly make her happy.

Of course, there was almost no chance she'd be admitted. There was even less chance that she'd get a scholarship, and it would be impossible for her father, a log truck driver, to pay the annual tuition listed on the Web site: it was twice what he earned in one year.

And yet . . . It was as if her very soul cried out that she at least had to try.

So she'd applied, in secret. Some hopes were better nurtured in private, where the words of others could not harm them, and where disappointment could be borne free of the pitying gaze of friends.

From the day she'd sent in her application, she'd been both dreading and eagerly anticipating an envelope in the mail, telling her whether or not they wanted her. It had been over two months now, making sorting through the mail every afternoon torture. No letter meant hope could live another day, but it also meant another night of dreading the inevitable disappointment to come.

"You quiet because you're thinking about Pete?" Jacqui asked, jarring Caitlyn out of her thoughts.

"Huh?" They'd come to Caitlyn's street. She hadn't heard a word either of her friends had said for the past fifteen minutes.

"Someone's lost in romantic daydreams," Jacqui said.

"Yeah, right."

Sarah and Jacqui laughed and waved good-bye. "See ya," Sarah said.

"Yeah. See you tomorrow." Caitlyn walked the last half mile

alone, her thoughts all on the letter that might, or might not, be waiting for her at home.

Ruin, salvation, or limbo: they were the three possibilities that the U.S. Postal Service could deliver to the mailbox any day but Sunday.

Which would it be today?

Caitlyn let herself into her house, stepping over the perpetual pile of her younger brothers' out-of-season coats, athletic gear, and shoes clogging the entryway. No one was home, but she knew the day's mail would be piled at the end of the kitchen island, like it always was.

Several white business envelopes were stacked on top of a pile of catalogs. Caitlyn chewed her upper lip and picked them up, forcing herself to go through them.

Cable bill.

Something from the grade school her three young half brothers attended.

Electric bill.

Credit card offer.

And one last envelope. She turned it over, her heart racing.

Mortgage statement.

Her shoulders sank in relief. Her hopes had been saved from execution, for one more day at least. With light steps she went to her room to drop off her backpack.

Tyler, Wade, and Ethan, her half brothers, were at their various sport practices and scouting activities. Her dad and stepmom were driving them in separate vehicles, engaged in the complicated ballet of boy pickup and delivery, pausing only to toss fast-food burgers and chicken parts to the boys as if feeding hungry lions. She had the house to herself for the moment.

She opened her door and was about to toss her backpack onto her bed when she saw it: a white envelope, already opened, set upon the corner of her bed. Her heart sank.

Caitlyn set her backpack down on the bed and picked up the letter, her dreams collapsing around her. A yellow sticky note was attached to the envelope.

What's all this about? We need to talk. —Mom

Great. Not only did she get rejected, but she got to look forward to the added pleasure of discussing with her stepmother, Joy, why she'd applied to a French boarding school. Joy probably took it personally, as if Caitlyn were fleeing from her in particular. She seemed to take every one of Caitlyn's moods personally.

Caitlyn's birth mother had been killed in a car crash when Caitlyn was only four. She had only the faintest memories of her, more imagined than real, and knew her face only from photos. She'd given Caitlyn her long dark hair, and—inexplicably—the tarot card of the Wheel of Fortune. She had tucked the tarot card under Caitlyn's pillow on the day she died. There was a family rumor that she had foreseen her own death, and that the tarot card had been her way of saying good-bye. Caitlyn's father refused to discuss it.

Joy had married Caitlyn's father by the time Caitlyn was five, and had embraced Caitlyn as her own child; Caitlyn had grown up calling her Mom. Joy was a simple, kindhearted woman, but the loving woman who had understood a lonely little girl was at a loss when dealing with a confused teenager who couldn't, even to herself, explain why she was so miserable. The less Caitlyn felt understood by Joy, the greater the gap between them grew.

Her dad, meanwhile, was grateful to have three uncomplicated, athletic young sons to deal with. Caitlyn became Joy's problem, not his. The few times Caitlyn had tried to talk to him about anything personal, he told her to go talk to her mom.

Caitlyn sank onto the end of her bed with the envelope in her hand, hopeless tears of disappointment filling her eyes. She couldn't face three more years of high school, she just couldn't. Something else had to be possible: a GED through the community college? Homeschooling? School online? Something. Anything.

She slid the single sheet from the envelope and unfolded it, snuffling back tears.

> *Dear Caitlyn,*
>
> *Thank you for your application. I am pleased to inform you that we can offer you both admission to the Fortune School in late January, and a full scholarship. Registration materials will follow under separate cover.*
>
> *Yours sincerely,*
> *Eugenia Snowe, PhD*
> *Headmistress, The Fortune School*

Caitlyn's breath froze in her chest. The letter seemed to float before her, held in hands that belonged to someone else.

She'd been accepted?

Full scholarship? For *her*?

She read the letter again to be sure she'd not misunderstood. "Oh. My. God," she said to the empty room. "Oh my God. *Oh my God!* Ohmigod, ohmigod, ohmigod, I'm going to France! *I'm* going to *France!*"

She leaped up onto her bed and jumped up and down, her

backpack sliding off the mattress to the floor, the bed frame squeaking. "I'm going to France! France! France!" she shouted. "I'm going to live in a castle! Castle! Castle! What do you think of that, huh?" she asked the portrait of Bia. "*What* do you think of *that?*"

Caitlyn dropped onto the mattress, rolled onto her back, and kicked her feet in the air like a manic puppy. She read the letter yet again, then lay it over her face and closed her eyes, savoring the moment of pure happiness.

She was leaving Spring Creek. Against all odds, she'd received her Get Out of Jail Free card. She sent an enormous *thank-you* out into the universe, to whatever force had guided the Fortune School to send her that initial e-mail.

Then a moment of fear hit her, and her eyes sprang open: What if her parents wouldn't let her go?

She shook the thought off. No, they'd be relieved to have her gone. Life would be easier and happier for them. They could focus on the boys and their sports, which is all they wanted to do, anyway.

In the meantime, Caitlyn would go out into the world, where the people would be new, where there was culture and history and varied ways of thinking. Where she'd live in a castle on a cliff. And where maybe, just maybe, she would find people like herself.

And if she was really lucky, maybe she'd find that guy of her dreams: the one who wasn't perfect, but who was, somehow, perfect for *her*.

The possibilities stretched before her, and she imagined in France a world full of sunlight and castles, art and laughter, and a boy who would see into her soul.

She was leaving Spring Creek, and life was never going to be the same.

CHAPTER

JANUARY 20

What was she forgetting? Caitlyn's tired gaze skipped over the shambles of her bedroom, trying to decide what else to cram into her makeshift luggage. Weariness and tension made decision making almost impossible.

Stuffed animal?

No. She'd look childish.

Favorite books?

Too heavy.

Her eye fixed on her bulletin board, and her heart skipped a beat. How could she have almost forgotten that? She plucked the tarot card of the Wheel of Fortune from the lattice of ribbons on the board. It showed a wheel floating in the sky, covered in esoteric symbols. Fantastical creatures surrounded it: a sphinx, a snake, Anubis, and four winged creatures in the corners of the card. In ballpoint pen, her mother had written a few cryptic words along the edge of the card: "the heart in darkness."

Caitlyn had always taken the words as a warning against bouts of melancholy. An uncle had once told her that her mother had been moody, given to dark thoughts and sometimes completely withdrawing into herself. Even though Caitlyn had been only four years old at the time, she wondered if her mother had seen hints of a similar personality in her, and had tried—however ineffectually—to warn Caitlyn to struggle against her nature.

Caitlyn had researched the card online, had even asked a fortune teller about it once, but she had never found an answer to why her mother had given it to her. The Wheel of Fortune's main meanings were "fate" and "change," which seemed about as ambiguous—or obvious—a message as you could leave a person on the day you died. Had her mother simply meant, "This is my fate," and then written the words about the heart in darkness to ask Caitlyn not to grieve?

But what kind of person left that type of message for a four-year-old? Only a madwoman.

Holding the card, Caitlyn sank onto the end of her bed, exhausted by packing and by her own nerves. It was almost one in the morning, and in a couple of hours she and her dad would start the two-hour drive to the airport. The rest of the house was quiet, her parents and brothers sleeping. She should be sleeping, too, but she knew she'd just lie staring at the clock if she undressed and crawled into bed.

She should have been ecstatic that she was almost on her way; that the day had finally come. Instead, she was haunted by a sense of loss and uncertainty. Her friendship with Sarah and Jacqui had started to weaken the day she told them she was going to France. As kids, she and Jacqui and Sarah had thought they'd be best friends forever. Caitlyn would never have guessed that those bonds could break so quickly, as they chose their separate paths through life. After she had told them, they'd been surprised and then excited, but as the weeks went by and they'd gotten used to the idea, they seemed to lose interest in both Caitlyn and her plans. It was almost as if they saw no point in investing further effort in her, since she'd be gone soon, whereas they still had boys and classes to worry about.

Or maybe it was the other way around, Caitlyn admitted to herself. Maybe *she'd* lost interest in *them*, for the same reasons.

Were all relationships so fragile at their core?

Her relationship with her family seemed to be. As she'd predicted, as soon as her father had understood that the Fortune School tuition would be free, he'd seen no reason not to let her go.

Joy had wept and asked why Caitlyn hated her home so much, but eventually had admitted that the educational opportunity was too good to pass up. "I just want you to be happy," she'd said, reproachfully, with the air of a martyr.

Caitlyn's half brothers cared only that there would now be one more bedroom available in the house, and began fighting over who would get it.

It hurt a little to see everyone's lives closing over the small hole that would be created when she left. They'd already started to move on.

But so had she, she realized. Part of her had already boarded the plane, flown over the pole, and landed in Europe. Spring Creek was no longer home.

But France was not *yet* home, either. She was in limbo, and it was eerily uncomfortable and disquieting. She was floating, untethered, between two lives. Caitlyn propped the tarot cart at the base of her bedside lamp and curled up on top of her bedcovers, trying not to think or feel. It was easier that way. Her eyelids gradually grew heavy, and between one moment and the next they drifted shut.

The jumbled images of half sleep crowded her mind, and then

they, too, gave way, and she slipped gratefully into the dark vastness of sleep. Somewhere in that darkness a dream began to form: a light shone faintly in the distance, and she floated toward it.

It grew larger as she approached, and then resolved itself into a familiar lamp beside an unfamiliar couch. Beyond the furniture there was only a blurry beige blankness hinting at the walls of a living room, but without depth or detail.

I know that lamp, Caitlyn thought, staring at it, puzzled. She'd seen it before . . . but where?

Your baby pictures, her unconscious answered. She had a photo of herself as a baby, being held by her mother, with this lamp in the background. It had been in the house where she spent the first four years of her life, just a few blocks from where she lived now.

Behind her, she heard the shuffling of cards and then the soft *snick, snick, snick* of cards being laid upon a table.

The hairs rose on the back of Caitlyn's neck, and she slowly turned.

Sitting in an easy chair, a TV tray in front of her, a young woman with hair as long, black, and straight as Caitlyn's own was laying out tarot cards.

"M-m-mom?" Caitlyn whispered hoarsely, afraid to believe what she was seeing.

The woman looked up, her pale gray eyes gazing straight at Caitlyn. Her face was preternaturally still, no emotion showing. She looked like a wax figure.

"Mom? It's me. Caitlyn." She took a cautious step forward, waiting for her mother's recognition, but afraid of that eerie stillness in her face. A small part of Caitlyn whispered in warning, *You're dreaming, she's dead, this isn't real* . . . But the voice faded under the power of the dream, and Caitlyn no longer questioned why she was standing in the middle of an out-of-focus living room, talking to her dead mother.

Her mother blinked, a hint of life coming to her features. "I know who you are," she said, her voice quiet, but with an underlying tension. Then her mouth crooked in a hint of a smile, and with a slightly shaking hand she shoved a loose lock of hair behind her ear. "I can certainly recognize my own daughter. You've grown into an attractive young woman."

"I look like you," Caitlyn said in mild wonder. She'd known from photos that there were differences in their faces and eye coloring, but in person, the set of her mother's shoulders and the way she held her head were echoes of Caitlyn's own posture, reinforcing their resemblance. It was like looking into a distorted mirror, watching another version of yourself moving and talking.

Her mother nodded. "You're your mother's daughter. In more ways than one, I think."

Caitlyn looked at her curiously. "What do you mean?"

Her mother's lips twitched, and she shook her head. "If you don't know by now, you'll know soon enough."

Caitlyn frowned, thinking about the hints of depression they might both share. "Do you mean the heart in darkness?"

A flicker of surprise raised her mother's brows. "Do I?"

"I don't know."

Her mother laughed, the sound more anxious than cheery. "Then that makes two of us, for the moment at least. No, I thought I meant something else. . . ."

Caitlyn shook her head, not following. "I don't know in what other ways we are the same. I don't predict the future, like you."

"What *do* you do?"

Caitlyn shrugged, feeling her failure to excel in any particular area. "I draw a lot."

"Mmm." Her mother looked at her expectantly. "But what do you do that's more . . . unusual?"

"Nothing, really," she said, feeling that the answer was inadequate, and suddenly fearing that she was a disappointment to her mother. "Well, except that I have strange dreams, but Dad gets upset if I talk about them."

Her mother rolled her eyes. "He's never been accepting of things outside his understanding. I mistook that for moral strength when I married him. It's strange how you can love someone and not be right for him. You'll figure that out for yourself someday." She sighed. "Too bad I couldn't figure it out for myself in time. But then, I never was any good at predicting my own future, only that of others."

"Is that what you're doing?" Caitlyn asked, pointing to the tarot cards and coming closer. She wanted to reach out and touch her mother, but something in the situation held her back. It was her mother's nonchalance, perhaps, or that hint of knowing wryness in her gaze. She offered Caitlyn no welcoming warmth.

"Yes, I'm fortune-telling."

"Dad won't let me buy a set of tarot cards. He says they're evil."

Her mother laughed again. "They're just pieces of paper and ink. The pictures help me give form to the future that I already know. The cards have no power of their own. But I see the future through many methods, not just the cards." She gave Caitlyn a sly look and set down the deck. "Tell me where life has taken you, Caitlyn."

"You don't know?"

Her mother shrugged one shoulder. "In some ways, I do. But I'd rather hear it from you."

"Oh. Well . . . Life hasn't really taken me anywhere, so far. But tomorrow I'm going to France. To boarding school."

Her mother's eyes opened wide. "*Really?* I didn't see *that* coming." She was silent a moment, as if unable to process the information, and then quirked a doubtful brow. "Really? France?"

Caitlyn nodded.

"I've always wanted to go to France," her mother mused. "But boarding school?"

"It's called the Fortune School. It's named after the castle that houses it, Château de la Fortune."

Her mother tilted her head, her gaze questioning. "You're happy about going?"

Caitlyn nodded. "Yes. A little scared, too," she admitted. "It has to be better than Spring Creek, though, doesn't it?" she asked hopefully.

Her mother's laugh was bitter. "It wouldn't take much, would it?"

Caitlyn chuckled, feeling a bond of like minds. She reached down to the TV tray and ran her fingertips over the cards that had been laid out, feeling curious and shy. "Could you do a reading for me?" she asked tentatively.

In answer, her mother gathered all the cards together and started to shuffle. Caitlyn inched over to her mother's side and perched with one hip on the arm of the easy chair, watching her manipulate the cards with practiced hands. And then, suddenly, everything began to fade into transparency. A dark blankness began to show through the scene, and a flush of panic went through Caitlyn. *No, stay!* her soul cried. *Stay with Mom!*

The scene solidified again, and Caitlyn found her mother staring at her, a fresh wariness in her eyes. She held the deck of cards out to Caitlyn. "Lay your hand atop it."

Caitlyn obeyed, and after a moment her mother took the deck back and started to lay out cards, facedown. When she was finished, she set the deck aside and closed her eyes for a long moment, breathing deeply. She opened her eyes, glanced up at Caitlyn, and then turned over the first card. "This card represents you, and the primary force working upon you."

It was the Nine of Swords. A woman sat up in bed, her face in her hands as if she'd been woken from sleep by an unutterable grief. On the black wall behind her were nine immense swords. "That doesn't look good," Caitlyn said doubtfully.

"Mm. Not good. Not necessarily bad. The cards have no set meaning; it changes based on what I feel in here," her mother said, holding her hand over her heart, "and what *you* feel in *there*." She reached out, her fingertips hovering an inch above Caitlyn's own heart. "You tell me: What do *you* think the card means?"

"The Screechers," Caitlyn said, the word coming out of its own volition.

Her mother raised a brow in question.

Caitlyn grimaced, embarrassed, obscurely afraid that her mother would think less of her. "It's what I call the nightmares I have."

"Those nightmares are important. Pay attention to them," her mother said pointedly.

Caitlyn frowned and bit her lip. Thinking about the Screechers made her tense and fearful. She'd rather forget them as soon as she woke and pretend they didn't exist.

"These next two cards are the people coming into your life." She turned the first one over: the Queen of Swords. A stern-looking woman with a crown of butterflies sat on a throne, holding a sword. "This is a woman of cold, efficient intelligence. She can help you, but if you cross her, she will cut you down without a second thought." Her eyes narrowed. "Be careful around her. She is seeking something. A heart that she does not have."

"Great," Caitlyn muttered.

Her mother flipped over the next card. "Maybe this is more to your liking?"

It was the Knight of Cups. An armored knight sitting astride a horse held up a golden goblet, a smile touching his lips. There were wings atop his helmet and on the heels of his feet, and his surcoat was patterned with water and fish. "A guy?" Caitlyn asked hopefully.

Her mother gave her a mischievous, knowing look. "A guy. A young man of imagination and emotion, who offers love."

Caitlyn grinned. "Yes!"

Her mother smiled, then pointed to the next three cards. "The upcoming situation, the near future." She turned them all over: the Three of Swords showed a red heart pierced by three swords, with storming rain in the background; the Fool depicted a young man with his eyes on the sky, about to step off the edge of a cliff and into an abyss; and finally, a skeleton in black armor rode a white horse, with the body of a king beneath the horse's hooves: Death.

Caitlyn squeaked in dismay.

"It's not quite as bad as it looks."

"What do you mean that's not as bad as it looks?" Caitlyn cried. "How could it be any worse? It ends in *death*!"

"It's not always literal. There are figurative deaths as well. But we have to look at the three cards together." Caitlyn's mother laid her hands over the cards and closed her eyes. When she opened them again, her pupils had dilated, giving her a look of blindness. Her face had gone slack. It was as if no one was inside her body. Or as if something *else* had entered it. Caitlyn shivered.

Her mother pointed to the heart struck through by three swords. "They seek to destroy the heart," she intoned, "but you must not let them." She pointed to the Fool, the young man about to step into the abyss. "The abyss waits for you. You stand upon its edge. To survive its depths, you must fully awaken to what is happening." Her hand moved to Death. "Death is the force that will create your new life. It is the mechanism of transformation. Welcome it."

"I *won't* welcome it," Caitlyn protested. "When has death ever done anything good for me?"

Her mother blinked several times, and when she glanced up again at Caitlyn, her pupils were back to their regular size, and her face normal. "There is no avoiding death, Caitlyn. Life cannot continue without it."

"That doesn't make any sense," Caitlyn muttered.

Her mother smiled softly. "You aren't yet ready to understand. But you will be, soon."

Caitlyn pressed her lips together. She didn't *want* to understand. Death was no friend to her. "Where's the Knight of Cups in all this? Shouldn't he be rescuing me from abysses and fighting off skeletons on white horses?"

"He'll be there. But not, I think, in the ways that you expect."

Caitlyn shook her head in confusion and frustration, and then pointed to the final card, facedown upon the table. "So what does this one represent?"

"This is the final outcome."

"Okay, let's see it. God knows it can't be any worse than what you've shown me already."

Her mother turned over the final card.

The Wheel of Fortune.

Caitlyn sighed a breath of wonder, and then looked at her mother.

"The *Rota Fortunae*," her mother said softly. "Fortune's wheel." She looked up at Caitlyn. "Destiny is at work in your life. That which seems random chance is not. You are at the edge of the wheel right now, lost in the chaos of a world that turns at maddening speed, but if you fulfill your destiny, you will journey to the heart of the wheel, where all is motionless and clear. You will journey to the heart. The heart. The heart," she repeated as if possessed, "the heart in darkness." Her eyes widened, and she stared at Caitlyn. "That is where you will find your true purpose."

Caitlyn struggled to make sense of what she was saying. "What *is* the heart in darkness? And why did you put this card under my pillow right before you died in that car crash? What did you mean to tell me?"

Her mother's brows puckered. "Car crash?"

"April 25, when I was four years old." Caitlyn frowned at her mother. "You haven't forgotten that you're dead, have you?"

Her mother looked flustered, her gaze darting around the room, her hands growing restless, touching and shifting the cards on the TV tray. One hand stopped on the card of Death, and then her face slowly filled with sadness. "Dead. And you so young." Her face contorted, her mouth turning down in an ugly grimace of grief, and then she violently swept the cards to the floor, the tray teetering and then falling with a clatter. She put her face in her hands and sobbed, becoming a living echo of the woman depicted on the Nine of Swords.

"Mom . . . ," Caitlyn said, reaching out a hand in tentative comfort. Just as her hand was about to connect with her mother's shoulder, Caitlyn felt a hand on her own shoulder, shaking her.

"Caitlyn? Wake up," her father's voice said.

Her mother started to fade into darkness, becoming transparent. "Mom!" Caitlyn screamed, struggling to reach her even as she seemed to be pulled away into darkness.

Her mother looked up, eyes red with tears, and then her face filled with panic. She lunged toward Caitlyn, trying to reach her. "Caitlyn! Don't go!"

"Wake up! Caitlyn, it's time to get up!" her dad insisted, shaking her harder.

"Mommm!" Caitlyn moaned, and was pulled against her will back into the world of the waking. Her mother vanished, and she opened her eyes. Her father, his face haggard from lack of sleep, was looking down at her.

He straightened up. "We have to get moving. You don't want to miss your plane, do you?" He walked out and closed her door.

She sat up, and picked up the tarot card on her bedside table. "Destiny," she whispered, and traced her fingertip in a circle around the edge of the wheel. The other images from her dream were quickly fading, along with the things her mother had said. She grabbed her art journal and sketched the tarot cards her mother had shown her. The clearest of them was the Knight of Cups.

"I knew you were out there somewhere," Caitlyn whispered to the knight, as with a few flicks of her pencil she crowned his helmet with wings.

"Caitlyn!" her father hollered from the hallway. "Come on! It's time to go."

She stuffed the art journal into her backpack, a smile tugging at her lips. Thanks to her mom, she finally felt ready to leave.

It was time to meet her fate.

CHAPTER

Caitlyn stared at the back of the driver's fat pink neck, white hairs sticking out of it like bristles on a pig. He smelled of wool and tobacco, the scents strong in the overheated Mercedes. He hadn't said a word to her since meeting her at noon outside baggage claim at the Bordeaux airport, his communications limited to grunts and gestures of his head. He was like a henchman in a James Bond movie, and she had a disquieting sense that he was delivering her to her doom.

She'd slept only in fits and starts on the four flights it had taken her to get from Oregon to the French city of Bordeaux, and her brain was fuzzy with lack of sleep, time confusion, and the high tension of leaving everything and everyone she'd ever known. Whatever comfort she'd gotten from her dream of her mother had long since worn off, erased by the torture of airplane seats, layovers, and long confused treks through airports to change planes. She was nauseated with a sour stomach, and had developed an annoying nervous twitch in one eyelid. She could feel it fluttering like a moth against her eyeball.

She'd never been chauffeured anywhere before, and had never been in a Mercedes. When she first got in, she'd felt like a celebrity, glancing around the airport parking lot, hoping someone would notice: Caitlyn Monahan of Spring Creek, Oregon, was being chauffeured in a Mercedes! But no one had spared her a look, and the small thrill of leather seats and a uniformed driver had been quickly forgotten as she'd taken her first real look at France, leaving the airport.

So far it was as gray, rainy, and dreary as Oregon had been thirty-two hours earlier. Bordeaux was near the southwest coast, and three hundred miles from Paris. Her driver had taken a highway around the outskirts of Bordeaux and then headed east into the countryside, passing through denuded winter vineyards, gently rolling farmland, and low wooded hills. The Fortune School was well over an hour's drive away, above the Dordogne River in an ancient region known as the Périgord Noir—called *noir*, black, because of the dark forests of pine and evergreen oak trees. Her travel book had pointed out the prehistoric cave paintings at Lascaux and Les Eyzies that were over fifteen thousand years old, and painted by some of the world's first artists. The Gauls had been here, too, and the Romans, as had the English, fighting with the French during the Hundred Years' War.

Despite those promises of a rich and dramatic history, the area was as rural as Spring Creek. She was five thousand miles away from home, and cave paintings or no, she was still surrounded by farms and dreary winter weather.

Brilliant.

Maybe coming here was the wrong thing for an unhappy girl with a possible mental disorder. That was what her parents had secretly feared, Caitlyn knew: that her bad dreams and depressed moods meant that she was on the verge of a breakdown. They could never understand that it was staying locked in the stale embrace of home that truly threatened to push her into the pit of despair.

Caitlyn remembered Joy's sad face and her long hug good-bye, and she felt her throat tighten. For a brief instant she wanted to ask the driver to turn the car around and take her back to the airport: she'd made a horrible mistake and she had to go home. But the words stuck in her throat, kept there both by her fear of the gruff stranger and her reluctance to admit defeat.

It wasn't just the exhaustion of travel that was eating at her. Even her complete ignorance of what it would be like to live and go to school in France was not what was making her feel almost sick. It was the anticipation of what her fellow students might be like.

A little Internet research had shown her that the Fortune School was meant for the daughters of blue-blooded, filthy-rich families, not for daughters of log truck drivers from Oregon. The girls at the Fortune School probably spoke several languages, skied in the Alps, vacationed on private yachts in the Mediterranean, and bought their clothes from shops like Chanel and Dior.

She had spent the last several months too engrossed in getting to France to worry about what would happen once she did. Now that the flights were over and she was on the ground, only an hour from the Fortune School, she finally began to wonder not just what *she* would think of the people she met, but what *they* would think of *her*.

And she knew they were going to think she was a hick.

She *was* a hick.

Her eyelid fluttered at the thought, and she pressed her hand against it. After all she'd gone through to get here, she would never forgive herself if she gave up on day one.

She closed her eyes and lay her head back against the headrest and tried to relax.

Suddenly, the brilliant glare of headlights pierced the rain and filled the car, a semi's horn blaring a warning. Caitlyn screamed as a massive truck bore down on them out of the gray drizzle, aiming straight for her in the backseat of the Mercedes. The truck's front grill filled her window, the headlights turning the driver's head into an abstract shape of white illumination and black shadow. There was a violent jerk, and then all went black.

The car was gone. As if in a dream, she was flying with the graceful ease of a bird, skimming low over summer-bleached farms and forests of oak. She saw the Dordogne River, wide, smooth, and green, with poplars and willows edging its banks and golden limestone cliffs rising roughly above on one side. Narrow honey-colored stone villages clung to the bottom of the cliffs, bounded by the river. The stone-shingled buildings looked centuries old.

She flew over a long-ago peasant family harvesting wheat by hand, flying so close that she could hear the mother's scythe as it cut through the stalks and feel the dust of the harvest in her nose. She left them and came up behind a group of riders on horseback, on a dirt road. They wore clothes out of a Shakespearean play: doublets and trunk hose, tall boots and plumed hats. As she approached, one of the figures turned in his saddle as if to stare at her: a beautiful young man with bronze curls, a straight narrow nose, and gently curved lips framed by a square jaw shadowed with stubble.

The Knight of Cups, something inside Caitlyn said. *You have found him.*

The young man's dark hazel eyes narrowed as she flew up close and hovered for a long moment mere feet from him, like a hummingbird examining a flower. Was this him, the one she had been waiting for?

She wanted to touch him; she wanted to feel that rough stubble on his cheek. She stretched her hand toward him, fingertips reaching for the plane of his cheek. He couldn't see her, his gaze going right through her, but his eyes were hard and suspicious, as if he knew someone or something was watching him. As if he knew that *she* was reaching out of the ether to touch him.

"Raphael, what is it?" one of the other men asked when her fingertips were an inch shy of his cheek.

The bronze-curled young man shrugged and faced forward. "Nothing."

Nothing? Caitlyn lay both hands on the back of his neck and ran her fingers up into his hair, knocking off his hat, and then flew beyond the chaos she had caused: Raphael jerked, his horse shied and crashed into the one to the right, voices shouted as the mounts danced and were drawn back under control.

A moment later she was past the riders, and when she looked back for another sight of the beautiful young man, the riders had disappeared, replaced by a vast army encampment of men, tents, and horses, with bedraggled women tending the cooking fires and squires cleaning armor. She could smell the smoke, the meat cooking, their unwashed bodies, the manure of animals. As they, too, melted away, vanishing like a vision, she looked forward and saw a field bisected by a column of Roman soldiers marching down a stone road, their leather-clad feet slapping the ground in drumlike rhythm. Their stone road sank away beneath green vegetation, taking the soldiers with it. A herd of strangely horned, enormous cattle grazed in their place beneath a sun that baked Caitlyn's skin, and when they as well faded away to nothing, Caitlyn felt a chill run over her body, and the landscape turned to blowing snow as far as she could see, as if an ice age had swallowed the land.

She jerked awake to the skittering sound of sleet on the roof of the car, the ice pellets scrabbling like the claws of frightened mice. She looked around in confusion, the scenes of her dream tearing apart like clouds in the wind, leaving her with only a memory of intense hazel eyes and a name: Raphael.

The Mercedes was moving smoothly along the road. Where was the semitruck?

"Excuse me?" she squeaked at the driver. "Er, *excusez-moi?*"

The driver's dark pebble eyes flicked up to look at her in the rearview mirror.

"Didn't we have an accident? *Un accident?*"

White brows drew down in a frown.

"With a truck?" she clarified. "*Camisole?*"

"*Camisole?*"

Shoot. That was an undershirt, not a truck. "Big car, for carrying things?"

"Ah. *Un camion.*"

"*Oui!* Did we almost have an accident with *un camion?*"

"I swerved."

"Oh." Of course he did. She remembered the jerk of the car. "Did I faint?"

He smirked, and turned his eyes back to the road.

She'd fainted, something she'd never done before. She rubbed her forehead and shook her head. Apparently, she was even more worn out than she'd thought.

At least she hadn't had one of her Screecher nightmares while she'd been out cold. Maybe, like the evil spirits of legend, the apparitions that visited her dreams couldn't cross over moving water and hadn't been able to pursue her over the Atlantic Ocean. She could always hope that the Screechers had been left behind with her old life.

Hazel eyes and a head of curly hair filtered up from her unconscious. *Raphael*, an inner voice whispered, and her heart tripped in response.

Caitlyn dug in her backpack and pulled out her art journal, flipping through to her last entry, where she'd drawn the tarot cards. The Knight of Cups sat on his horse in his winged helmet and armor, a cup held up in his hand. The only similarity to the boy in her dream was youth, and a horse. Raphael had worn no armor, had held no cup. She dug out a pencil and wrote *Raphael?* under the Knight of Cups. She turned to a fresh page and sketched the riders on the road, Raphael in their midst, twisting in his saddle to look back at her.

Her pencil hesitated over the blank of his face, the features already disappearing from her memory, leaving behind only a sense of how vivid they *had* been, mere minutes before. She tentatively shaded in shadows to give a sense of the proportions of his face, but the features themselves were lost to her. The effect of the shadows on her drawing ended up more ghostly than man-of-her-dreams, and she sighed in frustration. Her artistic skills had never been adequate to the vividness of her dreams. Never did she regret that as much as she did right now.

She flipped back to the beginning of her journal, and the first entry, from three years ago: a dark-faced Screecher with long black hair howled on the page, running toward her through a forest of twisted trees. Caitlyn had drawn the picture with a ballpoint pen, the marks violent and jagged on the white paper, and blotted with ink. The picture still gave her chills.

That first drawing, and the next half dozen in the journal, had been her attempt to exorcise the Screechers from her dreams, as if putting them on paper would exile them from her mind. It hadn't worked.

She flipped through the Screecher drawings. They were all humanlike, with smeared, indistinct faces. They clawed, struck, or cursed at her. They screamed and howled, and threw things. Worst of all, though, were the ones who did no more than silently, intently stare at her with their round, dead eyes.

She shuddered and turned the page. After several months she'd realized that drawing the Screechers wasn't making them go away, and to save her own sanity she'd turned her pens and pencils to recording images from her more benign dreams. She thumbed through those pages now, seeing her gradually increasing drawing skill more than the images themselves: hunters chased a dear; a pioneer girl rode a horse; teenagers loafed on a couch. On one page, a man stabbed his friend in a bar; on the facing page, a woman dressed for her wedding. There was no rhyme or reason to the dreams, no pattern that she could ever tell.

She turned to the drawing of the woman being burned at the stake, and paused. *That* had been an unusually creepy dream. It had lingered in her imagination far longer than was comfortable. It had felt so real, she almost wondered if she herself had once been a woman burned at the stake.

Caitlyn closed the journal and looked out the window, not wanting to think about flames and burning flesh. The countryside dressed in cold shades of gray was a welcome antidote to the hot orange flames licking at her memory.

The Mercedes was off the main road now, and they wound their way through a small village built into the base of a steep ridge of hills. They followed the black asphalt road upward as it clung to the edge of the hills and passed under dark, evergreen oak trees.

The driver suddenly cleared his throat, making her jump. His eyes met hers in the rearview mirror as he slowed the car and brought it to a stop in the middle of the empty road. He nodded to the right, where there was a break in the trees. "Château de la Fortune," he said, pronouncing it "shah-toe de la for-toon."

Caitlyn lowered her window, her sea-green eyes searching the landscape. The car was stopped halfway up the ridge. At the top of the next hill, a golden limestone fortress stood strong at the edge of a cliff, the stone of the earth merging with the foundations of the castle.

A tingling mix of excitement and fear ran over her skin, and a deep feeling of familiarity and recognition settled in her gut, as if she had at last come home.

CHAPTER

The Mercedes passed through a gate in a thick defensive wall and entered a parklike setting. The castle and grounds were on a headland jutting out above the valley, and the outer wall, complete with crenellations and towers, went from the cliffs that curved around the castle grounds on the south, to the cliffs curving around to the north, walling off the castle property from the dark forest that covered the rest of the hill.

The driveway continued through close-mown grass to the massive square castle, an archway piercing its center front. Gardens, riding stables, and outbuildings surrounded the castle itself. Caitlyn looked up as they rolled slowly through the archway and saw the iron points of an immense portcullis in the shadows above them; it was the first time she'd seen such a thing in real life. A shiver ran over her skin, as she realized she was really here.

The car came out into an immense courtyard in the center of the castle, and the thick-necked driver parked and shut off the engine.

Caitlyn drew a breath and got out of the car, pulling up the hood of her thrift-store parka. Her breath steamed in the frosty air, and as she watched it dissipate, she felt a curious dissociation from her body, as if she were an alien looking out of someone else's eyes. She'd had the same sensation before in stressful times.

Someone grabbed her shoulder, bringing her back to herself. She was shivering, and the smell of stale cigarette smoke in the driver's clothes filled her nose. He assessed her with narrowed eyes. "Are you sick?"

Her eyelid twitched and fluttered. She shook her head, then promptly bent over and retched, her airplane breakfast of omelet and orange juice spilling onto the cobbles and splashing his shoes. He swore in French and hopped out of the way. She was dimly aware of his leaving her, calling out, and knocking at a door. Hands on her knees, her long straight black hair hanging around her face, she stared at the ground and breathed deeply, trying to get the nausea under control, until female voices and hurried footsteps made her raise her head.

A plump middle-aged woman with short, fluffy blond hair trotted toward her, her rosy face puckered in concern. Behind her, moving more slowly, was a tall elegant woman in her thirties, with pale skin and dark red hair pulled back into a chignon at the base of her neck. Caitlyn recognized her from her photo on the school's Web site: she was the headmistress, Eugenia Snowe.

Oh, great! Good first impression you're making, Caitlyn. Way to shine. With a shaking hand she wiped her mouth and stood up straight, forcing a smile to her lips. Her eyelid twitched again. "I'm so sorry," Caitlyn said. "Is there a hose? I'll wash it away."

The chubby blond clucked in dismay, reaching her. "Child, it's not for you to worry about." She put her palm on Caitlyn's forehead and then lay the back of her hand against Caitlyn's cheek. "No fever. How long have you been unwell?"

"I'm okay, really," Caitlyn said, feeling a tingling in her skin where she had been touched. Her last traces of nausea seemed to have vanished, too. "The long trip . . . ," Caitlyn fibbed, unwilling to admit she was as tense as a guitar string. "Maybe a bit of carsickness?"

"And jet lag," the lady said. "It is very common with our students who come from a great distance."

Caitlyn nodded, glad for the excuse. She gathered her nerve and looked at Madame Snowe. She was afraid that the headmistress was already suspecting that she had wasted a scholarship on her.

The headmistress was looking at her with one auburn brow slightly raised, her dark brown eyes seeming to see through her. She was wearing a thin maroon sweater and a black pencil skirt, the clothes setting off her slender curves. She seemed not to feel the biting cold, despite the ice pellets dusting her hair and shoulders. "Are you quite recovered?" she asked, a hint of a French accent in her voice but not much concern.

"Yes, thank you." Caitlyn clasped her hands tight together, trying to still their shaking.

"Let's go inside then, shall we?" Madame Snowe turned to the driver. "The mademoiselle's bags, if you please," she said in French and, without waiting for an answer, headed back into the building, her posture as perfect as a ballerina's.

Caitlyn and the blond woman followed. Caitlyn heard the trunk of the car pop open and grimaced, remembering what was in there. She sent a fervent wish heavenward that Madame Snowe would abandon her for other duties before catching sight of her tattered luggage.

They went through a side door into a surprisingly mundane lobby that looked like a medieval dentist's waiting room. In front of a vast, empty stone fireplace a few pieces of tapestry-upholstered furniture surrounded a coffee table with magazines. To the left, a high counter and glass receptionist's window blocked off an office area. Beside that was a wall of antique post office boxes with glass windows and brass trim. On the opposite side of the room were two sets of double doors within gothic arches.

Madame Snowe brushed the ice off her sleeves, then loosely clasped her hands in front of her. "Now that we're out of the cold, let me be the first to welcome you, Caitlyn, to Château de la Fortune."

"Thank you," Caitlyn murmured.

"As you may have guessed already, I am the headmistress, Madame Snowe. It is my sincere hope that you will benefit from your time with us here at the Fortune School, and that you will take full advantage of all we have to offer. This is Greta," she said, nodding toward the middle-aged blond. "She is the house mother. She'll show you to your room. If you have any questions or need anything for your personal comfort, go to her."

The driver bumped his way through the door and plopped down Caitlyn's "luggage." Caitlyn watched Madame Snowe's eyes go to it, widening as she took it in. Caitlyn's cheeks heated.

Her "luggage" was a Vietnam War–era army green duffel bag, bought for a dollar at a garage sale. Cloud-shaped moisture stains mottled its faded surface, and jagged stitches of black carpet thread sealed a rip on one end, Caitlyn's clumsy needlework giving the mended hole the look of one of Frankenstein's scars.

"Is that all you brought?" Greta asked.

Caitlyn nodded, wishing the floor would swallow her.

"Very good. You will have no trouble unpacking, and then you can burn your bag, heh?"

"Reduce, reuse, recycle!" Caitlyn said with false cheer. "We're very big on living green in Oregon. Why buy a new suitcase when someone else's old duffel bag will do?"

"We'll see that it gets ... disposed of properly," Madame Snowe said dryly. "I will talk to you again in my office, at nine A.M. tomorrow morning, to give you a more thorough orientation to the school and to explain what I will be expecting of you as a scholarship student." She turned to Greta. "Greta, please see Caitlyn settled in her room, and see that she showers." With a nod she turned on her heel and left.

Caitlyn raised her arm and sneaked a sniff at her armpit. Was Madame Snowe saying she smelled? She caught Greta watching her and lowered her arm. "Just checking," she said sheepishly.

"Are you sure you are well?" Greta asked.

Caitlyn smiled crookedly. "I'm okay. Really. Just tired." Greta's warmth was a welcome contrast to the icy headmistress. Even Greta's German accent was somehow comforting, making it sound as if she'd next be offering warm apple strudel and hot chocolate.

"You will feel better after a bath, and perhaps some tea to settle your stomach. Try to stay awake until this evening; it will make the adjustment to the time difference easier," Greta said.

"Okay. Thanks." Caitlyn didn't know how she could possibly manage that. She was barely conscious as it was.

Greta patted her arm and smiled. "You'll be fine."

Caitlyn felt a small return of energy tingling through her arm as if from Greta's touch, and believed her.

"Now come this way," Greta said, and pushed through the double doors on the right side of the room. Caitlyn picked up her ecologically sound bag and followed her through an immense medieval hall with a stone checkerboard floor and walls painted in deep red scattered with gold fleur-de-lis; the ceiling high above was royal blue and

covered in gold stars. Yellow ocher columns ran down the center in
two rows, providing support to the arches above. The room was filled
with tables, benches, and the lingering odor of lunch. "The hall dates
from the 1140s," Greta said as she led Caitlyn out through another
doorway to a smaller room built of pale stone, and then up a wide
spiral stone staircase. The handrail was a rope as thick as Caitlyn's
wrist, strung between steel eyebolts sunk into the curved wall.

Caitlyn lagged a few steps behind Greta, in awe of her
surroundings. She'd spent hours poring over picture books
of castles; she'd seen them in movies, and read about them in
novels; but nothing had prepared her for the wonder of being
inside one in real life. Each stone step of the spiral staircase was
worn to a bowl by thousands of feet, and her own steps sounded
both muffled and loud at once; she could smell the faint, damp,
mineral-tinged scent of rock; her skin felt the chill of stone that
no modern heating system could vanquish. Her vision spun as
they wound higher and higher up the stairs, the rope rail under
her hand both rough with fibers and smooth with the oil of
hands. She was glad of the weight of the unwieldy duffel bag: its
reality kept her tied to earth.

"I hope Amalia has not gone out," Greta said over her shoulder.
"She can show you where everything is. She's a charming young
woman, a princess of Liechtenstein."

"A what?" Caitlyn said, stumbling on a stair.

"A charming young woman."

"No, a princess? A real princess?"

"Of course." Greta stopped and tucked in her chin, frowning at
Caitlyn as if she were a slow-witted child.

Caitlyn was too stunned to care. "And she's from where?"

"Liechtenstein."

"Ah!" Caitlyn had a vague notion of a tiny country somewhere near Germany or Austria. "Is it this princess's job to show new students around?"

Greta laughed. "No. But you are special."

"I am?"

Greta smiled. "You're her new roommate."

"Great!" Her eyelid fluttered. No pressure there. Not like a princess was going to notice she'd been stuck with an ignorant peasant for a roommate.

"Do you ride?" Greta continued.

"Ride what?"

Greta chuckled. "Horses."

"No."

"Ah, too bad. Amalia is a champion equestrienne. But never mind, I am certain you'll find you have much in common."

Oh, sure! Caitlyn's muscle twitched so hard her eye closed. "We'll be like peas in a pod."

Or like the princess and the pea, Caitlyn thought glumly. And it wasn't Amalia who was going to be the annoying vegetable stuck under a mattress.

CHAPTER
Five

Late that evening, wrapped in the navy blue Fortune School bathrobe she'd found in the armoire on her side of the room, Caitlyn sat cross-legged on her bed and leaned against the dark, carved headboard. She still hadn't met Amalia, but she had gotten to know the confines of her gothic, vaguely creepy room and its furnishings very well in the past several hours.

The room was a rectangle, with the door to the hallway centered in the wall on one end, and windows piercing the honey-colored stone wall on the opposite end. The two side walls were richly paneled dark polished wood, like something out of a manor house in a British costume drama. The floors were stone, covered in a worn, dark red Oriental carpet, while the ceiling was high above, crossed by massive beams blackened with age. They'd been charming during the daylight, but now, at night, Caitlyn's desk lamp couldn't pierce the darkness above her, giving her the uneasy feeling that anything could be clinging to the beams up in those shadows, watching her.

She and Amalia each had an antique wood bed, desk, chair, bookcase, and armoire. As she'd been told to expect, she'd found an entire Fortune School wardrobe in her armoire, in her sizes: socks, shoes, skirts, blouses, sweaters, even a wrap dress in a geometric print of the Fortune School colors of navy and burgundy. If she was lucky, maybe no one who mattered would ever see the old, comparatively ratty clothes she'd brought from home. Vintage clothing was daring in Spring Creek, but here her clothes felt like the castoffs they were, instead of a creative expression of her personality.

The room had two leaded-glass windows, set in deep embrasures that doubled as window seats. Caitlyn had opened one and stuck her head out earlier, before the sun had set, and seen a sheer drop of hundreds of feet to the treetops and rocks below. She'd clung to the edge of the window, absurdly afraid of falling out. Far below, the Dordogne River flowed in sinuous curves through the valley, with a patchwork of cultivated farmland on either side. She had seen two other castles far to the east, perched on cliffs, and a third castle to the west. Her guidebook to the region said that the Dordogne River had once been the border between France and the English region of Aquitaine, which explained all the defensive castles.

After pulling her head back in, she had looked over her absent roommate's belongings, seeking some hint of the girl's personality. On the wall above Amalia's bed hung a large, modern oil painting; Caitlyn had leaned in close to see the signature on it: Picasso.

A *real* Picasso. Big. In oil. It was probably worth several hundred thousand dollars, if not millions. She, Caitlyn Monahan, was sharing a room with a girl who used a Picasso as a dorm room decoration.

On Amalia's desk sat a framed photo of a horse. There were no other pictures: no parents, no friends, no goofy bunch of grinning girls squeezing together to fit in a photo. Caitlyn didn't think that boded well for the princess's social skills, but who was she to judge?

Maybe the princess was just private. Or maybe, like Caitlyn, a photo of family or friends suggested pain more than comfort.

Overall, this was the most luxurious bedroom Caitlyn had ever been in; it was the most historic, the most foreign, the most romantic, and the most likely to inspire gothic bouts of running down the hallway in a white nightgown during a thunderstorm, carrying a candelabra. The castle itself was the castle of her wildest fantasies, hovering as it did at the edge of a cliff, its walls a millennium old. However, all she wanted to do at this moment was cry.

Loneliness flooded her. For all that she hadn't thought that she belonged at home, and had felt tolerated rather than understood, at least she'd known deep down that her parents and her runty little brothers loved her.

She sighed as she sat alone on her bed. The laptop computer the Fortune School had provided was in front of her on the down comforter. She'd sent e-mails to her parents and even to her brothers, but no one had responded.

She blinked back the tears and stared at her empty in-box, willing it to fill with something other than the dozen orientation letters sent by school administrators, each with its own set of pdf files with maps, class lists, school rules, schedules.

As if on cue, her laptop softly pinged, striking her with a bolt of joy in the instant before she saw that the message was from Madame Snowe:

> Please thoroughly read all orientation materials before
> our meeting in the morning.
> —E.S.

Caitlyn shut the laptop. She'd make herself wait an hour before she checked again. How had anyone stood it, in the old days before e-mail? Imagine waiting a week for a letter; a month; a year or two, even, if you lived far enough away.

Never mind. She wasn't going to be lonely. She was lonely at this moment, yes, but that was to be expected.

She lay back on her bed and wrapped the plush comforter around her, closing her eyes as she relived her evening. After Greta had shown her to her room and shown her the communal bathroom down the hall, Caitlyn had unpacked, showered, drank the tea and eaten the cookies that Greta brought her, and then sat stewing alone in the room, wondering when Amalia would show up, and feeling too shy to explore the castle on her own.

At seven o'clock, hunger had forced her to gather her courage and go down to dinner. Classes would not begin for four more days, and according to Greta, many of the students had not yet arrived. Caitlyn had stood with her tray and surveyed the lonely dining hall, tempted to sit alone at a table. A spark of anger at her own cowardice finally made her ask a pair of German girls if she could sit with them. They'd agreed, and after asking a few politely inquiring questions in English, they'd slid back into German and held a long conversation with each other that they both obviously enjoyed very much. Caitlyn hadn't understood a word, and had been surprised by how much the unintentional ostracism had hurt. It had been a relief to scamper back to the safety of her room.

Alone on her bed now, Caitlyn told herself that things had to get better. She knew she wasn't a uniquely talented or extraordinary person, or particularly socially graceful, but neither did she think she was stupid or inept. People went to new schools all the time and made friends. She would, too.

Probably.

How different could blue-blooded rich girls really be from rural Oregon girls, after all?

A commotion of voices in the hallway made her sit up just as the door opened. Caitlyn quickly rubbed away any hint of tears and plastered a smile on her face as a trio of girls poured through the doorway, laughing and talking in rapid French.

A swarthy, imperious-looking girl with auburn highlights in her long, dark brown hair pulled up short and scowled when she saw Caitlyn. She hit a pudgy dark blond with the back of her hand, provoking a burst of annoyed noises.

The third girl, a brunette with pretty, conventional features and dark blue eyes, looked solemnly at Caitlyn for a long moment, then stepped forward, her hand outstretched. "You must be Caitlyn," she said, her voice betraying only the slightest of unidentifiable accents. "I'm your roommate, Amalia."

Caitlyn awkwardly shook Amalia's hand, wondering if she should stand or curtsy or say something formal and proper. "Hi," she said.

"This is Daniela and Brigitte," Amalia said, gesturing to the swarthy girl and the dark blond in turn. The two other girls nodded to Caitlyn.

"Nice to meet you," Caitlyn said.

"*Mucho gusto.*"

"*Enchanté.*"

They stared at her, eyes roaming over her loose hair and Fortune School robe, as if seeking keys to her character. Did they know she was here on scholarship?

And even if they didn't know, could they sense her poverty as easily as she could sense their wealth? Daniela wore black leggings, long loops of a pearl-and-gold necklace, and a wool minidress in an oversize black-and-white houndstooth weave that Caitlyn could swear she'd seen in an ad in the *Vogue* she'd thumbed through at an airport newsstand. Amalia wore a short, tailored black leather jacket over a silk blouse with shades of blue that drew out the dark hue of her eyes; designer jeans; and leather boots. Brigitte had on magenta tights and a strange, unflattering magenta sweater dress with random ruching and wide sleeves, but the fine knit and elaborate workmanship hinted at "cashmere" and "designer," just as the sparkle at her ears said "diamond."

"You're American, yes?" Daniela said.

"Yes."

"New York?"

"Oregon."

"*Dónde?*" Where?

"It's a state on the West Coast."

"Near Los Angeles?" Brigitte asked.

"North of there. Just south of Canada."

All three sighed, "Ah."

"You're from the ends of the earth," Amalia said, a teasing smile on her lips.

"Not quite *that* far!"

"Almost!" Brigitte said. "There are still wild animals and cowboys, and naked savages running through the forest, *oui?*" she asked, laughing.

Caitlyn smiled awkwardly, a little taken aback by the teasing. "There *are* cowboys, at least at rodeos. And bears and cougars in the mountains. And if by 'savages' you mean descendants of the Umpqua tribe, then yes to that, too. My great-grandfather on my mother's side was a full-blooded Umpqua," Caitlyn said proudly. She saw Brigitte's mouth pucker in surprise and her cheeks turn pink in recognition that her jokes may have verged on offensive.

"Although I don't believe he ever ran naked through the forest," Caitlyn amended, and smiled to soften the blow. "The weather doesn't encourage streaking."

"The rest of your ancestors, are they equally exotic?" Daniela asked, her brow arched. "I can trace my ancestry to Ferdinand of Aragon, who sent Columbus to discover your continent." A smug smile played on her lips. "Perhaps that gives us a connection, of a sort."

Of what, conqueror to conquered? Daniela's comments didn't sound as innocent as Brigitte's.

Caitlyn shrugged, affecting nonchalance. "We don't put much stock in genealogy where I'm from." Caitlyn grimaced as if hating what she had to say next, then went on in an apologetic tone, "It's assumed that you're kind of a loser if you have to sink to boasting about your family in order to impress people."

Daniela gaped at her, then shut her mouth and narrowed her eyes.

Caitlyn met her glare and held it. She might be a little nothing from nowhere, but she'd be damned if she'd let herself be talked down to by a girl who had nothing but other people's ancient accomplishments to brag about.

Brigitte giggled nervously, the sound only adding to the tension in the room.

Amalia cleared her throat. "We are all tired. Maybe it is time for bed," Amalia said, and ushered her friends toward the door.

"*Bonne nuit, petite Americaine,*" Brigitte said brightly, wagging her fingers in farewell.

"I hope she is not one of the 'ugly Americans,' ignorant and loud!" Daniela whispered to Amalia, but loud enough for Caitlyn to hear. "It will be too bad for you, to have to live with someone like that."

"Enough!" Amalia hissed, pushing her out the door.

"Good night, sleep tight," Daniela called mockingly to Caitlyn, the familiar idiom sounding strange in her faint Spanish accent.

"*Buenas noches*," Caitlyn said, glad she remembered a few basic phrases from the one Spanish class she'd taken. "*Que descanses.*" She was rewarded with a flare of surprise in Daniela's eyes, and then the girls were gone and she was alone with Amalia.

"I am so embarrassed," the princess said. "Daniela—" She shook her head. "Anyway, I meant to be here when you arrived, but then Brigitte arrived, and I had to go out to dinner with them in Sarlat. It is Brigitte's first day back after . . . well, after some very difficult times, but you do not want to hear about that now."

Amalia sat on the foot of Caitlyn's bed, her dark blue eyes looking hopefully into Caitlyn's own. "We can begin anew, yes?"

It was the faint hint of uncertainty in Amalia's eyes that softened Caitlyn's heart. "Yes, let's," Caitlyn said, smiling.

Amalia grinned. "I promise, tomorrow they will be very ashamed of themselves, but they will be too embarrassed to admit it and apologize."

"Have you known them long?"

"A year and a half, but friendships grow quickly here. We are so isolated; there is very little for distraction."

Caitlyn laughed ruefully.

"What is it?"

Caitlyn shook her head. "I thought that all of France would be like the movies I've seen of Paris: full of people riding bicycles down cobbled streets, a baguette tied on behind."

"And a little red beret?" Amalia laughed. "Maybe an accordion player singing *La Vie en Rose*?"

Caitlyn grinned. "Yes. Museums and cheese shops on every corner, and castles everywhere. I didn't know the rural parts were so . . . rural."

"But at least you were right about the castles, even here, among the farms," Amalia said. "You have not been to Europe before?" she asked tentatively, as if afraid of causing offense.

"I hadn't been on a plane before yesterday."

"*Vraiment?*" Truly?

"*Oui, vraiment.* Truly. You won't tell *them*, though, will you?" Caitlyn asked.

Amalia shook her head, then got up and started getting ready for bed. "What made you decide to come here? Or did you not have a choice?"

"You make it sound more like a penitentiary than a school."

Amalia made a face and shrugged her shoulder. "I like it well enough, but some of the girls, they feel as if they are in prison. They miss boys and the city, shopping, clubbing. Which is perhaps why some of them were sent here by their parents."

Caitlyn's shoulders sagged dramatically. "I've sent myself to reform school."

A laugh trilled from Amalia's throat. "No, no, it's not like that! Or not *completely* like that. Think of it more like a convent."

Caitlyn's mouth turned down, making Amalia laugh again. "Would you believe that I came here for the education?" Caitlyn said.

Amalia climbed into bed and turned off her lamp. "It is a good school. Not perhaps the very best academically, but if you want a good education, you can get one here."

Caitlyn put her laptop away and crawled under her covers. When she turned off her own bedside lamp, the room fell into darkness, broken only by the gray rectangles of the windows and the green digital display of her clock. Caitlyn pulled the covers up under her chin and rolled onto her side, facing the shadows where Amalia lay. "Did you have a roommate last term?" she asked, hoping Amalia was not done talking for the night. Caitlyn already liked her, and was eager to form some sort of friendship.

"She was expelled."

"Why? What did she do?"

"She brought her boyfriend into our room for a weekend while I was away."

Caitlyn was shocked. "Oh."

"Madame Snowe is very strict about such things."

"I have to meet with her tomorrow morning."

"Agree with everything she says. Don't question anything. The sooner you escape, the better."

In the dark, Caitlyn couldn't tell if Amalia was joking. "She's that bad?"

"Life is easier if you do not attract her attention. Now we must sleep, or else you will not wake in the morning and you will be late, and that would be very, very bad."

With that unhappy threat lingering in her thoughts, Caitlyn rolled onto her back and forced herself to close her eyes, convinced that sleep would never come. She lay for what felt like hours.

And then the noises started.

CHAPTER
Six

Caitlyn lay frozen, listening, not yet daring to open her eyes.

There were murmuring voices, snippets of words, coming from the foot of her bed. Footsteps. A door closing.

Amalia?

But then she heard water, like someone pouring it from a height into a basin or pool.

There was no sink in their room.

Humming, an unfamiliar tune. Under the breath.

Male.

Caitlyn's eyes popped open.

Orange light flickered in reflections off the paneled walls. She heard a crackle and pop, and smelled woodsmoke.

Fire?

Fire!

She sat bolt upright. Over the foot of the bed she saw orange flames on the floor across the room. It took her a long moment to realize that they were confined within the stones of a fireplace.

Relief ran like warm water over her skin . . . until she remembered that there was no fireplace in her room.

Where was she, then?

A shadow moved, and she heard a trickling splash of water again. Her line of sight was blocked by the corner of the curtained four-poster bed she was in—an unfamiliar bed, not the small twin in which she'd gone to sleep. She crawled cautiously toward the foot of the bed to take a look.

A naked young man slouched inside a round wooden tub, knees drawn up, his eyes closed, a sea sponge loosely clasped in one lax hand atop a knee. The water could not fully tame his hair, its bronze curls lying thick around his face. Firelight touched his features, and Caitlyn had a flash of memory: this boy, riding a horse across the countryside with a group of companions, turning to look in her direction as if he knew he were being followed. *The Knight of Cups.*

"Raphael," she whispered, the name emerging from her throat before she even recognized it. Of course. She was with Raphael. With the logic of a dreaming mind, she accepted her presence in his room as something that made sense.

"What is it now?" Raphael said in Italian, eyes still closed.

He'd heard her! Her dreaming mind knew that she didn't speak Italian, but for some reason the meaning of his words was clear to her, forming in her head as he spoke.

"Please, I told you. I'm not hungry," he said. "If you've brought food, take it away. All I need is some time to myself."

Caitlyn hid behind one of the curtains by the post at the end of the bed, her heart racing. She peered out at Raphael. What was he going to think if he caught her in his bed, spying on him in his bath? He might think she was infatuated with him. Her soul cringed at the embarrassing thought. She had to get out of there before he saw her.

The fire crackled. Raphael's brow puckered and he opened his eyes. "Beneto?" He turned around in the tub, water sloshing, and searched the shadows near the door. "Ursino?"

Finding nothing, he shrugged to himself and sank down lower in the bath, closing his eyes again. "Wonderful. Now I'm hearing things."

This might be her only chance. She slid off the edge of the bed, dropping to all fours. She started to crawl toward the door, cursing silently as her long white nightgown got caught under her knees.

She made it five feet, ten feet, fifteen . . . She could see the handle of the door, a wrought-iron lever with a decorative spiral of metal at the end. She started to get to her feet, her back hunched.

"Stop!" Raphael shouted, and there was a sloshing splash of water.

Caitlyn yelped and sprang for the door, looking over her shoulder as she reached it and yanked on the latch.

He was right behind her, wet and angry, a towel loosely hung around his waist. He was fast—too fast. Caitlyn shrieked, and fumbled with the latch.

"I said, stop!" He switched to French. "Stop!"

The handle turned and she started to pull open the heavy door, but then he was upon her. He slammed the door shut with the side of his body, drops of water from his wet hair hitting her face.

Caitlyn yelped and danced out of his reach, running toward the bed like a frightened rabbit. She jumped onto the mattress and scrambled across.

The mattress *whumphed* as he leaped onto it, and then his hands were on one of her ankles. With one strong jerk he pulled her back to the center of the bed, her nightgown riding up her legs, and threw himself down on top of her, pinning her. He grabbed her wrists and held them above her head in one strong hand, while with the other he roughly searched her body.

"What did you take? Were you trying to steal the heart? Who sent you?"

She panicked. "Get your hands off me!" she cried with a French fluency unknown in her waking life, and bucked beneath him. "Stop it!" She raised her head and tried to bite him, snapping her teeth at his neck.

"Enough!" he shouted at her. He ceased his search and put his palm against her forehead, using it to pin her head down and keep her teeth far from his neck. He stared into her eyes, the force of his gaze turning her panic into something deeper and more frightened. She went still, sensing something dangerous in him.

"Who are you?" he asked in French, his voice low, but with a current of intensity in it that warned her she must answer.

"Caitlyn," she gasped, her breath hard to find beneath his body weight and her own fear.

"Why are you in my room?"

She goggled at him. What could she possibly say?

He gave her a shake. "Why are you here?"

"To . . . uh . . . ," she fumbled, and then inspiration struck. "I, uh, I'm a servant and thought you might need help with your bath."

He stared at her a long moment, and then the severity of his face softened into doubt. His hand on her forehead eased its pressure, and then slid gently down the side of her face, caressing her cheek. "Who sent you? Was it Giovanni? Or Philippe? Did they tell you I needed company?"

"No one sent me."

A loud rapping at the door interrupted them. "Raphael?" a male voice called. "Are you all right?"

Panic flushed anew through Caitlyn, irrational thoughts of Madame Snowe and the rules against boys flooding her mind. "Don't let him see me! I can't be found alone with a boy! Please, I'll be in so much trouble!"

He released her, and she climbed off the opposite side of the bed and hid in the shadows and curtains at the head, standing stiff as a bedpost within the brocade drapery. She closed her eyes and wished the person at the door away.

There was silence in the room. Caitlyn waited to hear Raphael or the other's voice, but the seconds stretched into minutes and there was no sound. They were gone.

She realized with a sinking dread that she wasn't in the room with Raphael anymore. She couldn't hear her own breathing anymore, or feel her heart in her chest. She was somewhere else, somewhere bad.

No, not again . . .

Cold seeped over her skin, like frost on glass. She had the vertiginous sensation of falling, and spread her arms, grabbing for something to hold. She gripped something cold and damp that gave way beneath her fingers, and even though she knew what was waiting for her she opened her eyes.

The moment she did, the sound hit her: screeching screams of terror, ripped from an abyss of the soul. This time they came from a thin girl as transparent as smoke. Her hair hung in wet tangles around her pale face, her mouth stretched wide as she screamed. She clawed at Caitlyn, her fingers bent like talons, her scrawny arms moving with fierce, desperate speed.

Caitlyn screamed.

The sound of her own voice broke through her sleep, knocking her abruptly into the waking world. She could feel the tail end of her scream in her throat even as she sat up and fumbled for the switch on her lamp.

Amalia was already out of bed and halfway across the room toward her. "Are you okay? *Mein Gott,* you gave me a fright!"

"Sorry! I'm so sorry! I was having a nightmare." She steadied herself and tried to calm her rapid breathing.

"I should think so! Are you all right?"

"Yes, yes, I'm fine. I'm sorry I woke you."

Amalia waved away the thought. "We cannot control our dreams."

Caitlyn rubbed her face with her shaking hands, feeling the cold slick sweat of fear.

Amalia went back to her bed. "Do you want to talk about it? What was it about?"

Caitlyn bunched up her pillow and held it to her chest for comfort. "It wasn't really about anything. It never is."

"You have these nightmares often?"

Caitlyn shrugged one shoulder. "I had hoped not to have any here," she evaded. "Maybe I'll need to buy you earplugs?" she joked.

Amalia settled back into her pillow. "If it becomes a problem, you can take sleeping pills, yes?" she said, and again Caitlyn was not sure whether she was serious or joking.

"It shouldn't be a problem," she said, hoping it would become the truth. "I'm just tense. New place, new people. You know."

"I sometimes dream that I have an exam for which I'm not prepared, and once I even dreamed that a tiger was trying to eat me, but I don't think I've ever had such a bad dream that I woke up screaming. What is it that scares you so badly?"

"Things ... that want to hurt me."

"What things?"

She shook her head. "I don't know what they are, really."

Amalia's eyebrows rose. "But you suspect?"

"They *look* like some type of . . . well, some type of ghost, or evil spirit. Just in my dreams, of course. I know they aren't real," she fibbed. She wasn't sure of that, at all.

"It's good they aren't real. You'd be in trouble, if they were." Amalia smiled. "Castles are always full of ghosts."

"Then thank heavens these exist only in my imagination," Caitlyn said faintly. She turned off her light and lay back down, staring into the dark, trying to shove the Screechers out of her mind and think instead of the fragment of dream she remembered from *before* that screeching, clawing girl had made her appearance.

Raphael.

It was the second time she'd dreamed of him in the space of a day, and each time she'd thought of the Knight of Cups. For a moment she could hear the rich timbre of his voice, and see his hazel eyes staring intently into her own. She could feel the heat of his palm pressed against her forehead, his touch softening to a caress along her cheek.

Who was he? And was he real?

And how could he possibly be her Knight of Cups if he existed only in her dreams?

A tear trickled out the corner of her eye. It didn't matter.

The Screechers had followed her. An ocean hadn't stopped them. Nothing ever would.

CHAPTER
Seven

"*Entrez!*"

Caitlyn put a restraining hand over the twitch in her eyelid, willing it to stop, then pushed open the heavy oak door to Madame Snowe's office. It was nine A.M., and she was right on time for her appointment. She stepped into a space whose warm coziness was at odds with the icy composure of the headmistress.

Oriental carpets in deep reds and blues covered the stone floor. One long wall was composed of leaded-glass windows looking out over the castle grounds and, beyond, the valley of the Dordogne. Two of the other walls were paneled in dark wood, like Caitlyn's bedroom.

The remaining wall was taken up by an immense fireplace, in which flames burned merrily. On the tall stone overmantel hung a gold-framed portrait of a woman in historical dress: a strawberry-blond noblewoman, her braided hair pinned up in a coronet, pearl drop earrings dangling from her lobes. Her face was a perfect oval, her dark eyes filled with knowledge, a hint of a smile playing on her lips. She wore a rose satin dress with puffed sleeves, a ruby-and-gold necklace, and on her lap a book lay open, one of her long-fingered hands holding her place.

Caitlyn was drawn to the portrait, her feet taking her toward it in complete and inadvertent disregard for Madame Snowe, who was waiting behind her desk. The portrait was obviously an original and must have been several hundred years old. Something about it teased at her memory: a feeling of a dream forgotten, or a place she had been.

"You like the painting?" Madame Snowe asked, getting up from her desk and coming to join Caitlyn at the fire.

"It reminds me of something. I can't think what." Caitlyn cocked her head, and then suddenly the answer came to her. "I know!"

Madame Snowe studied her face. "You do?"

"I have a poster in my room at home, of a painting hanging in a museum in Italy. It's a portrait of a girl in white, named Bia. It was painted by someone called Bronzino, and it's called *The Pearl*."

"*La Perla*," Madame Snowe said, her expression as coolly composed as that of the woman in the painting above the fire, but intense interest was dancing in her eyes.

"Yes!"

"This painting was done by Agnolo Bronzino as well, in 1559."

Caitlyn felt a bubble of delight and was pleased with herself. She wasn't such a hick, after all! "Really? I must have recognized something about the style."

"Or perhaps it was the sitter you recognized. *La Perla* is a portrait of Bianca de' Medici as a girl. This, too, is a portrait of Bianca de' Medici, as a woman."

Caitlyn stared at the portrait. It was kind of a dramatic coincidence. *Hey, Bia. Are you following me?* "Who was she?"

"Art historians know *La Perla* as a courtesan in sixteenth-century Florence. She was more than that, though: she was an illegitimate child of Cosimo the Great, the man who was once head of the de' Medici family of Italy. She was burned at the stake for heresy in 1572."

Caitlyn's eyelid twitched. "Heresy?"

"In her case, it meant witchcraft. Her wealth and high-powered connections could not save her from Pope Pius V. He was the one who ordered her burning."

Caitlyn remembered the image she'd drawn in her journal on the day she found out she'd been accepted to the Fortune School: a wise woman, being burned at the stake. A shiver ran up her spine, and she broke her gaze from that of the painting and looked at Madame Snowe. "What did Bianca do that made him think she was a witch?"

Madame Snowe's lips twisted wryly. "Bianca had become the mistress of Cardinal Rebiba, Grand Inquisitor of the Roman Inquisition."

Caitlyn's eyes went round. "She was sleeping with a *cardinal*?! I thought they were supposed to be celibate."

"They were, but even some popes were known to have mistresses and children. People looked the other way; at least, until Pope Pius came into power. He was a different breed, much more strict, and unfortunately for Bianca, Pius believed that only a witch could turn a man such as Cardinal Rebiba away from his vows to God. He was, after all, a Grand Inquisitor. He was supposed to be above tawdry scandals." Madame Snowe paused thoughtfully, then asked, "Do you believe in witches, Caitlyn?"

"If you mean pointy black hats and flying on broomsticks, and cursing the neighbor's cow so it won't give milk, no," Caitlyn said, still lost in shock over the idea of cardinals and popes having mistresses.

"If you mean women who might have intuitive abilities that go beyond the understanding of most men, then yes."

"Do you think that *you* have any such abilities?"

Caitlyn frowned and shook her head, surprised by the question. "Not that I know of."

"Oh." The single sound held a world of disappointment. "*Tant pis*. Too bad. I've always thought it would be useful to have such gifts, haven't you?"

Caitlyn murmured a noncommittal sound, thinking of her mother. Being able to tell the future hadn't seemed to do her very much good.

Caitlyn turned back to the painting, admiring Bianca de' Medici's luminous skin and utter self-possession. She glanced at Madame Snowe. "You look a little like her."

Madame Snowe flashed a smile, the first genuine one Caitlyn had seen on her. "I do, don't I?"

"Is she an ancestor?"

"Everyone in Europe is related to one another; we're all just an extended family," she said lightly. "I've heard that at least half of us can claim descent from Charlemagne! So Bianca could be as closely related to me as she is to you. But enough of this. Come, sit down."

Madame Snowe returned to her broad, ebonized desk with ornate gilt legs. Its surface held a flat-screen computer monitor, a sleek phone, and nothing else. It was as perfectly elegant as Madame Snowe herself. Today she wore a dark green tweed skirt suit and ivory blouse, with long strands of amber and coral beads falling in cascades around her neck. She gestured to an ebony chair in front of the desk.

Caitlyn sat on the edge of the chair's gold satin cushion, her back straight. She'd woken at six this morning to study the rules and general information of the Fortune School. She'd even memorized the offenses that would result in immediate expulsion from the school, certain that Madame Snowe would test her.

"I trust you have settled in?" Madame Snowe asked.

"Yes, ma'am."

"Good." She pressed her fingertips together, almost as if praying, and tapped the points lightly against her chin as she studied Caitlyn for a long moment. "You are an exceptionally fortunate young woman, Caitlyn, in being chosen to be the first scholarship student this school has accepted."

Caitlyn's lips parted in surprise. "The first?"

Madame Snowe dropped her hands. "We—and by 'we' I mean the Sisterhood of Fortuna, who are the regents of the school—see a unique potential in you, a potential that seemed unlikely to emerge under the tutelage of your public high school teachers in Oregon. It will be your responsibility to prove us correct, and not to make us regret our choice. We have high expectations of you."

"Er, exactly what type of potential do you see in me?" Caitlyn asked, both confused and flattered. She'd never shown the least flash of brilliance at anything.

"It is not easily quantifiable. It is a combination of character traits and aptitudes that we feel is uniquely suited to the goals of the Fortune School."

"Really? My parents think I'm maladjusted and antisocial."

Madame Snowe chuckled. "I suppose they'd prefer you to try out for the basketball team and run for student council?"

Caitlyn nodded. "They'd be thrilled."

"The students who enjoy such things will find their own way in the world. But those who are fundamentally different in their outlook—like you—are the ones who can bring unique talents into play, if given the proper opportunities. There is a price to these opportunities, however." Madame Snowe met and held Caitlyn's gaze for an uncomfortably long moment.

"What is it?" Caitlyn asked nervously, her voice quavering.

Madame Snowe smiled slightly. "The price is a loss of choice about your future. You will take the courses that the Sisterhood has chosen for you, and when you leave us you will attend the university of our choice—at our expense—where you will also study what we choose for you."

"But why would you want to do that?" Caitlyn asked, bewildered.

"We don't want to see our investment in you wasted."

"You don't think I can choose for myself what my future should be?"

"We will not make choices that are antithetical to your nature. As likely as not, they will be the same choices you would make for yourself."

"But if they're not?" Caitlyn asked, growing alarmed. She was feeling the bars of restriction closing around her.

Madame Snowe folded her hands on top of the desk. "I am asking you to make an adult decision right now, Caitlyn. You can take the free, superior education we offer, and with it our guidance, or you can return to Oregon and make your own way."

Caitlyn's stomach dropped. She couldn't go back to Spring Creek. "Why didn't you tell me this before I came? I don't remember seeing anything about this in all that paperwork."

"We did state that you must accept our decisions about your curriculum, both present and future. I am simply elaborating upon that clause."

"I thought you meant how many math classes I had to take, or credits of PE!" She frowned. "Wait a minute. Did I hear you just say you'd pay my college tuition?"

"And room and board. A 'free ride,' I believe you call it in the States."

Caitlyn let the words sink in. She'd always thought that her path to a higher education would be two years at a community college before transferring to a state school. Part-time jobs, school loans, roommates, and cheap apartments: she knew that that was what lay ahead if she went back home.

Having everything paid for by someone else would be so much better.

"It's the same decision the children of the rich are often forced to face," Madame Snowe said. "Should they accept their parents' money and live according to their rules, or seek the freedom of fending for themselves? Money is power, whether we like it or not, and it can persuade us to take actions we find abhorrent."

"You don't sound as if you're trying to persuade me to stay."

"As I said, Caitlyn, I'm asking you to make an adult decision. I will also expect you to abide by that decision, once made. There will be no going back on your word. You will be expected to give your full energies to the work we set before you. There will be no slacking off. Do you accept?"

Caitlyn hardly needed to think about it. Surely she could bear the educational control of this Sisterhood of Fortuna for a few years; they did, after all, think she had potential.

They believed in her. No one else ever had.

"I accept."

Madame Snowe smiled. "Good girl."

"So do I have to sign a blood oath or something?"

"We're a modern institution. A DNA swab will do."

Caitlyn laughed, but Madame Snowe's face remained impassive as she went to the wall and pressed a spot in the paneling that popped open a hidden cabinet door. She retrieved a narrow tube with an oversize Q-tip-style swab inside, and handed the swab to Caitlyn.

"Rub this on the inside of your cheek, please."

Caitlyn gaped at it. "Are you serious? Why?"

"It will allow us to run tests to determine if you are vulnerable to several diseases, and to take preventive measures if necessary. We would have gathered this information when you had your routine physical in Oregon, with your regular doctor, but your father refused to sign the release we sent."

Uneasiness squirmed inside Caitlyn, and a grudging respect for her father and his instinctive paranoia. "I didn't sign away my privacy, you know. I don't see what my genetic code has to do with my attending the Fortune School."

"You refuse to do this simple thing for us, when it could save your life?"

"You really meant it about protecting your investment, didn't you?" Caitlyn asked, reluctantly taking the swab and rubbing it in her mouth before returning it to Madame Snowe.

"You have the potential for a long, rewarding life ahead of you. You may have come from nothing, but fifty years from now—yes, fifty; you should still be vital and active then—you may find yourself to be a woman of influence in the world. Perhaps you will lead a country, or be an adviser in a government cabinet. You may head a charity organization that saves the lives of hundreds of thousands. Or perhaps you'll move in circles where your opinion is whispered into important ears, and subtly shapes international events. It would be a great loss to the world were you to die young."

"Those are kind of big expectations."

"To us, they do not seem so. You see, then, why the Sisterhood will be choosing your courses for you. You know neither what you're capable of, or what you were meant to do."

"Isn't that something most people figure out on their own? I thought it was part of growing up, to find your passion."

Madame Snowe chuckled. "That's a pretty bubble of myth that needs popping. Most people never feel a calling for a specific career. They stumble upon work that is more or less compatible with their personalities and abilities, and rise as far as their competence—or incompetence—will allow them.

"The Sisterhood, however, does not wish to see you stumble into a position of mediocrity. We will help you live a life of consequence, and you will repay tenfold to the world that which we give you now, in your youth."

Caitlyn bit her lip. This Sisterhood thought she was capable of far more than seemed realistic, but what was she going to do? Turn down a couple hundred thousand dollars' worth of education because of self-doubt? She wasn't stupid!

Madame Snowe pulled a keyboard shelf from under her desk and tapped a few keys. She slid it back and turned the monitor to face Caitlyn.

The screen showed the home page of the Fortune School. There was the familiar picture of the castle, the name of the school, and beside the name the figure of a blindfolded woman in a blue gown, her hand on a large wooden wheel. A sash floated across her torso, inscribed with a Latin phrase:

Fortuna Imperatrix Mundi

Caitlyn had noticed the figure before, but hadn't paid it any attention. Her eyes had all been for the castle.

"Do you understand the meaning of this figure?" Madame Snowe asked.

Caitlyn shook her head.

"She is an ancient symbol, going back to the Greeks in recorded history; although she assuredly originated long before that. The Latin translation is, 'Fortune, Empress of the World.' What does that say to you?"

Caitlyn looked closely at the image. Fortune was a woman? And she stood beside a wheel.

Fortune and her wheel. Fortune's wheel.

The Wheel of Fortune.

A chill ran over Caitlyn's skin. How had she not seen it? It was so obvious! The tarot card from her mother; it had been telling her that she was meant to come here, to the Fortune School!

"Fortune, Empress of the World," Caitlyn said, repeating Madame Snowe's translation of the Latin on Fortune's sash. "I think it means that we are all subject to the whims of Fortune."

"Yes, we're all on the *Rota Fortunae*, Fortune's wheel," Madame Snowe said. "The message is that even the mightiest may be laid low, and the lowliest rise. *Fortune rota volvitur*: the wheel of Fortune turns. We intend for you to ride the wheel upward, Caitlyn."

"Was the castle named for Fortune's wheel?"

"No. The castle has been Château de la Fortune since the thirteenth century. One of the early owners, Simon de Gagéac, was a Knight Templar—"

"A Knight Templar owned the castle?" Caitlyn interrupted. "They were something to do with the Crusades, weren't they?" They'd come up in several historical novels she'd read, and in *The Da Vinci Code*.

Madame Snowe nodded. "Their original mission was to protect pilgrims on the way to the Holy Land, but they also joined in the Crusades. Simon de Gagéac, legend says, brought home an immense treasure from the Holy Land. He became convinced that the treasure was cursed, though, and hid it somewhere in the castle, swearing that he would protect the world from its evil influence."

"Cool!" Caitlyn said.

"Perhaps the treasure *was* cursed, though. Simon de Gagéac went insane."

"What happened to the treasure?"

"*Alors*, that's how the castle got its name. The castle and the secret of the treasure's location was passed down for several generations, but then the family line died out, and with it the location of the treasure."

"So it's still here?"

Madame Snowe raised a brow. "It is a story, Caitlyn. The world is full of tales of buried treasure, and few of them have proved true." Her face softened. "But still. I do like to believe that there is something special here at Château de la Fortune, something *hidden at the heart of it*," she said with special emphasis, "that gives strength to what we of the Sisterhood try to achieve for the young women within these walls." She looked at Caitlyn expectantly.

Hidden at the heart . . .

Were you trying to steal the heart? Caitlyn heard the words in her head, spoken roughly by Raphael.

A shiver went through her body.

Madame Snowe narrowed her eyes. "Is something the matter?"

She shook her head and tried to smile. "No." Her eyelid twitched. "But I'm not sure that a treasure with a curse on it is such a great thing to have as the heart of your castle."

Madame Snowe's expression tightened in disapproval. "We consider it an inspiration. 'Fortune' can mean great wealth, or it can mean fate. We of the Sisterhood of Fortuna choose to educate young women so that they may control both their wealth and their destinies. We wish them to turn their own wheels of fortune to their best advantage, and to the advantage of the world we live in. We expect *you*, Caitlyn, to become a force for change in the world, and not a hapless victim on the rim of the wheel."

Caitlyn swallowed, feeling small beneath the force of Madame Snowe's convictions. "I promise to do my best not to become Fortune's roadkill."

"An apt, if not particularly lovely, metaphor," Madame Snowe said, her lips twitching. "We seem to understand each other. You may go now."

Caitlyn blinked, surprised that the interview was over. "You don't want to go over the school rules, or any of that?"

"Did you read them all thoroughly?"

"Yes, of course."

"Did you have any questions about them?"

"No."

"Then I see no need to review them, do you? You may go."

Taken off guard, Caitlyn rose and started to leave, then stopped and turned halfway around. "I—"

"Yes, Caitlyn?"

"I want to thank you, and the Sisterhood of Fortuna, for giving me this chance. It means . . . everything to me. I will do my best not to disappoint you."

"We know you will. I want to make this clear, though: you have been given a great opportunity, and we expect your efforts to be equally as great in return. If you disappoint us, you will be expelled. Do you understand?"

Caitlyn's eyelid twitched. "Yes."

Madame Snowe shooed her out with a flick of her fingers.

Caitlyn went, eyes rising to meet those of Bianca de' Medici as she passed the portrait. The noblewoman's supercilious expression seemed to ask, *Are you sure you can fulfill those big expectations?*

No, not at all, Caitlyn silently answered. *But I'll work until my dying breath, trying.*

Caitlyn fled the room, sure of only one thing: she could not afford to disappoint Madame Snowe.

CHAPTER
Eight

The next two and a half weeks passed in a blur for Caitlyn. Amalia took her under her wing and gave her a tour of the school, introduced her to girls whose names Caitlyn promptly forgot, and showed her how to take care of everything from her laundry to refreshing her toiletry supplies.

Once classes started, Caitlyn immediately found herself drowning in a sea of reading and homework. Amalia showed her quiet places to study and, by her own studious example, helped Caitlyn buckle down to the work and plow forward.

Caitlyn was so frightened of disappointing Madame Snowe, she barely allowed herself time to breathe between waking and sleeping. She devoted herself to schoolwork with an obsession that would have stunned her teachers back home. It was only in the stolen, solitary moments—while taking a shower, or when she lay down her head at the end of the day—that her thoughts would drift to Raphael, and she'd feel a tug at her heart. She hadn't dreamed of him again, and each morning when her alarm clock went off, she awoke with the sense of an opportunity lost.

The Screechers, unfortunately, were more eager to pay her visits. Three more times, she'd woken Amalia with her screaming nightmares. The princess's remarkable patience was showing signs of wearing thin; Caitlyn was certain she'd heard Amalia mutter some very rude words the last time she'd been woken.

There had been no other dreams that she could recall, and she wondered why. Stress? The rigidity of her study schedule was starting to chafe, and she had reached her limit on adjusting herself to a new way of life. The term *culture shock* had new validity for her. The food, the people, the classes, the physical environment: everything was new, and it was wearing her out.

Take her class schedule: instead of having the same six or seven classes every day like at her high school, the Fortune School followed a plan similar to universities. On Mondays, Wednesdays, and Fridays Caitlyn had algebra, world history, French, and geology for an hour and a half each. On Tuesdays and Thursdays she had two hours each of English, French conversation lab, and art. And just to make things especially confusing, on Saturday mornings she had a riding lesson.

How was she supposed to keep track of all that?

Was it her fault that somehow, when she'd finished her lunch a few minutes ago, she'd gotten it into her head that today was Friday, not Thursday, and had gone to her geology classroom instead of the art studio?

And that, having realized her mistake, she got lost trying to find her way to her art class, and was now running around like a rat in a maze? Lost! After living in the castle for two and a half weeks! Madame Snowe was not going to like hearing that she'd been late to a class.

Caitlyn swore under her breath and dashed up the southeast spiral staircase; or at least she hoped it was the southeast staircase. There were four grand stone stairways in the castle, one in each corner, and she still wasn't sure which was which.

She blamed her mental breakdown on the horrible *salade Périgourdine* she'd had for lunch. For each meal, the Fortune School students took their plastic trays and filed through the kitchen at the end of the Great Hall. A menu, in French with no translation, was posted on the wall, and it was each girl's choice what she wanted to order. The cooks were local women with limited English, and a gruff impatience with girls who timidly mispronounced *cassoulet* or *soupe de chou-fleur*, or who asked what *ris de veau* was. Caitlyn quickly learned to get in line behind confident French speakers and copy whatever they said. Getting unknown food was better than holding up the line while a stocky, red-faced woman repeatedly said, "Eh?"

And thus the *salade Périgourdine*. The plate of lettuces, walnuts, tomatoes, dark meats, a slice of something that looked like light brown cheese, toast, and the little cup of jammy-looking stuff had seemed enticing. She'd sat down by Brigitte and dug in, spreading the soft brown cheese and jam on a piece of toast and taking a big bite.

Only, the brown stuff wasn't cheese. The taste of liver had filled her mouth, its texture as unctuous as butter. Caitlyn had gagged, but at Brigitte's questioning glance she twisted her grimace into a smile, chewing with what her grandmother had called "long teeth." It didn't stop the oozing liver from finding its way into every corner of her mouth, though, and the jam—a chunky fig concoction, the fig seeds popping loudly between her molars—was little help. At long last she swallowed, rinsing it down with half a glass of water.

"What is that?" she asked hoarsely, pointing to the remainder of her tan "cheese."

"It is *pâté de foie gras*. The best in France comes from here, the Périgord."

"But what is pah-tay deh fwah grah?" Caitlyn asked, mimicking Brigitte's pronunciation.

"It is a sort of paste of fatty goose or duck liver. Delicious, *non?*"

"Fatty liver?" Caitlyn chewed her lip, looking at the *pâté* still on her plate. "Do you want mine?"

"*Oui!*" Brigitte scooped it up with the point of her knife, then ate it off the blade. "And that is *magret de canard fumé*," she said, pointing to the paper-thin slices of meat still on Caitlyn's plate. "Smoked duck breast. And that," she said, pointing to small chunks of meat, "you must try that. My brother Thierry used to love it, and made me bring him cans of it whenever I came home."

Caitlyn warily stuck her fork into one of the chunks. It looked innocent, like regular meat. She put it in her mouth and chewed, and was immediately thrown back to childhood, when one Thanksgiving she'd been curious about what was cooking on the stove and, lifting the lid of a small pot, had stuck her nose into the steam and taken a huge sniff, only to discover that it was a collection of giblets being boiled for the cat.

"*Gésiers!*" Brigitte cried happily.

"Geh-zee-ay," Caitlyn repeated unhappily. It could only mean "gizzards."

"You are so lucky to come to the Périgord Noir for school. You will eat very well! None of your American 'amburgers and 'ot dogs here, only duck, duck, duck!" Brigitte quacked, and dissolved into giggles.

Hungry and with no prospect of normal food anytime soon, and with an apparently insane dining companion, Caitlyn had wanted to cry. It was the final straw in her load of culture shock. After that, was it any wonder that she hadn't been thinking straight, and got the days confused, and then gotten herself lost in the castle while trying to find her art class?

Caitlyn came to a tiny landing stuck to the side of the curving staircase wall and pushed open a heavy old oak door, its age-blackened beams banded with hammered iron. She jogged down the stone hallway beyond, looking for the double doors into the art studio.

She eventually reached the end of the hall, but there weren't any double doors. She squeaked in frustration and dashed halfway back down the hall, double-checking. Had she been mistaken about the double doors?

And where was everyone? She couldn't hear a single voice.

Caitlyn chose a random door and pushed it open. Gray light from the windows revealed a storage space packed with dusty bookshelves, boxes, and a dozen of the school's wooden chairs with attached small tables for taking notes.

Caitlyn whimpered. No wonder she couldn't hear any voices. Where the heck was she? She dashed through the furniture to the window, hoping to orient herself, her heart thudding in her ears.

The window looked out on the courtyard. The château was shaped like a hollow square, the cobbled courtyard taking up the middle. A few cars were parked there, and an elaborate stone well with an iron frame to hold the bucket sat toward one corner. The entry arch pierced the center of the east wing, and from the looks of things that arch was three stories down and directly beneath her window. The south wing of the castle, to Caitlyn's left, had a series of immense skylights in one section of the slanting roof that faced the courtyard.

The art studio.

Her heart lurched and thudded. "Crap!" She was in the wrong wing altogether! Her heart raced with panic, the sound of it filling her head and seeming to vibrate in her skull—*thu-THUMP, thu-THUMP!*—and then her vision dimmed, and she started to see stars.

Caitlyn dropped to her knees and put her head down, resting her forehead on the cool stone of the floor, hoping to prevent a faint. For a moment her heartbeat seemed to expand, the sound so loud that it felt like it was coming from *outside* her body, as if the heart belonged to someone else. She sensed a presence in the room, living inside that impossibly loud heartbeat . . . *and it was coming for her.*

Caitlyn whimpered again and squeezed her eyes shut, wrapping her arms over her head.

A deafening *thu-THUMP* filled the room, and then an utter silence that rang in her ears. A moment later Caitlyn's heart seemed to regain its usual quiet beat, and she released her pent-up breath. The feeling of light-headedness went away, and she cautiously peered out from under her arms. When she saw nothing but the storage room full of furniture, she got back to her feet, her hands shaking.

What had *that* all been about? What had that presence been?

As soon as she thought it, she started to doubt it. *A presence? Really, Caitlyn? It's probably just a panic attack.*

But reason couldn't chase the chill from her flesh. She scampered from the room, glad to shut the door behind her.

Five minutes later, out of breath but relatively composed, she slid between the double doors of the art studio and tried to blend into the milling herd of her classmates, who were adjusting easels and gathering drawing boards and paper from a rack.

"It's good of you to join us, Caitlyn," Monsieur Girard said without turning from the plywood platform where he was arranging a chair and pillow. He was a squat man with a round face and curly brown hair that made a thick doughnut around his bald spot. Like all her teachers except her French instructor, he spoke in English, it being the common language of the international student body.

"Sorry. I got lost."

He made a show of looking at the clock. "Lost in the woods, perhaps? Or on the road to Paris?"

77

"Sorry," she murmured again, shoulders hunched.

He sniffed dismissively. "Get set up," he said, and turned back to the chair and pillow.

"*Oui*, Monsieur," she agreed, relieved that a disdainful sniff was the limit of the repercussions for her tardiness. She looked around, trying to figure out exactly how she was supposed to be setting up. A couple easels to the left, Daniela was smirking at her.

Caitlyn looked away. She ate dinner every night with Amalia, Brigitte, and Daniela, and of the three Daniela was the only one who made subtly snarky comments apparently designed to keep Caitlyn in her place. Instead of being eager to broaden Caitlyn's experience, as Brigitte had proved herself to be at lunch, Daniela mocked her lack of sophistication. "You have never been to the Louvre?" Daniela had said. "You cannot count yourself a human being until you have spent at least a week there." "You do not ski? So what do you do in winter? Do you content yourself with building snowmen with children?" "English is a language lacking in poetry. It is a pity your native tongue is not beautiful, like Spanish. At the very least you should learn to speak French properly. Your accent is atrocious." Caitlyn couldn't decide if Daniela saw her as a threat to be neutralized, or a weakling to be tortured with the same glee with which a little boy would pull the wings off a fly.

The other students in the class hailed from Japan, Laos, Dubai, New Zealand, Sweden, France, and Bermuda. A girl with smooth ebony skin and hair in hundreds of tiny, waist-long braids caught Caitlyn's confused gaze. "Here, take this easel by me," the girl said in an English accent. She was from Ghana. Caitlyn could remember everyone's home country better than their names.

"Thanks!" she said gratefully.

"I'm Naomi."

"Caitlyn."

Naomi grinned. "So I hear."

Caitlyn groaned. "Why is Monsieur Girard so grumpy?" she whispered.

"You haven't noticed? It's his natural state."

Naomi showed her what she needed to set up. The last three sessions had been anatomy lectures and PowerPoint slide shows on art history; Monsieur Girard hadn't let them do any art. "So we're drawing today?" Caitlyn asked.

"Monsieur feels that we need to stop talking about art and start doing."

"It's about time! I've been dying to start drawing. It's about the only thing I'm any good at."

"Pride goeth before the fall," Naomi said wryly. "According to Monsieur Girard, no one can draw. Last term we did still-life drawings, and you should have seen his fury over an improperly shaded sphere."

Caitlyn swallowed hard. "So he's not the gentle, supportive sort of art teacher."

Naomi laughed. "No."

Monsieur Girard turned and glared at them, pinching his fingertips together in a Shut-it! gesture.

Caitlyn shut her mouth and exchanged a sidelong look with Naomi, whose eyes widened in a mock I'm-scared! look.

Caitlyn smothered a giggle.

Monsieur Girard closed the shades on the skylights and turned on a spotlight aimed at the platform, throwing the lines of the chair and the pillow into dramatic lights and shadows. The lighting simplified the lines and masses, and Caitlyn felt a spark of hope that she might not make an utter fool of herself trying to draw the chair, no matter how critical Monsieur Girard might be.

The door to the studio squeaked open, admitting one of the plump, middle-aged cooks from the kitchen. She was dressed only in an old cotton bathrobe, her hair still in its lunchroom bun. Caitlyn stared at her, alarmed. Had the woman gone mad?

Monsieur Girard welcomed the cook and then addressed the class. "We begin with thirty-second gesture drawings. I shall demonstrate. Madame Dupont, *s'il vous plaît?*"

Madame Dupont took off her robe, laid it on a stool, and stepped naked onto the platform. Caitlyn goggled, her mouth dropping open in shock. Madame Dupont's expression, however, was as blandly unconcerned as if she were fully clothed and standing on a street corner waiting for a bus.

Caitlyn was too stunned to do more than gape as embarrassment washed over her. She kept her eyes glued to Madame Dupont's face, but then the cook made eye contact with her, and Caitlyn felt herself flush an even deeper red. Her gaze skipped wildly over the danger zones of the cook's body, settling at last on the relative safety of her feet.

"*Allez,*" Monsieur Girard said. Go.

Madame Dupont stuck one leg in the air and spread her arms like an oversize bird in flight, utterly unconcerned with her exposed body. She didn't seem to care that the folds of her belly were out for all to see, that her breasts were unsupported, nor that her dimpled thighs had taken on a pitted look from the high contrast spotlight.

Caitlyn slowly shook her head in disbelief. This was *so* not like her high school art class back home.

"*Changez,*" Monsieur Girard said.

Dupont squatted and arched one arm above her head. Thirty seconds later, at Girard's order of "*Changez,*" she laid on her side. She was in her fourth pose before Caitlyn calmed down enough to look at what Monsieur Girard was doing.

At his easel, Girard was making wild scribbles of charcoal that loosely captured the shape of Dupont's positions. "It is the feel of the movement that you want to capture," Girard said, his arm moving in sweeps as he covered the paper with continuous black lines. "What is the spine doing? Where is the center of gravity? Which way does the head turn? What is the feeling of the pose? You must exaggerate. Do not give me this," he said, demonstrating a rigid up and down stick figure. "Give me movement."

Embarrassment began to give way to interest. Caitlyn and the other girls crowded around Monsieur Girard, watching rapt as the ungainly figure of the cook was translated into graceful looping lines on paper. Dupont's heavy belly and thick thighs became living lines that spoke of voluptuous grace and the glory of womanhood. Girard's skillful hand made obvious what Caitlyn had been too blind to see: the beauty of Madame Dupont.

Then it was their turn to draw. Caitlyn picked up her charcoal and stared hard at Dupont's body, no longer seeing private parts and varicose veins. She sought instead the line of Dupont's spine, the tilt of her hips, the lyrical swoops of her arms. She wanted to draw forth the beauty of the cook, just as Girard had done.

"Do not draw with your hand!" Monsieur Girard said, coming up beside Caitlyn and gripping both her wrist and shoulder. "Gesture drawings come from the shoulder!" He forced her into the movement he wanted, wielding her arm like a giant paintbrush. "You see? Much better."

"*Oui*," Caitlyn squeaked.

They moved on to a longer pose, Monsieur Girard working his way around the room to torment each student in turn.

"What are these ugly scribbles?" Caitlyn heard him saying to the Laotian girl.

"Shadowing?"

"You must unify your lines. Draw them all in the same direction. Parallel."

Caitlyn looked at her own drawing, full of scribbled shadows, and quickly went over them with parallel lines.

Girard moved on to his next victim. "You think that is the size of her head? Really?" he asked Daniela. "You think it is one tenth the size of her body? You are paying no attention to proportion. The head is one seventh to one eighth the height of the body."

"Of course. I know that. I'm just having trouble putting it on paper," Daniela said. "I'm a very good artist, but it's all locked in my head."

Monsieur Girard snorted quietly, then more loudly, the snort turning into a guffaw of derisive laughter. Caitlyn glanced up as he tapped Daniela on the forehead. "Locked in your head! I have a classroom of brilliant artists, but the art is locked in their heads! Ha! The only true artist who ever lived here was Antoine Fournier, for a brief time in the 1870s. It was he who put in the skylights for the studio. He did the painting of Fortuna in the Grand Salon, upon which the symbol for the school is based. Of course, Fournier said that it was that painting that forced him to leave the château."

The bait dangled for several seconds until Caitlyn finally bit. "How could a painting make him leave?"

"Because! Fournier said that his model for Fortuna was a ghost, a spirit who haunted him while he worked in his studio. She told him what to paint." Monsieur Girard threw up his hands. "*Alors!* What painter wants to be told what to put in his picture? There is such a thing as inspiration, as a muse, but a ghost goes too far."

Caitlyn froze. *A ghost. There* was *a ghost in the castle. It had been a real presence she'd felt!* Chills moved up and down her arms, and she felt the hair standing on the back of her neck.

Monsieur Girard grinned at the effect his story had had, and moved on, grunting disparagingly at another student's efforts. As he approached her, Caitlyn went back to work, afraid to be caught slacking. He came to stand behind her, watching her attempts, and despite her best efforts her arm slowed and then dropped as she was overcome with self-consciousness.

"Do you, too, have a brilliant artist locked in your head?" he asked.

"No. I'm beginning to think I don't know a thing about art."

"Class! Do you hear? She knows nothing about art! And she proves it in her drawing."

Caitlyn cringed.

"This," he went on, laying his hand upon her head, "is the proper state of mind for learning to draw. Your mind must be blank of your old ideas and old ways of seeing. You must start fresh, like a baby who has never seen the world." He dropped his hand from her head and pointed to the area she'd shaded with parallel lines. "This is nice."

"Thank you," Caitlyn said in soft surprise.

He nodded in acknowledgment. "Keep listening. With open ears, you will be one of the few who learn."

Caitlyn felt a stab of pride. Monsieur Girard's smallest compliment was worth a dozen times more than the gushing praise of a gentler person.

After class, Caitlyn and Naomi walked together back to the dormitory wing of the castle. It took up the top three floors of the west side of the box, which was the only side that came right up to the edge of the cliff. The other three sides of the square château were surrounded by formal gardens, a kitchen garden, riding stables, an open meadow, and, just to the south of the castle, a chapel perched atop the cliff. It was a world unto itself, sequestered inside the outer defensive walls. The village of Cazenac was a half mile from the base of the cliff, and the larger, historic town of Sarlat-la-Canéda was close enough that any girls with money for a taxi could go there for a day of shopping and restaurants.

"We have geology together, too, don't we?" Naomi said.

Caitlyn nodded. She liked Naomi's casual confidence; the girl didn't seem to care what anyone thought of her, and that made her strangely comfortable to be around. "How long have you been at the Fortune School?" Caitlyn asked, seeking a way to prolong the conversation.

"This is my second year. I'd gone to a boarding school outside London since I was ten, but my parents decided I'd be safer here."

"Safer from what?"

"Who knows!" Naomi rolled her eyes. "The evils of London, I assume. They imagine drug pushers and drunken parties, and don't want to see me in a tabloid, falling out of a car without my knickers."

"Why would anyone put you in a tabloid?"

"They wouldn't, I'm sure. But my mother is queen of the Ashanti tribe, and she thinks that everyone is looking at our family."

Caitlyn's brows shot up. "Queen? Jeez, everywhere I look around here there's a princess!"

Naomi laughed. "Which tells you we're nothing special. Being a princess is overrated."

Caitlyn doubted that.

"I'm first in line to be queen, but I don't want to be," Naomi went on, as blandly as if she were discussing not wanting to go into the family shoe repair business. "I want to go to university in the States, and then to law school. Someday I'd like to do international work for the rights of women."

"Wow." Caitlyn was impressed. It was such a noble goal, and Naomi would give up being queen for it! All she'd ever aspired to was getting away from Spring Creek; she hadn't spent a lot of time considering what she wanted to move *toward*.

What *did* she want to do with her life?

Of course, now the Sisterhood was going to decide that for her. It might not be her choice; she'd signed it away before she'd even begun. She frowned at the thought.

"What about you? How did you end up here?" Naomi asked.

"Scholarship," Caitlyn confessed.

"So you're a genius?"

"Far from it!"

"You're being modest. Why else would you get a scholarship?"

"Madame Snowe thinks I have potential."

"Then you must," she said simply.

Caitlyn smiled wryly. "If so, it's been thoroughly hidden for fifteen years."

Naomi laughed. "What about art? You did better than anyone else in class today. Maybe you'll be the next Rembrandt!"

Caitlyn shook her head, rejecting the compliment. "All I could see in my drawing was what I'd done wrong."

"That means you're a true artist: you're never satisfied." Naomi smiled and waved a casual good-bye, and headed to her room.

Caitlyn watched her go, then turned her feet toward her own room, lost in disquieting thoughts. What if she did decide that she wanted to study art seriously, and become an artist? Would the Sisterhood of Fortuna allow that?

Caitlyn was beginning to get an inkling that in agreeing to the Sisterhood's scholarship, she may have sold her soul to the devil.

Thoughts of the Sisterhood, though, reminded her that they were the Sisterhood of Fortuna, and it had been a *ghost* who told Antoine Fournier to paint the portrait of Fortuna in the Grand Salon.

Caitlyn had seen the painting before, but had not looked at it carefully. She was suddenly sure, though, that there was more there than had met her eye.

It was time for a second look.

CHAPTER
Nine

"What are you doing here so late at night?" someone asked.

Caitlyn jumped, and looked up from her book, squinting across the dim light of the Grand Salon. A moment later she smiled in pleased relief: it was Naomi.

"Are you hoping to win the blue ribbon for most diligent student?" Naomi asked.

"I didn't know there was one."

"There isn't." Naomi dropped one pajama-clad hip onto the edge of the desk where Caitlyn sat.

The Grand Salon was a vast living room on the second floor of the dormitory wing. The room had French doors going out to a wide balcony cantilevered out over the cliff. A massive fireplace was centered in the long wall, big enough to roast an ox in. At one end of the room was a flat-screen TV, while the other was dominated by the large painting of Fortuna by Antoine Fournier. In between the two ends, thick Oriental carpets, a grand piano, several desks, and three groupings of sofas and chairs filled the space. Bookshelves displayed the leather bindings of ancient tomes likely never touched by the Fortune School students, who used the space either for watching TV or studying.

"Amalia goes to bed early and can't sleep if I have my desk light on," Caitlyn said, which was true but only part of the story.

"It's past two A.M." Naomi looked at Caitlyn's book. "I *know* that *Northanger Abbey* is not engrossing enough to keep you awake this late."

"I'm enjoying it."

"You're going to start looking like this if you don't get enough sleep," Naomi said, and with her fingertips dragged down the skin beneath her eyes. "And you're pale."

Caitlyn closed the book and sat back. "Okay, I confess. I'm not awake just because of schoolwork. I have trouble with insomnia." Which was another way of saying that she was reluctant to turn out the lights and lay her head down, for fear that sleep would bring another visit from the Screechers. Another visit would mean more screaming, which would mean destroying the last ounce of patience that Amalia possessed.

Naomi's brows rose. "Then we have something in common."

"You're an insomniac, too?"

Naomi flashed a smile. "How else would I have found you here?"

"What keeps you awake?"

"My mother says I was born nocturnal." Naomi shrugged. "Who can say? But all night my mind churns. If it produced something worthwhile, I wouldn't mind."

"You don't take sleeping pills?" Caitlyn asked.

Naomi wrinkled her nose. "They leave me more groggy during the day than lack of sleep. You?"

She shook her head. "I'm prone to nightmares. The last thing I want is to be less likely to wake up from one."

"I've heard."

"Amalia told you?" Caitlyn asked, embarrassed and a little angry.

"Not me. Someone, who told someone, until everyone knew. That's how it works here. It's not easy to keep a secret."

"I suppose I should have expected that." There were only fifty-five girls in each grade. Class sizes averaged fifteen students, which meant no chance of sliding under the radar if you hadn't done your reading or if your incomprehension of quadratic equations was showing on your face. There were times in the past several days when Caitlyn had missed the relative anonymity of her public high school. "On the other hand, how many secrets worth keeping do a bunch of teenage girls locked up in a castle without boys actually have?"

Naomi chuckled. "More than you might think."

"Really? Spill!"

Naomi shook her head, her thin, long black braids sliding over her shoulders. "You'll have to discover them on your own. I listen to gossip, but I hoard it for myself." Naomi made a motion of zipping her lips and throwing away the key.

"You're just saying that to get me to tell you something juicy," Caitlyn said doubtfully, suddenly tempted to tell Naomi all about the Screechers, Raphael, her mother and her tarot cards, and anything else that she'd ever kept to herself.

"You've seen through my cunning plan."

Caitlyn laughed uneasily, feeling too aware of the temptation to tell all. "Did you come in here to study the painting by the great Fournier?" she asked, hoping to change the subject before she gave in to temptation. She felt like she could trust Naomi, but words once spoken couldn't be unsaid.

"The haunted painting. Ha! Monsieur Girard told that story last term, too." Naomi twisted to look at the painting, but it was hanging in shadows. She slid her hip off the desk and walked toward it.

After a moment Caitlyn followed. She had already had a quick second look at the painting, but nothing had sprung out at her, and the presence of other girls in the Grand Salon had made her too self-conscious to examine the painting closely. As the hours of the evening had crept onward and the other girls had left the Grand Salon for the night, shutting off lamps as they went, a disquieting awareness of the painting had begun to lurk in the back of Caitlyn's mind. By the time she was alone, she'd been afraid to cross the room to look at it again. It felt safer to hunker down with her book.

Naomi found the switch to the light aimed at the portrait and turned it on.

The painting, four feet wide by six feet tall, emerged from the gloom in a burst of pale pinks, turquoise, and gold. Fortuna in her flowing robes stood on a cloud beside a tall black wheel with twelve spokes. Gold disks marked both the hub at the center and the terminus of each spoke on the rim. Each disk along the rim was studded along its edge in a different color of gemstone, and had a different female face embossed in its center; for the second time, Caitlyn leaned close to see how the artist Fournier had created the illusion of three-dimensional faces and jewels with his oil paints. The disk at the hub of the wheel had no face; instead, a large ruby was set at its center.

Fortuna floated in a sky lit by the magic hour before sunset, cumulus clouds roiling behind her. On the ground beneath, to the left, the land shot up in a golden cliff, Château de la Fortune perched upon its edge. On the ground to the right, a black chasm opened in the earth, from which a dragon emerged. A knight in shining armor fought the dragon from the back of a horse, a white shield with a red cross on his arm, his lance piercing the dragon's throat.

Caitlyn's heart skipped a beat. The Knight of Cups? But no, this knight was warlike and had none of the beauty of Raphael.

Caitlyn took in Fortuna's strong body in her flowing light blue robes and *Fortuna Imperatrix Mundi* sash. Fortuna's pink lips were parted, as if about to speak, but the blindfold erased any hint of what she might have said. Her dark hair was coiled around her head in an elaborate arrangement of braids, except where a few long tresses floated free between her neck and shoulders, echoing the lines of the clouds. "Who do you suppose the knight is?"

Naomi expelled a breath of disbelief. "It's Saint George, of course."

"Hey, there's no 'of course,'" Caitlyn said, defensive. "I'm not religious. I don't know saints."

"Sorry! He's just so famous in Europe. He's the patron saint of England and a couple dozen other countries. You know, Saint George killing the dragon, et cetera." Naomi pointed to the shield. "The red cross of Saint George. You'll see it on the surcoats of the Knights Templar."

Caitlyn's ears perked. "The Knights Templar. So Saint George is in the painting because of that legend about a Templar having once owned the castle, and burying his stolen, cursed treasure under the château."

Naomi shrugged. "Yeah, I assume so."

"It would be cool if the treasure was still here, wouldn't it?"

"Sure, why not?" Naomi looked up at the painting, a hand on her hip, her head cocked. "You know, I'd wager that the entire idea of the Woman in Black got started right here, with this painting and Fournier's story about being haunted by a ghostly woman."

"The Woman in Black?"

Naomi gave her a sly look. "I'm not sure I should tell you about her, this late at night. You might never get to sleep. Are you afraid of ghosts?"

Caitlyn giggled nervously, thinking of the Screechers and the peculiar heartbeat in the storage room. "You have no idea. Positively terrified."

"Good!" Naomi switched off the portrait's light and went to the couch in front of the fireplace, curling up at one end.

Caitlyn joined her, tucking her feet under her and pulling a throw over her knees. She'd built a fire in the hearth earlier, keeping it stoked with the wood from the bin to one side. A primitive part of her hoped that fire would ward off evil spirits.

If nothing else, the light might. She'd learned years ago that her sleep was slightly less likely to be disturbed by apparitions if there was plenty of light; maybe it kept the Screechers away, or maybe it did something to her sleeping brain that didn't allow them to appear.

"So who is the Woman in Black?" Caitlyn asked.

"No one is quite sure," Naomi said in a quiet voice, as if afraid of being overheard by the shadows. "All anyone knows is that in the dead of night there is the sound of silk skirts rustling in the hallway, as of a woman walking quickly, searching for something or someone that she can never find."

"Silk skirts?" Caitlyn asked. Not heartbeats?

"Rustling. *Shh, shh, shh . . . ,*" Naomi said, her eyes dramatically wide. "The most popular version of the story is that she was a young woman waiting for her lover to come back from war, but he was killed in battle and his enemy took the castle, and then took her, too. She threw herself off the battlements to escape him, and now roams the castle for all eternity, dressed in the black of mourning and searching for her lost love, Raphael."

Caitlyn's breath stopped. *Raphael!*

She gaped at Naomi, and then the fire popped and she shivered.

"It's not *true*, Caitlyn!" Naomi said, laughing. "There's no such thing as ghosts."

Raphael. That name couldn't be a coincidence! Caitlyn pulled the throw blanket up to her chest, feeling chilled. "Has anyone seen the Woman in Black?"

"Well . . ." Naomi bit her lower lip. "First you must solemnly swear never to repeat this."

Caitlyn nodded. A mischievous smile curled on Naomi's lips. "Sometimes when I can't sleep, I wander all over the château. And you know how the halls are only dimly lit this time of night?"

Caitlyn nodded again.

"Well, Daniela caught sight of me once: she was on her way to the bathroom, and I was at the far end of the hall, almost in the dark, wearing dark blue pajamas and standing still. She stared at me with that cautious, rabbit-ready-to-run look of someone alarmed by what they see, but not quite certain *what* they see, you know? I remembered that she wore contacts, and realized that she had probably taken them out before going to bed. I must have looked like nothing more than a blurry, dark, human-shaped shadow to her. She stared and stared, and I don't know why, but I didn't say anything.

"And then I started walking toward her. Very slowly, you know, walking on the edges of my feet, not making a sound except where my satin pajamas rustled the slightest little bit."

Caitlyn leaned forward, appalled and curious both. "What'd she do?"

"She backed away a few steps, making a sort of gibbering sound, then turned and ran back to her room. The next morning it was all over the school that Daniela had seen the Woman in Black."

"Naomi, that's awful!" Caitlyn said, even as a small part of her was glad of Naomi's trick.

Naomi put the fingertips of one hand to her lips and widened her eyes in mock horror. "It *was* wicked of me, wasn't it? I don't think she's gone to the bathroom in the middle of the night since."

"Why'd you do it?"

"You've *met* Daniela."

"Yeah. Okay. I guess I don't need an explanation."

"Anyway, I didn't do her any harm. She's been milking the story for a year, eclipsing Mathilde Obermann, who was the last girl to have seen the Woman in Black."

"So there really *is* a ghost here?"

Naomi shook her head. "Mathilde's Woman in Black was no more real than Daniela's, I'm sure. She seems suggestible, and maybe not too bright. I'd think *I* would have seen the Woman in Black by now if she was real, considering all the time I spend wandering these halls in the middle of the night."

"You have a point," Caitlyn admitted.

Naomi yawned. "What do you think? Make a go at bed?"

"You go ahead. I'll wait until the fire's died down a bit more."

She shrugged. "Suit yourself. G'night."

"'Night."

When she was gone, Caitlyn wrapped herself in the throw blanket and scrunched down on the couch, watching the fire. Her eyelids grew heavy, and her mind went back to what Naomi had said about the Woman in Black calling for Raphael. What did it mean? It seemed like there should be an explanation, if she could only think of it.

Who was the Woman in Black?

Who was Raphael, for that matter? And why had she dreamed of him, and felt so certain that he was her Knight of Cups? It made no sense.

Despite the tumult in her mind, her eyelids drooped.

And then she heard his voice.

CHAPTER

Ten

Caitlyn found herself standing in shadows beneath wooden scaffolding up against one side of the castle, in the courtyard of Château de la Fortune. She recognized the well in the corner, with its distinctive wrought-iron dome housing the winch and bucket. It was sunset, the sky above painted in pale orange, and she could smell horses and stone dust, straw and woodsmoke. For a moment she was confused, but then her dreaming mind accepted her surroundings, making its own sense of her being there.

"You should have come with me, Ursino!" Raphael called out.

Caitlyn sucked in a breath and peered out around a beam of scaffolding. Raphael stood a couple feet away in doublet and trunk hose, and leather riding boots up to his knees. He had his hands on his hips, his face turned up to an open window on the second floor of the castle. A groom was leading his horse away, its hooves *clip-clopping* on the cobbles.

"It was a perfect evening for a ride," Raphael continued, unaware of her watching eyes. "You spend too much time indoors, reading!"

A man about ten years older, with brown hair and a narrow,

94

cadaverous face—Ursino, apparently—leaned out the upstairs window. "Better to fill my head than to leave it as empty as yours!" he taunted back.

"Women would rather a man had a full life than a full head, Ursino!"

"That shows how little either of you know," said an elegant, slender, black-haired man holding a rapier as he walked out of a doorway into the courtyard, followed by a shorter, stockier man. "It's a full purse they want."

The men all laughed, including Raphael. Caitlyn smirked. She wouldn't begrudge *Raphael* his laughter. With his shoulders relaxed and the smile on his lips, he looked gloriously alive and carefree.

The sound of laughter woke an elderly man, sitting on a bench near the wall, whom Caitlyn hadn't noticed earlier. He coughed and stirred, then looked around with the confusion of the freshly woken.

Ursino retreated back into the room beyond the window above, and Raphael turned his attention to the old man on the bench, walking over to him. Caitlyn shrank back into the shadows under the scaffolding, choosing to wait for Raphael to be alone.

"Beneto, you should go inside," she heard Raphael tell the old man. "It's not good for your bones to sit out here on cold stones. They'll ache tomorrow."

"The stones were being warmed by the sun when I first sat here," old Beneto said, a spark in his voice. He was bald except for wisps of white hair around the bottom of his skull, and he had a large hooked nose.

"But now the sun has gone," Raphael said gently, and Caitlyn could see that he cared about the old man. *Who were they to each other?* she wondered.

Beneto looked up at the sky. "So it has."

Raphael squatted down and picked up a stack of paper, a board, and a piece of red chalk from the ground near the bench and handed them to Beneto as the old man stood. Caitlyn caught a quick glimpse of a sketch upon the top sheet of paper; was the old man an artist? Beneto nodded his thanks as he took the things from Raphael, and then went slowly indoors, his movements stiff, his back bent with age.

Caitlyn heard a clanging and scraping of metal, and turned to watch as the slender black-haired man and the stocky one began fencing with rapiers in the center of the courtyard. They were both in their twenties, but the black-haired man moved with the grace of a dancer, making his opponent look like a lumbering ox in comparison.

Caitlyn glanced over at Raphael. He, too, was watching the men fence.

The stocky man lunged, but at the same moment the black-haired man stepped aside, twisted his wrist, and sent the other man's sword flying through the air. It landed with a clatter on the stones.

"Where did you learn *that?*" the stocky man complained, his face sour with defeat.

"From one of your countrymen," the slender man said. "Everyone knows that Italians are the finest swordsmen in the world, Giovanni."

Giovanni's expression lightened. "This is true, Philippe. We Italians are much better than the French," he said. "Generally speaking. Not today, perhaps." He put out his hand with a hint of reluctance, and the two men shook.

"Now it's your turn, Raphael!" Philippe said, suddenly spinning around and pointing his rapier at Raphael. Caitlyn gasped.

"Perhaps tomorrow, when I haven't just come in from a long ride," Raphael said.

Philippe advanced toward him, making feinting motions with his rapier. "When those assassins make another try for you, they will not care if you are tired or in the wrong clothes. If you do not practice, you will make it easy for them to dispatch you. Is that what you want?"

"God forbid you make it easy for an assassin," Giovanni said as he scooped up his sword and handed it to Raphael. "You wouldn't want to bore him."

"That *would* be a tragedy," Raphael agreed, taking the sword and tossing his hat aside. It landed at the base of the scaffolding, a few feet from Caitlyn. He got into position facing black-haired Philippe, and raised his blade. Caitlyn put her hands to her cheeks, almost afraid to watch.

"I agree with Giovanni. Assassins should at least break a sweat before they skewer you," Philippe said, and then he and Raphael engaged swords, the blades dancing against each other in short, violent flurries of motion. Caitlyn held her breath, but then just as suddenly as they'd begun, the two of them stepped out of each other's reach, each assessing the other's movements.

"I don't know"—Raphael said between breaths, his eyes locked on Philippe's every move—"of any assassin"—Raphael parried and thrusted, only to have Philippe dance aside and make his own thrust—"who attacks his target"—he lunged at Philippe. Philippe grinned as he knocked the sword from Raphael's hand, but the grin disappeared as Raphael continued toward him and his other hand appeared holding his dagger, the point of it held now at Philippe's throat—"with a rapier, when a dagger will do the job with much less effort," Raphael concluded.

Giovanni hooted in glee. Caitlyn silently cheered.

Philippe's look of surprise turned to one of appreciation. "You have a point," he said, but then in three quick moves knocked the dagger from Raphael's hand, twisted his arm behind his back, and kicked his feet out from under him. Raphael fell to the ground.

Caitlyn winced, and Giovanni grimaced.

"But in case of a dagger attack, you should know how to defend yourself even if you are without a weapon." Philippe's brow rose sardonically. "So as not to bore the assassins, of course."

Raphael rolled over and sat up, shaking his head but smiling. "You'll have to show me how you did that."

"Ah, I have interested the pupil at last! *Bon!* Tomorrow I will teach you. Right now, I want my dinner."

Raphael returned Giovanni's rapier, and Giovanni and Philippe headed into the castle. "Are you coming?" Giovanni asked Raphael from the doorway.

"In a minute."

"The colors change the same way every night," Giovanni said, nodding to the sky.

Raphael shook his head. "Then you have no eyes to see them."

Giovanni shrugged, and the two men disappeared inside. Raphael went to the center of the courtyard and, tilting his head back, watched as the orange sky darkened into greens and deep blues. Caitlyn watched him, entranced herself by the wonder on his face. She didn't want to disturb him.

At long last he lowered his gaze, and then his eye was caught by his hat, forgotten on the ground near the scaffolding. He came toward the scaffolding, and her. Caitlyn nervously clasped her hands together, trying to think of what to say to him. And then he was just a few feet from her, bending down to pick up the hat.

As he reached for it, Caitlyn heard a scraping sound of stone sliding on wood overhead. She looked up just as one of the boards of scaffolding above her came loose and its end tilted toward Raphael.

Her heart caught in her throat and she acted without thought, leaping from the shadows and shoving Raphael out of the way. He yelped in surprise and stumbled backward as a board and large stone block tumbled from above. Caitlyn felt the cold passage of air as they skimmed by her and smashed to the ground.

Raphael's shocked gaze focused on the shattered stone, and then rose to her. "You!"

Ursino instantly appeared again in the window above. "What was that?" he cried. "Raphael! Are you all right?"

Caitlyn instinctively sank back into the shadows under the scaffolding.

"It's nothing!" Raphael called back, his voice quavering. "An accident."

"Holy Mother, did that stone almost hit you?"

"It was an accident."

"You've been cursed with too many near-miss accidents of late!"

"Or blessed with protection from them."

"The workmen should be whipped for leaving that stone so precariously placed. I'm coming down to look at it."

"As you wish."

Raphael turned and sought Caitlyn in the shadows. His expression was impossible to read, but when he put out his hand to her, she hesitated for only a moment and then took it. It was warm and strong, and lightly callused.

He pulled her with him through a doorway and grabbed a

candle lantern just inside. Hurrying, he lit the way up a familiar spiral staircase, pulling her along at a run. Caitlyn grabbed up her rose satin skirts in her free hand to keep from tripping on the wedge-shaped, worn stone steps as she struggled to keep up.

A faint feeling of puzzlement flitted through her, and she glanced down at the satin in her hand. Was this her dress? She felt like she'd seen it before, on someone else. But who? When?

There was no time to figure it out. Raphael rushed her down a corridor and up another flight of stairs, dragged her halfway down a hallway, and then pushed open a door into a small storage room devoid of furnishings except for a few leather trunks banded with metal. For a brief moment, Caitlyn's mind filled it with old desks and chairs, bookshelves and boxes, and the sound of a beating heart. She shook her head to clear it, and the room returned to its near-empty state.

Raphael pulled her in and shut and barred the door behind them. Caitlyn was panting from the long dash up the stairs and down hallways, and from the sheer unexpectedness of what was happening.

Raphael lifted the lantern and looked at her. "You saved my life," he said in French. He had spoken Italian to the other men.

He thought she was French, she realized. Which made sense, since they were *in* France.

"Either that," he continued, "or you just tried to kill me."

Caitlyn shook her head, winded from the stairs, her heart pounding in her chest. "No! I pushed you out of the way!" she answered in French, with easy fluency. It felt as if she'd spoken it from birth.

"But had you tilted the board, first? That's what I want to know."

"No! Why would I?"

Raphael set the lantern on a trunk and stalked toward her, as slow and stealthy as a cat. She backed up, afraid of the look on his face. He did not look so carefree now; he looked instead like he might strangle the truth out of her. The pounding in her chest grew stronger.

"I wouldn't have expected a female assassin. Who sent you?" he demanded, standing virtually on top of her.

"No one!"

"Was it Pius?"

"Who?"

He snorted. "'Who?' Who do you think?"

A memory surfaced, the name of the man who had sentenced Bianca de' Medici to the pyre. "Pope Pius?"

"Is he the one who sent you?"

"No! No one sent me!" Caitlyn cried. Her heart felt as if it would explode from her chest.

"Was it that de' Medici witch?"

Her ears rang, and she felt light-headed. "Bianca?"

Raphael's face went white. He clenched his fist, and for a moment Caitlyn thought he was going to strike her. She threw up her arms to defend herself.

Seconds passed, and then she lowered her arms and saw him backing away from her in slow, stumbling steps. He suddenly sank to his haunches and dropped his face into his hands. Caitlyn heard him take a deep, rasping breath. His shoulders shook.

Was he crying?

She inched forward, uncertain whether to flee or to stay and comfort him. "I didn't have anything to do with that block falling," she said quietly. "I wouldn't hurt you."

The shaking of his shoulders stilled. He dropped his hands and looked up at her, assessing, and then his gaze dropped to her satin gown. A frown creased his brow, and he slowly shook his head as if unwilling to believe what he was seeing.

Caitlyn looked down at her bright skirts, and then smoothed them under her palms, puzzled at what the dress might mean to him. "I would like you to trust me," she said.

"I'm supposed to trust you, aren't I?" he asked hoarsely. "That's why you're wearing that dress. It's a message." He met her eyes. "Who *are* you?"

"I'm Caitlyn. I told you that before."

He shook his head and stood, then sat on one of the trunks. He stared at her, as if expecting her to do something.

She fidgeted under his gaze. "Er, the stone falling *was* an accident, wasn't it?" she asked.

"There have been a lot of accidents these past few months. I've either become distracted and clumsy, which is possible," he said with a weak smile, "or someone is helping ill fortune in her efforts to dispose of me."

"Someone's trying to kill you?! Who? Why?" Caitlyn's heart beat in sudden fear for him. The sound of it made an uneasy drumbeat in the back of her skull. *Thu-thump, thu-thump . . .*

"I'm not sure who's behind it," he said, but she sensed that he had an idea. "Tell me, how did you get in and out of my room two weeks ago?" he asked abruptly. "I didn't see you arrive or leave."

Caitlyn struggled to recall those moments in his bedroom. "I was hiding in the bed curtains, and then . . . I don't know what happened next. It was dark," was all she could think to say. She frowned. She knew that she *had* been in his room, and that she had then somehow *not* been in it, but she could not clearly recall any life or existence beyond the moments she had spent with him.

Who *was* she? He had asked her that question, but she suddenly realized that she did not know.

Raphael looked at her carefully, and then held out his hand, palm up, in invitation.

Caitlyn hesitated, and then inched forward. She laid her hand on his own. His thumb stroked over her knuckles, sending a shiver up her forearm. She met his eyes, deep and unfathomable in the dim light of the lantern. He tugged her toward him. She came, and stopped only when her skirts brushed against his knees. Her heart pounded so hard she thought he'd be able to hear it himself. *Thu-thump, thu-thump, thu-thump!*

"You're good at moving around in the shadows," he said softly, as if he didn't want to frighten her. "But you're not a servant, like you claimed. I asked around about you. No one knows of a servant named Caitlyn, or even of a servant with straight black hair."

She bit her lip. "I'm not a servant."

"I didn't think so. What are you?"

Her mind struggled to find an answer as he gazed at her, but she was distracted by his closeness.

"Do you even know?" he asked.

"Of course I know what I am," she lied. An answer suddenly came to her out of thin air. "I'm a student. Here."

"From the convent outside Cazenac?" he asked in surprise.

Caitlyn nodded slowly. Maybe that was right. She had a faint sense that she went to school with a bunch of girls. It was hard to think, though: the beating of her heart now seemed to be two hearts, out of synch with each other: *THU-THUMP thu-thump . . . THU-THUMP thu-thump THU-THUMP thu-thump . . .*

"Why did you come to me?"

"You're the Knight of Cups," she said without thought, the words emerging from her mouth of their own volition.

He blinked in surprise. "What does that mean?"

She shook her head. She didn't know what the words meant, only that they were true. "I didn't want you to see me, last time I was here. I didn't *mean* to spy on you in your bath. It just ... happened."

His mouth quirked. "How long *did* you spy?"

Caitlyn's cheeks heated. "No longer than I could help."

He chuckled, and tugged her a hair closer. Her knees bumped against his. "Last time you were here, you said you'd seen me earlier. When? Where?"

Her ears rang, the sound of two heartbeats almost drowning out her own voice as she spoke. "In the valley, riding with the others. You lost your hat."

His face went still. "I didn't see you."

"No. You couldn't."

"I felt someone watching me. You must have been hiding in the field, or the trees near the river."

"No, I was right behind you. I knocked your hat off."

The hand holding hers went cold, as if drained of blood. "The *wind* blew my hat off."

She didn't answer. Instead, she pulled her hand free of his and circled around the chest he sat on. He twisted to watch her, as far as he could, and then when he could turn no farther she rushed toward him and ran her fingers through the back of his hair, from nape to crown.

He shot off the chest and spun around, staring at her with his mouth agape.

"*I* knocked your hat off," she said with pride. "Not the wind!"

"She *did* send you," he whispered in awe.

The sound of the double heartbeats tolled in her head, a hundred times louder. Caitlyn winced and held her hands over her ears. She shook her head, trying to clear it of the sounds. The heartbeat that seemed to be her own was fading, but it left behind that second, alien percussion. Its volume rose.

"What's the matter?" he asked, his voice coming to her as if from a great distance. "Do you hear something?"

"A thumping sound."

"I don't hear it." He came close to her, examining her, as if looking for a key to who or what she really was.

She started to feel light-headed. The beating got faster, as if it was approaching. *THU-THUMP THU-THUMP!*

"Do you know who Bianca was?" he asked. His hazel eyes held hers.

Caitlyn anchored herself for a moment to that gaze, trying to block out the thumping heart sounds. "I know that she was burned as a witch."

"And?"

Caitlyn held out her hands, palms up, not knowing what he wanted her to say. The heartbeat came back full force, pounding against her eardrums, and she winced. "You really don't hear anything?" She looked around the room, seeking the source of the noise. It was driving her half mad. *THU-THUMP THU-THUMP THU-THUMP . . .*

"I hear nothing."

She tilted her head toward a wall. No, not there. She approached a chest. Not there, either. "Earlier, who did you mean by the de' Medici witch?" she asked.

"Catherine," he spit out. "Queen mother of France. Who else?"

"You hate her," Caitlyn said in uneasy wonder.

"Shouldn't I hate her? She holds my sisters captive."

"Why?"

He ignored the question. "*What* are you looking for?"

105

"The source of that thumping! It can't just be in my head!"
THU-THUMP-THU-THUMP!

"I still don't hear anything," he insisted.

"Why don't you rescue your sisters and take them somewhere safe?" she demanded. The heartbeat, she had to find where it was coming from and stop it!

"Take them where? It would have to be the ends of the earth, to escape Catherine's grasp."

THU-THUM-THU-THUM-THU-THUM! Caitlyn squeezed her temples with her fingertips, trying to block it out. "Why not take them there?"

"Where?"

Caitlyn made herself stand still. She tried to look sane.

"The ends of the earth. The Pacific coast of America. The New World."

He laughed. "There's nothing there but Spaniards and savages. I would do better to kill my sisters than bring them to such a place."

The "savages" comment piqued her. "There must be *somewhere* safe."

"England might be. But I need to find a fortune first."

"The Templar's fortune. Of course."

"You know about that? What do you know?" He grabbed her upper arms, holding her still. "Tell me!"

"*Where* is that noise coming from?" she wailed. "It's like there's an enormous heart in the middle of the room, beating, beating, beating! Can't you hear it?"

Raphael's face paled. "What did you say?"

A voice in the corridor called Raphael's name, and then in Italian, "Are you up here?"

"In here, Beneto!" Raphael shouted, and then to Caitlyn, "What did you say about a heart?"

"The beating! Where's it coming from?"

Beneto started to pound on the wood planks of the door. "Open up! Ursino told me what happened!"

Frustration filled Raphael's face, and then with a grunt of exasperation he let go of her arms and turned to open the door. "One moment, Beneto! I have someone in here who has information we can use."

As Raphael went to the door, Caitlyn dashed to the chest on which he'd been sitting earlier. The sound of the beating heart filled her head and chased out all thought. The black chest was half covered with ornate decorative bands, handles, and latches. With nimble fingers she pressed a series of hidden buttons and inconspicuous curlicues, her hands inexplicably knowing what to do. She could hear each touch move a mechanical part somewhere inside the chest. A moment later she flung open the lid, revealing the elaborate locking mechanism, a cage of wheels and sprockets that covered the entire underside of the lid.

A wool blanket covered the contents of the chest. With the heartbeat banging in her ears, her very body trembling with the force of sound, she tossed the blanket aside. In the depths of the chest, something softly glimmered.

Silence instantly consumed her, and the world faded to black.

CHAPTER
Eleven

Caitlyn felt a hand on her shoulder, and jerked awake.

"Child, did you spend all night here?" a German-accented voice asked.

Caitlyn's vision flickered between two scenes: she saw Greta's concerned, motherly face, and then the blanket coming away from the contents of the chest, revealing—

"Child?" Greta's face again filled her vision.

"Mmm?" Caitlyn mumbled, and tried to cling to sleep.

"It's almost eight. You have class in half an hour."

Caitlyn felt her mind shift into full consciousness, and with it the dream began to shred, its elements floating away from her grasp. As the meaning of "almost eight" sank into her brain, Caitlyn swore, scrambled off the couch, and dashed to the desk where her things were. She grabbed a pencil and her journal and sketched down images, desperate to capture the details of her dream before they disappeared entirely.

"Is there a problem between you and Amalia?" Greta asked.

Caitlyn put up her left hand, a finger raised to beg a moment.

Catherine de' Medici, she wrote on the edge of a page.

Beneto

Ursino

Falling stone

Sisters captive

Beating heart

When she had all she could think of, she finally looked up at Greta. "No problem with Amalia. I fell asleep studying, is all."

"Good sleep is as important as books. You will do better for your brain by sleeping in your own bed, at a decent hour."

"I'll try to remember that." Caitlyn gathered up her stuff. "And thank you for waking me."

Greta harrumphed. "You have no time for breakfast, even."

Caitlyn smiled. "I'll be okay." She hurried to her room to get dressed, her mind reviewing over and over the fragmented scenes she'd captured in her notes. She willed herself to remember them.

All through her algebra class, she replayed the scenes of her dream in her mind. She was surprised by how hard it was to remember, and by how much of what she did remember seemed tied to her waking life: the rose satin dress that she now recognized as identical to the one Bianca wore in the portrait in Madame Snowe's office; going to school with girls at a "convent"; the storeroom and the sound of a beating heart; the Templar treasure.

Catherine de' Medici, queen mother of France, however, was a name she didn't know, but it was one she could research. Had there been such a person? Or had Caitlyn's sleeping mind taken Bianca de' Medici's name and with it formed another?

Google would soon tell.

She had to wait until lunch to slip in a search on Catherine de' Medici, but the results came quickly. She was real.

Married to Henry II of France in 1547, and in power until her death in 1589, the Italian-born Caterina Maria Romula di Lorenzo de' Medici was despised by everybody, accused of murdering Jeanne d'Albret, Queen of Navarre, and of ordering a massacre of Huguenot guests who'd come to Paris for her own daughter's wedding. Her enemies called her a witch, a devotee of the dark arts who would consort with the devil to keep herself in power.

The confirmation sucked the wind from Caitlyn's lungs. She stared at the computer screen, almost not believing it.

She'd never heard of Catherine de' Medici before last night; she'd swear to it.

How had her dreaming mind known the name? How had she known Catherine was called a witch?

If the information hadn't come from her brain, it had to come from outside it. Raphael was the one who had given her Catherine's name.

Who *was* Raphael?

Maybe even more important, *what* was Raphael? He couldn't be a figment of her imagination who existed only in her own mind, if he'd told her about Catherine de' Medici. So what possibilities did that leave?

Caitlyn frowned. There weren't any possibilities. Not rational ones, anyway.

Was Raphael a real person? He'd have to be, if he was her Knight of Cups and they were meant to be together. If he was real, then where was he? Maybe he was a living person, meeting her in her dreams. Maybe she was having a psychic connection with some guy here in France, who was right this moment sitting at his own computer, trying to figure out who Caitlyn was. Maybe the dream world was their own virtual reality game, where their avatars sometimes met.

It was an idea, anyway.

There was another possibility, of course. Maybe Raphael *had* been a real person, but wasn't any longer.

A sensation like a cold wet hand slid down Caitlyn's spine. Could Raphael be a ghost?

She was tempted to talk to Naomi about it. If nothing else, Naomi would keep her thoughts grounded. On the other hand, Naomi might decide Caitlyn was a complete flake and not worth getting to know better, and Caitlyn could say good-bye to their friendship. Same with Amalia: Caitlyn was already on thin ice with the Liechtenstein princess, given all the times she'd woken her with her nightmares. Sharing fantasies of meeting sixteenth-century ghosts in her dreams didn't seem the right way to strengthen the bond between them.

Brigitte would probably be delighted by the story, but would not provide any help in figuring it out. And then she'd repeat it to everyone, not out of malice, but out of natural chattiness.

Talking to Daniela was out of the question.

Caitlyn sighed and felt a pang of loneliness. A moment later she put her fingers back to work on the keyboard. A search for Catherine's name with Raphael's turned up no obvious connection; hits all seemed about the Renaissance artist Raphael and his ties to the Florentine de' Medicis.

She didn't have time to investigate further. She wolfed down a lunch of seared duck breast and asparagus and hurried to her French class, her mind lost over four hundred years in the past.

"Caitlyn, *s'il vous plait!*" Madame said, whacking the blackboard with her stick, its end pointing to the irregular verb *devoir*, "to have to." She wanted Caitlyn to conjugate it.

Caitlyn felt the class's attention turn to her, and a clammy sweat broke out in her armpits. Her brain stopped in its tracks, unable to move under the pressure. A vague sense of having known how to speak French in her dreams tickled at her brain, but the skill was as lost to her in the waking world as was Raphael.

"*Devoir*," Caitlyn croaked. "Er. *Je dev? Tu dev?*"

Madame gaped at her, horrified.

Caitlyn shook her head; she knew those words were wrong. "Er . . . I mean, uh . . ." And then out of nowhere came, "*Egli deve, lei dovrebbe . . .*" These words felt right. *He must, she must . . .*

Several girls burst into laughter.

"*What?*" Caitlyn demanded.

"You're speaking Italian!" one girl shrieked, and collapsed into hysterical giggles.

Madame rolled her eyes and heaved a put-upon sigh.

Caitlyn shrank in her chair, confused and humiliated. She didn't *know* any Italian.

Madame wrote out *devoir* on the board and, whacking each conjugation with her stick as if by so doing she could beat the words into Caitlyn's brain, angrily enunciated each form and made Caitlyn repeat them, over and over, while the rest of the class snickered.

When the torture was over, Caitlyn subsided into the misery of the linguistically ungifted and struggled to focus on the lesson. Her disobedient mind, however, kept abandoning French grammar in favor of two unnerving questions: Who was Raphael? And why was he haunting her?

CHAPTER
Twelve

Caitlyn's riding lesson the next morning, Saturday, was destined to be even worse than the disastrous French lesson.

The day started well enough. With her mind still half lost in thoughts of Raphael, Caitlyn walked with Amalia through the chill morning air to the stables, where Amalia would practice dressage and Caitlyn and the other novices would get their first chance to saddle and ride a horse. The lesson the week before had been focused on the care of horses and tack, and Caitlyn was both excited and nervous finally to get to mount a horse.

"You've truly never ridden before?" Amalia asked her.

"Not in real life, but I used to have a recurring dream that I was friends with a pioneer girl in the 1800s, and we'd ride bareback together on her horse through the woods and fields."

"A dream doesn't count!"

"It felt very real at the time," Caitlyn said with mock seriousness. "I'm sure I learned all about riding a horse. How hard could it be?"

Amalia clucked her tongue and shook her head.

"I thought you were going to Sarlat today, with Daniela and Brigitte," Caitlyn said, changing the subject. Daniela had invited Amalia and Brigitte on the lunch and window-shopping outing during last night's dinner, then looked at Caitlyn and added, "You can come, too, *if* we can all squeeze into the taxi."

"*Bien sûr*, she'll fit!" Brigitte had said. "You *have* to come, Caitlyn. It is a very charming town."

A taxi and lunch would have meant money, though, and Caitlyn didn't have any. She'd murmured an excuse about having too much homework.

Amalia shrugged. "I'd rather stay here and ride. And Daniela . . ."

Caitlyn tilted her head. "What about her?"

"Sometimes she forgets to show her better side. She is a good person, but has a bad home life. At the start of every term, it is the same. After a winter break with her family she is full of unhappiness, and makes herself unbearable to others. In a few weeks she will settle in, though, and you will see her true self."

"I hope so," Caitlyn murmured. "Brigitte seems nice, though."

"She is . . ." Amalia nibbled her upper lip.

"But?" Caitlyn asked curiously.

"Mm. It's a little embarrassing."

"What?"

"I went out with her brother Thierry a few times, just to annoy my mother and show that I was a rebel at heart."

Caitlyn couldn't help laughing. "A rebel? You?"

Amalia looked mildly annoyed. "Rebellion is a relative thing. You have not met my mother. She's German, so for her the way to show affection is to control me, for my own good." Amalia shuddered. "She calls me on my cell every Sunday to talk about the dog, her travel plans, and everything I'm doing wrong."

Caitlyn smiled wryly. "I get to read e-mails about the cat, my brothers' sports, and questions about whether I'm emotionally able to handle being here."

"Our parents are not so different, then."

"I guess not." *Give or take a couple billion dollars,* Caitlyn silently added. "So what's Brigitte's brother like?"

"Thierry? He's a player. Or he was, anyway," she added in a mumble.

"Is he cute?"

"Gorgeous. But he was also a complete jerk. I only went out with him to prove that I wasn't . . . How do you say it? A log in the mud?"

Caitlyn giggled. "Stick. Stick in the mud."

"Stick, yes. Thank you. Despite my best efforts, though, I can't seem to escape being the type of orderly, controlled person who is afraid to act on impulse. I have no spontaneity."

"That's not necessarily a bad thing," Caitlyn protested. "I'm sure it keeps you out of trouble."

"Thierry told me I was cold. He wasn't the first boy to say that, either."

Caitlyn winced. "Ouch."

Amalia turned toward Caitlyn. "I wish I could be more like you."

"*Me?* Are you kidding? Why?"

"You let your emotions show on your face. They're right on the surface, for all to see."

Caitlyn grimaced. "I thought I'd learned to control that."

"See?" Amalia copied her grimace. "Right on the surface!"

"Mmph," Caitlyn grunted unhappily.

"Mmph," Amalia copied.

Caitlyn threw up her hands in defeat, then cast a quick warning look at Amalia. "Don't you do it!"

Amalia chuckled.

They'd reached the stables and parted ways. As Caitlyn headed toward the small group of girls waiting for their riding instructor, she went over the conversation with Amalia, feeling bemused.

How strange it was that a beautiful, wealthy, intelligent princess would want to emulate the very trait that had once earned Caitlyn the hated nickname Moan-n-Groan. Amalia seemed so perfect to Caitlyn's eyes, she'd never have guessed that she had her own share of insecurities.

Princesses really were just people, weren't they? Who knew?

She joined the other girls, all of them looking tense. The small, wiry, bad-tempered riding instructor, Madame Pelletier, was no one's favorite. Caitlyn and her classmates were wearing burgundy breeches, tall boots, navy sweaters, black helmets, and had their hair pulled back in French braids. They were finally going to ride. The thought sent a fresh shiver of excitement through Caitlyn. She'd never been on a horse, but some hidden part of her insisted that it would come naturally to her. To paraphrase Daniela and her comment in the art class, she felt like she had a good horsewoman locked inside her.

Unfortunately, that lock was the size of a bank vault, as Madame Pelletier soon made clear.

Before she would allow anyone to mount her horse, each girl had to lead the horses out of their individual stalls and into the wide corridor that ran down the center of the stables, where ropes attached to both walls were tied onto the horses' halters, to keep the animals in place. Then they had to groom their horse, clean its hooves, properly attach a saddle, and fasten on a bridle.

Caitlyn struggled with the terror of being kicked as she lifted each hoof of her horse in turn and used a pick to clean out bits of dirt and gravel wedged between hoof and metal shoe. When the last hoof was clean, she released it with a sigh of relief and rested her head against her mount's warm neck, breathing in the comforting scent of the horse. The smell tickled a distant memory, buried somewhere in her brain and associated with good feelings, even though she'd never been this close to a real horse before.

The good feelings dissipated as she struggled with the riding gear. The hornless English saddle and bridle were a confusion of leather straps and bits of steel, and the more Caitlyn fussed with them, the more her mount began to dance sideways, growing nervous with Caitlyn's ineptitude.

"Caitlyn!" Madame Pelletier barked, and strode toward her. Her black slashes of eyebrows drew down in a frown. "What are you doing? You have the bridle inside out!"

"I'm sorry!" Caitlyn cried, and removed the tangle of straps from the horse's face.

"Settle down! You are alarming your horse." Pelletier glared at her, her hands on her angular little hips. "Have you no sense of animals? Eh?"

Caitlyn cringed under the assault; it seemed unfairly harsh. "*Non*, Madame!"

Madame Pelletier inspected the saddle that Caitlyn had put on her mount, a chestnut named Rosamund. "You have the saddle pad backward. Take this off and start over. From the beginning."

Caitlyn's heart sank. "*Oui*, Madame."

Madame moved on to the next student, and Caitlyn heard her voice soften as she instructed the other girl.

Caitlyn put the simple halter back on her horse and tied it to the walls, using the special quick-release knot they'd been taught. "Sorry, Rosamund. I think Madame Pelletier has it out for me."

The other girls had finished and were leading their mounts to the arena when Madame Pelletier came back to inspect Caitlyn's work once again.

"What is this?" Madame asked incredulously, and flicked her fingers at the saddle.

"What?" Caitlyn asked in alarm, her nerves on end. "What'd I do wrong this time?"

"*Regardez!*" Look!

Caitlyn looked. It took a moment, but then the scale of her mistake hit her. This time the saddle itself was on backward. Her shoulders slumped. "Crap."

One of Madame's eyebrows rose. "There is no 'crap' in France, mademoiselle." Her mouth twisted. "In France, there is only *merde.*"

"*Merde!*" Caitlyn repeated, growling the R sound. "*Merde, merde, merde!*" This was one piece of vocabulary she would remember.

"At least you have learned *something* today. I must go to the other girls now. If you ever get Rosamund properly tacked up, lead her to the arena. But if you do not manage in the next twenty minutes," Madame said, glancing at the dusty clock high on the stable wall, "then you will not be riding today."

The threat sent a bolt of panic through Caitlyn's heart, and she set to speedy work. The more she hurried, however, the more mistakes she made, and the more jittery Rosamund became, her movements making Caitlyn's work harder. With each twisted strap and wrinkle in the blanket, Caitlyn became more desperate and closer to tears.

She pulled all the gear back off Rosamund, determined to get it all right from the start. She wanted to ride. She didn't want to have to wait another week, the sole student too clumsy to put a saddle and bridle on a horse.

Caitlyn looked up at the clock: eighteen minutes had gone by. She wasn't going to make it.

"Rosamund, what am I going to do?" Caitlyn asked, her vision blurring with tears.

The horse nickered and shifted her weight.

Caitlyn closed her eyes and took a deep breath, accepting that she was defeated. She wouldn't be riding. She had no natural horsewoman locked inside her.

With the acceptance came a strange peace. Caitlyn gave up struggling and thinking. With vague intentions of putting Rosamund back in her stall, Caitlyn undid the ropes tied to her halter and then removed the halter itself. She felt curiously calm, as if she were floating slightly outside herself, watching as her hands took a plain rope from a peg and looped it into an odd configuration. She slid the looped rope over Rosamund's nose, then draped the ends over the horse's neck, like reins.

As if in a trance, without consciousness of her own actions, Caitlyn grabbed a handful of mane in one hand and put the other hand on Rosamund's broad back. In one easy motion she pulled herself up, lying across Rosamund's bare back before swinging her right leg over and sitting upright.

Caitlyn gathered the rope reins and nudged Rosamund forward, riding her down the corridor and out into the arena with its soft floor of sand and sawdust. She was dimly aware of her fellow students gathered in the middle of the arena with Madame Pelletier, practicing mounting and dismounting. Advanced riders were a distance away, tracing figure eights. As if the others did not exist, Caitlyn nudged Rosamund from a walk to a trot, and a moment later nudged her into a canter. Caitlyn moved with easy, flowing grace along with the rolling gait of the horse, guiding Rosamund less with the rope reins than with the balance of her own body.

The lost memory that the scent of the horse had stirred in her came suddenly to life, melding with Caitlyn's vision of the arena.

Caitlyn was mounted behind a pioneer girl named Emily, her hands wrapped around Emily's waist as the two of them cantered bareback down a dirt road. Emily's long cotton skirts were gathered around her thighs, her dirty bare legs hanging down the horse's sides in front of Caitlyn's. There was dust and noise up ahead; Emily guided the horse onto the grassy verge as they passed a man driving a wagon pulled by a team of oxen.

"Emily!" the man called. "Get yourself home, girl! You should be helping your mother, not riding to hell and yonder!"

"In a bit, Pa!" Emily called over her shoulder, and shared a secretive look with Caitlyn. "I haven't had a good run in days!"

Caitlyn looked back to see the man shaking his head, a reluctant smile on his tanned face. She turned forward again as Emily urged the horse to greater speed, the two girls bending low as the wind whipped their faces and the world flew by in a blur.

Madame Pelletier intruded upon Caitlyn's vision. "*Arretez! Arretez! Mon Dieu, qu'est-ce que vous faites? Arretez!*" Stop! Stop! My God, what are you doing? Stop!

The country road vanished, and the arena appeared before Caitlyn's eyes in startling clarity. The other novice riding students were frozen, watching her.

The advanced riders had halted, Amalia among them, all staring with the same horrified fascination. "You know, she's from the

American West," Caitlyn heard Amalia say. "Riding bareback is in their blood!"

But with the loss of her trancelike state, the horse beneath Caitlyn's thighs became an alien motion, out of synch with Caitlyn's balance and movement. Caitlyn panicked and pulled back on the reins, making Rosamund come to a bouncing halt just as Caitlyn began to lose her seat.

"*Merde,*" Caitlyn muttered, and in a long slow descent into shame, she fell.

CHAPTER
Thirteen

Caitlyn was glad her French comprehension was poor. It made listening to Madame Pelletier's infuriated ranting about the bareback fiasco more bearable. Pelletier had dragged her to Madame Snowe's office mere moments after Caitlyn had fallen off Rosamund.

Caitlyn was sitting in front of Madame Snowe's ebony desk, slouched down in her chair as the riding instructor shouted, gesticulated, and pointed at her shameful student. Caitlyn had never been sent to the principal's office before. It was humiliating, and she hoped it didn't happen again.

Fortunately, Caitlyn hadn't been hurt in her fall. It had been more embarrassing than anything else, especially with Amalia watching.

Madame Snowe made understanding noises to Pelletier, and she said some firm words in French that seemed to calm her down. Snowe walked the woman to the door, no doubt letting her know that the miscreant would be dealt with severely.

Caitlyn felt something itchy on her stomach and lifted the hem of her sweater. A bit of sawdust from the arena fell out onto her thighs. She brushed it off, then grimaced as it formed a pale smudge on the Oriental carpet. Caitlyn surreptitiously rubbed it in with the tip of her boot.

Caitlyn peeked over her shoulder to see if anyone had noticed, and found her gaze caught by *La Perla*. Bianca looked amused. *It's not funny*, Caitlyn silently told her. *I might get kicked out for this whole horse thing.*

"Caitlyn?" Madame Snowe said. "Is there a reason you are glaring at that portrait?"

"What? No!" She turned forward again and straightened her posture, trying to prepare herself for the dressing-down Madame Snowe was about to deliver.

Snowe—in a midnight blue shantung silk suit—rested one slender hip on the edge of her desk and looked down at Caitlyn. "Would you like to tell me your side of the story?"

"I'm so sorry! I don't know what came over me."

"But something did 'come over' you?"

"I never meant to disobey Madame Pelletier, or to ride bareback, I swear! I wanted to ride so much, though, and I didn't think I was going to be allowed to, and then . . ."

"And then?"

Fear took hold of Caitlyn's tongue, silencing it. She remembered how her father and Joy had reacted to her stories about the vivid dreams that felt so real, she sometimes confused them with reality and claimed she had done things that she had, in fact, only imagined. Her parents had accused her of lying at first, but as time went by they started to worry that something might be wrong with her. Maybe, like a schizophrenic, she couldn't tell what was real and what was not. A psychiatrist her parents talked to said that it wouldn't be out of keeping with schizophrenia that Caitlyn's symptoms had started with puberty.

Caitlyn learned to keep her dreams confined to the covers of her journal.

"And then I made a simple bridle and mounted Rosamund, and went for a ride," Caitlyn said dully.

"How did you know how to make the bridle?"

"I didn't. It just came to me."

"Someone must have taught you at some time. It was an improvised hackamore you made, Madame Pelletier said."

Caitlyn's heart thumped. "What's that?" she asked. She had learned something *real* from one of her dreams?

"It's a Spanish type of bridle, seen mostly in Western riding. So it seems likely you made one before, or saw someone make one."

Caitlyn shrugged, trying to hide her interest. This would be the second time she got *real* information from one of her dreams!

"And then there was your ability to ride. Madame admitted that if she hadn't been so startled, and so frightened for you, she might have admired your seat. You rode with a natural grace, she said. Until you fell, of course." Madame Snowe lifted Caitlyn's chin with her long, cold fingers, forcing her to meet her eyes. "*Alors.* Tell me the truth. You have ridden before."

Caitlyn hung on the precipice of truth and lies, not knowing which would save her. The intensity of Madame Snowe's gaze, though, threatened that the headmistress would sense a lie. Caitlyn almost imagined that she could feel Snowe's will, forcing her to tell the truth. "Only in my dreams," Caitlyn squeaked.

"Ah?" Snowe released Caitlyn's chin. "These must be very vivid dreams."

Caitlyn nodded.

"And do you have other dreams where you learn to do things like ride horses bareback?"

124

Caitlyn thought about Raphael, then shook her head. She didn't want to share him with the headmistress. "Or at least, I don't know if I do. Like anyone else, I rarely remember more than snippets of my dreams."

Madame Snowe tapped her lower lip with a fingertip, thinking. "I suppose cryptomnesia could be the explanation for your riding skill," Madame Snowe mused, almost to herself.

"Crypto-what?"

"Cryptomnesia. It's when you forget how or when you learned something, and even forget that you know it, until it suddenly pops into your mind. It tricks some people into believing they have psychic or other paranormal abilities. Has it done that to you?"

"No. Of course not," she semi-fibbed. She *had* been thinking there was something unusual going on with her dreams, that might find an explanation in the paranormal.

"*Bon.* You may have learned to ride by watching other people, or movies, and then incorporating that knowledge into your psyche by dreaming that you yourself were riding."

"I guess so," Caitlyn said, although the explanation was a letdown. It was so . . . mundane.

"If you have any more of these cryptomnesiac spells, I want you to tell me. I have a doctorate in psychology, and I find them . . . fascinating. Will you do that? Will you tell me the details, the next time something like this happens?"

"You don't think . . . ," Caitlyn started. "I mean, you aren't worried that . . ." Caitlyn circled her finger around her ear and crossed her eyes.

"That they're a symptom of a mental illness?"

Caitlyn nodded. "It's not a symptom of schizophrenia?"

Snowe exhaled a short breath of laughter. "No. You are not crazy.

You are, instead, *unique*, Caitlyn. Be content with that, as I am."

Caitlyn blinked in surprise. She was beginning to accept that Madame Snowe truly *did* believe that she was special. It seemed that the traits that had made her an unhappy oddball in Oregon were now the things that made her valuable in Madame Snowe's eyes.

Maybe there hadn't been anything wrong with Caitlyn all these years; maybe she'd just been in the wrong environment, with the wrong people.

Caitlyn smiled. "I think I can be content with uniqueness." But she still didn't want to talk about Raphael with Madame Snowe.

"Good. And don't forget to tell me the next time this happens. I want all the details. Promise?"

Caitlyn smiled and nodded, and hoped she wouldn't be struck down for the lie.

CHAPTER

Fourteen

Breakfast was the quietest meal of the day in the Great Hall, although as far as the food went it was Caitlyn's favorite. This morning, a long buffet was laid out with croissants, *pain au chocolat*, butter, cheese, sliced deli meats, yogurt, fruit, muesli, milk, tea, orange juice, and hard-boiled eggs, and Caitlyn was free to take whatever she wanted. She didn't have to talk to a single cook. Girls came down from the dorm still half asleep and in their pajamas, or dashing in just before the kitchen closed to scoop up a couple croissants from the buffet. Some girls never came down at all, valuing sleep more than food.

Caitlyn put her bowl of yogurt and fruit at an empty space at a table, next to Mathilde Obermann, the girl who had seen the real Woman in Black.

Caitlyn had been thinking about talking to Mathilde for several days. She wanted to hear the story of her encounter with the Woman in Black, and whether or not Mathilde had heard the ghost calling for her lost love, Raphael.

Madame Snowe's talk of cryptomnesia made perfect sense as an explanation for Caitlyn's dreams that seemed to have a basis in fact. She must have read or heard about Catherine de' Medici before. Maybe she'd seen a show on the Discovery Channel or the History Channel, a show unmemorable to her conscious mind that nonetheless left an impression on her unconscious. She'd been happy with that explanation until she'd suddenly remembered that the first time she'd dreamed Raphael's name had been in the car coming from the Bordeaux airport, *before* she'd arrived at the school. Where could she possibly have heard Raphael's name, then?

Maybe Mathilde's encounter with the Woman in Black could shed light, however feeble, on the question.

Caitlyn was pleased to have found Mathilde alone. The Austrian girl had frizzy red hair that stuck out in a halo around her pale face, and her eyebrows were so light they were invisible, giving her a look of perpetual fright.

"Hi," Caitlyn said.

"Hello."

"I'm Caitlyn."

Mathilde grinned. "The Wild West girl who rode bareback! Yes, I know. The whole school knows! Can you shoot a gun, too?"

Caitlyn's cheeks heated in embarrassment. "Urg," she gurgled, "no."

"I would have liked to have been there for Madame Pelletier's reaction. I heard she was furious!" Mathilde waved her arms over her head and made an angry, ranting face. She dropped her arms and chortled. "I would have liked that very much."

"It wasn't so great from my end."

Mathilde smiled, her cheeks dimpling. "But now you have a good story."

"Like you do. I heard that you saw the Woman in Black, a year or two ago."

Mathilde's smile faded. She dropped her gaze and picked up her croissant, shredding it between her fingers. "That was very frightening for me."

"As scary as Madame Pelletier?"

Mathilde flashed a smile. "Maybe not."

"I was wondering if maybe you could help me?"

"How?"

"I have to write a paper on Jane Austen's *Northanger Abbey*, which is sort of a ghost story; I thought maybe I could work your encounter into my essay." Which was true, and it was also a good excuse for being so curious about the Woman in Black.

Mathilde frowned. "I read that book. There's no ghost, only a heroine who imagines things. I didn't imagine the Woman in Black."

"No, of course not! That wasn't the angle I wanted to take. I wanted to contrast a real ghost encounter with a fictional one."

Mathilde thought for a moment, then popped a piece of croissant in her mouth and smiled. "Okay."

"Start from the beginning."

"It was the middle of the night. I'd gotten up to get a glass of water," Mathilde said.

"So you were out in the hallway?" Caitlyn asked. "Which floor?"

"Third floor. I heard a sound behind me, like heavy silk skirts. The sound they make, what is the word . . . ?"

"Rustling?" Caitlyn supplied.

Mathilde nodded. "Rustling, the way long skirts do when a woman walks. I was very surprised, of course. *Who is this?* I thought. *Who would be dressed in long skirts and coming down the hall at this hour?* So I turned around."

"And?" Caitlyn asked, her hands clenched tight together. "What did you see?"

"Nothing! No one there."

Caitlyn's shoulders sagged in disappointment. Maybe Mathilde's ghost encounter was as false as Daniela's. Rustling noises could have been anything from mice to the wind.

"The noise, though—it did not stop," Mathilde continued darkly.

Caitlyn blinked. "What?"

"It got louder, and closer. I could feel the cold air moving in front of her as she came down the hall. I could not move."

Caitlyn's pulse raced. "And still you saw nothing?"

"Nothing! I just heard that rustling sound: Shh, shh, shh. Getting closer and closer."

"What did you do?!"

"I stood, right there. My legs would not run. It was like being in a dream, you know? And all the time, Shh, shh, shh, getting closer."

"And?"

"When she was right next to me, when my skin had gone cold from her closeness, the sound stopped. The lights flickered, and as they flickered, in the moments of darkness, I saw her standing in front of me."

A shiver ran down Caitlyn's spine. "What did she look like?" she half whispered.

"She was dressed all in black, and had a black veil draped over her head, but through it I could see the whiteness of her face. She stared at me. And then the lights went all the way out, and all I could see was the misty white of her face, only it wasn't really a face, it was just a smear of white against the darkness, and I heard a terrible scream." Mathilde's eyes went wide, and she put her hands up to her ears and shook her head, as if to shake away the memory. "Then the lights suddenly came back on, and I saw I was alone."

It took Caitlyn a moment to free herself of the image, so like the Screechers, and gather her wits. "Did anyone else hear the scream?"

Mathilde shook her head, then dropped her hands and ate another piece of croissant.

"The Woman in Black didn't say anything?"

"No. I know people in the past have said she calls for her lost lover, but I did not hear that. But those stories are from long ago; maybe the ghost has given up finding him."

"I wonder why she stays around."

Mathilde shrugged.

"Thank you for telling me your story."

"You have enough for your paper?"

"Absolutely."

That evening Caitlyn was still trying to figure out what it all meant, if anything. She went and stood in the hall on the third floor of the dormitory, where Mathilde had seen her ghost, and tried to picture what it had been like for her. The walls were paneled in wood, and set with sconces every fifteen feet or so, midway between the doors to the bedrooms. Their shaded bulbs cast only a dim golden glow that did little to illuminate the dark corridor.

It had to have been terrifying, to stand here alone and hear the *shh, shh, shh* of rustling skirts approaching, and yet see not a soul.

Why hadn't the Woman in Black called for Raphael? Mathilde's idea that she'd stopped looking for him seemed out of keeping with most ghost stories; ghosts didn't change their behavior, did they?

Whatever the reason, Caitlyn was glad of it. Raphael was *hers*, and she didn't want to share him. She hated the idea of a long-lost lover roaming the halls of the castle, looking for him. It meant there was someone else in his life.

She was, she realized, jealous.

That's stupid! How can I be jealous of a ghost, over a guy who might not even exist?

And yet, there was no other word for what she felt. Since the moment she'd seen Raphael riding in the valley, her heart had claimed him as her Knight of Cups.

She rubbed her forehead and closed her eyes, not believing her own thoughts. She really was half nuts, wasn't she? She was getting a crush on a guy she'd seen only in a dream.

A memory surfaced of the feel of his hand holding hers, the pad of his thumb stroking over her knuckles, and she felt a rush of warmth pour down her body. Raphael's eyes, looking into hers as he tugged her closer, until her knees bumped into—

A bedroom door creaked open, making Caitlyn start and turn.

"What are you doing, standing there?" Daniela asked, leaning against the frame of the open door, her arms crossed over her chest.

"Trying to imagine seeing the Woman in Black!" she said, a little too quickly. "I'm putting Mathilde's experience into a paper I have to write about *Northanger Abbey*."

To Caitlyn's surprise, Daniela's eyes lit up. "Did you know that *I* saw the ghost, too?"

"I'd heard something like that," she said, remembering the trick Naomi had played on her.

"You should put my story in your paper, too. Do you want to hear it?"

"Er, sure."

She followed Daniela into the room she shared with Brigitte; it was the first time Caitlyn had been invited in. If listening to a fake ghost story was the price for being treated civilly by Daniela, she'd pay it. Maybe Amalia was right, and Daniela was beginning to show her good side.

Caitlyn couldn't help her eyes roving over the room, taking in the hints of the girls' lives beyond the walls of the château. Brigitte wasn't there, but her personality was: *Hello Kitty* knickknacks, a bright pink comforter cover, a menagerie of stuffed animals crammed in among the books on her shelves. On the wall beside her bed hung a framed poster of a mermaid combing her hair. The rest of the wall was covered in framed photos of family, friends, and of Brigitte herself grinning beside celebrities. Her father was a famous character actor in French films.

Caitlyn pointed to a black-and-white professional photo of Brigitte and a fair-haired, handsome young man who looked a few years older than her. "Who's that?"

"Brigitte's brother Thierry," Daniela said, sitting down on her own bed with its duvet cover of dark gold silk shantung. She had shimmering gold Klimt posters on her wall, a black fur throw at the foot of her bed, and one onyx-framed photo on her desk, of herself. "Thierry got the looks, but Brigitte got the heart."

Caitlyn gave Daniela a censorious look. "I think Brigitte is adorable."

"I know she is. I'm not the one who said that about her looks; she is. Besides, better to have a heart than to be a heartless pig."

Caitlyn raised her brows in question.

"Thierry's a playboy: you know the type. Treats women like garbage," she said, echoing Amalia's assessment. A shadow moved over her face. "Or at least he did. Not anymore."

"Is he dead?"

"He's alive enough," she said, and then smiled with false brightness. "Unlike . . . the Woman in Black!"

Caitlyn sat on Brigitte's desk chair and listened to Daniela embellish her encounter with Naomi in the dark hallway. Some of her details were obviously cribbed from Mathilde's story, but Caitlyn pretended to be fascinated anyway. She wouldn't be the one to tell Daniela that she'd been tricked: Daniela seemed delighted to have seen the ghost.

"So the castle really is haunted," Caitlyn said.

"Eh! All of Europe is, but I think this area here is especially bad. You know about the *gouffre*?"

"The goof? What's a goof?"

"*Gouffre*. It is a—how do you say . . . A big hole in the ground, very deep, that sometimes goes down to water."

"A pit?"

Daniela shook her head. "Big. Deep."

Caitlyn had a sudden picture of the dragon emerging from a chasm in the ground in the painting of Fortuna. "Chasm? Abyss?"

"Maybe abyss is the word. *Gouffre* in French. There is a large *gouffre* in the forest near the château, and it is haunted. There is a story that it is the door the devil uses to get to and from Hell, but I don't believe that. I think it is something more primitive than that, something dark in Nature herself. You know the French expression for being almost in despair, almost in disaster?"

Caitlyn shook her head.

"*Je suis au bord du gouffre.* 'I am on the edge of the abyss.'"

Caitlyn's mouth went dry. She had a mental flash of her mother reading the tarot cards, with the Fool about to step into the abyss. *The abyss waits for you. You stand upon its edge.*

"The expression might as well have come from the *gouffre* here," Daniela said.

"Why? What happens there?"

"Brigitte could tell you—"

"I could tell her what?" Brigitte asked brightly, coming into the room with Amalia.

"Why the—" Caitlyn started.

"Why I tell the story about the Woman in Black so many times," Daniela interrupted, giving Caitlyn a warning look.

"She loves the attention!" Brigitte laughed. "You didn't make Caitlyn listen to it, did you?"

"She asked. It's her own fault."

"If you'd given me a euro for each time you told that story, I'd have a new handbag by now, and you *know* I only like expensive handbags."

"I'm writing an English paper on real ghost stories in contrast to those in *Northanger Abbey*," Caitlyn explained.

Amalia dropped onto Brigitte's bed and kicked off her shoes. "Did you choose the topic because of the ghosts in your nightmares?"

Brigitte and Daniela turned to stare at Caitlyn. "What ghosts?" Brigitte asked.

Caitlyn cast an accusing glare at Amalia, who had the grace to grimace. Her eyes pleaded for forgiveness.

"They're just in my nightmares. They're not so interesting," Caitlyn said.

"Tell us anyway," Brigitte said, crawling onto her bed beside Amalia.

"There's not much to tell." Caitlyn shifted in her chair, uncomfortable with their avid attention. This wasn't something she liked to talk about. She wanted to make new friends, but she was never going to get close to any of them if she walled herself off.

Besides, if Daniela could tell ghost stories, why couldn't she?

Caitlyn took a deep breath. What the hell. "In the middle of the night I'm visited by . . . *things*. I call them the Screechers."

All three girls stared at her with wide eyes.

"They look like people," she went on, "but they're usually in black and white, and sort of smeared, like a bad photo. There's usually only one at a time, but sometimes two or three. They come in the night, while I'm asleep, and scream at me in my dreams. Sometimes they try to scratch or beat me, or throw things at me."

"*Mon Dieu*," Brigitte said. "What are they?"

"I don't know. I wish I did. Maybe I could get rid of them."

"Are they real?" Daniela asked. "Or are they dreams?"

Caitlyn shrugged. "No one else sees them."

Amalia nodded confirmation.

"That means they're in my head, doesn't it?" Caitlyn said.

"Or it means that they're real and no one else is sensitive enough to see them," Daniela said. "Like the Woman in Black: only a few people ever see her. They say abilities like that run in families, especially in women."

Caitlyn's lips parted, her face going still with realization.

"Caitlyn?" Amalia asked. "What is it?"

"My mom. My real mom, I mean, not my stepmom. She died in a car wreck when I was four, so I never really knew her, but she used to tell fortunes."

"You see?" Daniela said, delighted to be proved right. "It runs in your family! How about your mother's mother; did she have any special gifts?"

"I don't know; she died before I was born. A cousin told me that she once saw the Umpqua Maiden, though."

"The what?" Amalia asked.

"The ghost of an Umpqua girl, supposedly the daughter of a chief; but they're always daughters of chiefs, in the stories."

"Like princesses in fairy tales," Brigitte said, and nudged Amalia.

"Mmph," Amalia grunted.

"Anyway, the Umpqua Maiden has been seen in Spring Creek

for centuries, since even before the pioneers came to Oregon. There are several versions of her story, but the most popular one is that an evil spirit killed her beloved and took on his form, and then tricked her into marrying him. On their wedding night, she discovered his trick and tried to run away, and the evil spirit was so angry that he killed her. Now she roams the earth, forever looking for her true beloved, but never finding him."

"What does she look like?" Daniela asked.

Caitlyn shrugged. "I've never seen her, but most of the stories say she appears as a horrid, deathly pale face floating in the darkness, watching you. They say that if you see her, it means you're going to die soon."

"And *do* people die soon after?" Brigitte asked, breathless.

Caitlyn smiled. "Given that there are some people walking around Spring Creek right now who claim to have seen her, I don't think so!"

"Why does it always seem to be," Amalia asked, addressing the room in general, "that female ghosts spend all their time looking for men they can't find?"

"They can't take no for an answer?" Caitlyn said, and earned a chuckle from the girls.

"Because there's nothing on TV?" Daniela suggested.

"Because the male ghosts are out drinking with their friends?" Brigitte offered.

They all laughed.

"If any of you die an untimely death," Amalia said, "make me one promise."

"Anything!" Caitlyn said.

"Promise me you won't spend eternity looking for a guy who doesn't want to be found!"

CHAPTER
Fifteen

Three weeks later, Caitlyn sat in the library surrounded by a pile of books on the de' Medicis and felt like she *was* spending eternity hunting a guy who didn't want to be found. She hadn't dreamed of him in twenty-one nights, and there was not a single mention of Raphael in anything she'd read.

The reading wasn't a complete waste, though, as it was research for the term paper she was writing on Bianca de' Medici, for her world history class. It gave her a perfect excuse to spend endless hours in the library, poring through old mildewed books whose contents had never reached the Internet. What she wouldn't give for a Search function on some of those books.

Each night that went by without a dream of Raphael, his face in her memory grew a little fainter, even as she found him consuming more and more of her thoughts.

Was he a ghost?

If so, had he lost interest in haunting her?

If he wasn't a ghost, what *was* he, and why did she feel such a strong pull toward him?

Whatever he was, when would she see him again?

She wished she had more control over her dreams. Maybe Raphael was impatiently waiting for her in the dream world, and *she* was the one who was somehow failing him by not appearing. She knew nothing of how to dream herself into a place on purpose.

Neither had she had any of those cryptomnesiac dreams that Madame Snowe was so interested in, where she learned to ride horses or do useful things like master quadratic equations or keep straight the difference between metamorphic and igneous rocks. The dream fragments she remembered were vivid, but unremarkable, barely worth a few quick sketches in her journal.

The Screechers had made two appearances, though. The first one had come while Caitlyn dreamed she was walking down a wooded path at twilight, her bare feet silent on the earth. The next moment a guttural roar had shaken her, and a massive thing had dashed at her, swinging a blade three feet long. Caitlyn screamed as the thing shouted and grunted, its figure whirling. She'd caught only a glimpse of its face—male, and covered in dark hair—before Amalia's hand on her shoulder woke her.

The second appearance had left fewer details in Caitlyn's memory, but was no less horrible for that. All she could recall of the dream was lying on a bed, and then a furious banshee appearing, screeching, and flailing at Caitlyn as if trying to destroy a demon from Hell.

With these disturbances, Caitlyn was spending more nights staying up late in the Grand Salon, to allow Amalia to sleep. Naomi was often there with her for a couple hours, and they would chat or study, or do a little of both, and then Naomi would go back to her room and Caitlyn would crash on the couch. She'd come close, several times, to telling Naomi about her obsession with the dreams of Raphael, but had then chickened out at the last minute. She didn't want to mess up the friendship it felt like they were slowly building between their art and geology classes, and the nightly hanging out in the Grand Salon. She couldn't believe that Naomi would still like her, if she knew how little Caitlyn's thoughts were grounded in present-day reality.

"I'm starving," Brigitte whispered across the library table, startling Caitlyn out of her thoughts. Brigitte sat surrounded by a pile of books on the early history of French cuisine, which was the subject of her own term paper. The entire class was in the library, doing research the old-fashioned way, with books.

"Forty-five minutes till lunch."

Brigitte groaned under her breath. "And me here, reading about the history of bread. It's unbearable."

Caitlyn chuckled, and went back to her books.

In her attempts to find Raphael, her reading had taken her on a long, circuitous route through the Knights Templar, de' Medici family history, and the history of Château de la Fortune itself. Her notes were a jumbled mass of information more about those things than about Bianca herself, who had made only a small impression in the pages of history.

Caitlyn went back over her notes, trying to pick out the bits of information that might be pertinent to her search for Raphael.

Her notes on Bianca's distant cousin, Catherine de' Medici, were extensive. Catherine had been married off to the future Henry II, King of France, when she was only fourteen years old. Henry fathered nine children with her but otherwise shunned her, devoting all his attention to his mistress. When Henry died during a freak jousting accident, there were some who accused Catherine of witchcraft.

After Henry's death Catherine's sons inherited the throne

of France, but she controlled her sons and was the ruling force of France almost until her death in 1589. She ruled, however, over a country at war with itself over religion, Catholic versus Protestant Huguenots. Her ruthlessness became legendary as she struggled to maintain control of her country and keep her sons on the throne, using any means necessary, no matter how underhanded.

Caitlyn's research on the history of Château de la Fortune, however, turned up only a single mention of the treasure of the Knights Templar, and the legend that it was hidden somewhere within the castle.

The last lord of the castle to hold the secret, Gerard, died without issue in the fourteenth century. He had bankrupted the château with an extravagant refurbishment of the fortress and its chapel, using Christian motifs throughout in an apparent attempt to expiate unnamed family sins. Shortly before he died he wrote a letter to a friend saying, "Only the light of God will guide you to the true treasure," the true treasure being salvation.

An unusual sundial had been the most notable element of Gerard's refurbishment, although the information on the Web neglected to mention what made it so fascinating. Caitlyn had spent an entire weekend searching all over the château and grounds and found nary a sundial.

Poor Gerard. His one achievement of note had been erased from the earth. Perhaps the treasure *was* cursed, after all.

Caitlyn got up to stretch, feeling an ache in her back from hunching over books and notes. She went to a window to lean her hands against its stone sill as she gently stretched the backs of her calves. Brigitte soon joined her, apparently glad of a distraction. The other students were beginning to stir, gathering together books and notebooks: the clock said they had only five minutes of class time left.

"I love these panels of stained glass, don't you?" Brigitte asked.

Caitlyn followed Brigitte's gaze to the square of painted, fired glass set into the center of the window whose sill she was using to stretch. It depicted a brilliant yellow sun over painted blue waves, with the Latin words *Fiat Lux* in the corners. Caitlyn had no idea what the words meant.

"My favorite is the one in the chemistry lab," Brigitte went on. "It's a woman in a gown, spreading flowers on a path."

"I haven't seen that one yet." The painted panes were only a foot tall and about eight inches wide, each one set in the center of a leaded-glass window. There were dozens of them throughout the castle, each one different: a portrait of a man, a city on a hill, a shield and sword, a griffin. "I feel like they all have meanings I can't decipher."

"Most are probably religious," Brigitte said. "I think they're more mysterious and beautiful if you don't know what they mean."

"Maybe you're right."

They were both quiet for a moment, and Caitlyn got the feeling that Brigitte was working up the courage to say something.

"Amalia tells me that your nightmares are still bothering you," she finally said.

Caitlyn grimaced. "Yeah. I feel bad for her, having to put up with me."

"I might know of something that could help."

"Really?" Caitlyn asked with interest. "What?"

"My parents sent me to a therapist in Paris for a time, when I was having bad dreams and . . . trying to deal with some other things." She picked at the leaves of the potted plant on the stone windowsill beneath the stained-glass sun. "She had me try something that in English is called 'lucid dreaming.' Have you heard of it?"

"No. What is it?"

"When you are dreaming, you try to realize that you are dreaming.

And then, without waking up, you change the dream so that it goes the way you want."

"But how do you realize you're dreaming? I never figure it out until I wake up!"

Brigitte ceased her abuse of the potted plant. "There are tests you can do in your dream, like looking at your face in a mirror: if your reflection is not normal, you're dreaming. Or pinch your nose shut," she said, demonstrating. "If you're asleep, you'll still be able to breathe without opening your mouth."

"But I'd have to know I was dreaming before I could try the tests," Caitlyn said doubtfully. Nor did she think she'd have the presence of mind to try them when the Screechers came.

"There is another way to try it."

"Yeah?"

"It works best if you're not too sleepy, so the middle of the day works well. You try to go from awake to dreaming, keeping your mind conscious the whole time."

"How do you do that?"

"It's hard to explain, but when you try for yourself, you will see. When you're trying to fall asleep, aren't you aware for a few moments when you start to have strange, dreamlike thoughts or visions?"

Caitlyn nodded. "Yeah."

"That is the feeling you must hold on to. Let yourself go deeper into dreams, but keep a small part of yourself awake, and watching. Remind yourself to stay in control. With practice, you can master this. Once you do, you can change anything that happens in the dream. When you start to have a nightmare, you can stop it and change it to something happy."

Caitlyn tilted her head, considering. It seemed barely possible. If it was, then not only could she control the Screechers, but she might be able to find Raphael! She wouldn't have to wait for dreams of him to come to her: *she* could go to *them*. A fresh wave of excitement went through her. "Were you ever able to have a lucid dream?"

Brigitte bobbed her head this way and that, and leaned back, resting her elbows on the windowsill. "Yes and no. When a dream started that I didn't want, I told myself that I wasn't going to dream that; I was going to dream that I was decorating a big house, instead. Sometimes it worked." She smiled. "I decorated a lot of houses in my sleep."

"You had a lot of bad dreams that needed redecorating?"

She nodded slowly. "My brother, Thierry. He almost died this past September. It has been very hard on my family."

"What happened?"

Brigitte straightened, knocking the plant off the windowsill in the process. It hit the stone floor and disgorged half its dirt. "*Merde!*"

Both girls crouched to scoop the dirt back into the plastic pot. "It was an accident," Caitlyn said, meaning the plant.

"My poor brother. Yes, it had to have been an accident." Brigitte shook her head, tears starting in her eyes. "He didn't try to kill himself. It was an accident, his falling into the *gouffre*."

Caitlyn looked up. The *gouffre*. Caitlyn felt a chill run over her skin. The one time Caitlyn had had a chance to speak to Daniela alone and ask her to finish what she'd been saying about the abyss in the forest, Daniela had pressed her lips tight together and shaken her head. "I should not have said that. Please don't mention it to Brigitte."

"What happened to Thierry at the *gouffre*?" Caitlyn asked softly.

Brigitte's jaw tightened. "He'd come down here with some of his friends, to hang out with me and Amalia and Daniela, before classes started in September. One of his friends had heard about the *gouffre*, and they decided to go see it—there's a path from the château that goes right to it. His friends tell me that when they got there, they messed around throwing things in and listening to the distant splash, normal things like that, and then they noticed that Thierry was standing right at the edge of the *gouffre*. Just standing, for a long time, staring into the depths. And then, without warning, he tilted forward and fell." Brigitte met Caitlyn's eyes. "He didn't jump. He didn't scream. He just ... tilted, and fell. One of his friends said it was like watching a tree fall."

"Why'd he do it?" Caitlyn asked, bewildered.

"I don't know. I thought he was doing all right; he'd had some trouble with drugs, but he was better. It could have been an accident, couldn't it?" Brigitte pleaded, as if Caitlyn could have an answer.

"I guess so."

Brigitte nodded, then went on, "It took half an hour to get help down to him. He survived, but something happened to his brain. He can't remember any of his life from before the fall. He can't remember any of *us*." A few tears ran down her cheeks. "He's a different person now. The doctors say he must have brain damage from being underwater for so long, but they can't find it on their scans."

They rose, and Caitlyn put the plant back on the windowsill, centering it on a square of scarred black metal embedded in the stone. She felt obscurely guilty for all the fuss she had made over her bad dreams. She had nightmares. So what? Brigitte's brother had tried to kill himself, and emerged from the experience with brain damage.

Je suis au bord du gouffre, Caitlyn thought. I am at the edge of the abyss. The psychological and literal meanings had come together in Thierry.

"I'm sorry about your brother," Caitlyn said, not knowing what else to say. "I hope he gets better."

"Thank you." Brigitte sniffled, and then gathered her composure. "Anyway, all this is the reason I ended up going to a therapist. Do you like the lucid-dreaming idea?"

"I do, very much. I'll try it tonight, and tell you what happens."

"*Bon.* You can tell me how you decorate your house."

Caitlyn only smiled in answer. It wasn't home decorating she was going to pursue in her dreams: it was Raphael.

CHAPTER
Sixteen

After dinner, while Amalia was watching TV in the Grand Salon with Daniela and Brigitte, Caitlyn plumped the pillows on her bed, turned out all the lights except her desk lamp, and lay down on top of her duvet. She folded her hands over her abdomen and tried to relax: an impossible quest, given her excitement. She was going to see Raphael again, and *this* time she'd be in control!

Passing voices in the hall outside her door seemed unusually loud and distracting: Soma, a girl from India, was telling Japanese Kaori that she'd gained a kilo in the past month and was going to try a new coconut-oil diet to lose weight.

Caitlyn groaned in frustration and flipped on her alarm clock radio, tuning it to the white noise between stations. The sounds of the hallway quickly became indistinct under the wash of static.

Dream but stay in control, she told herself.

After several minutes she finally felt herself sinking into the first layer of sleep, awareness of the room around her fading.

Raphael. I want to dream about Raphael.

She imagined his face and loose curls, and his hazel eyes.

The deliberate effort briefly brought her closer to the surface of consciousness, but as she held his face in her mind she began once again to sink toward sleep.

A thrill ran through her as Raphael's face suddenly came to life. He and the old man, Beneto, whispered near a leaded-glass window with a painted panel in its center. Moonlight spilled through the glass, tracing their profiles in silver and glimmering softly on a box Raphael held in his hands. Caitlyn stood a few feet away, in shadows untouched by the moon, and unnoticed by either man.

"We have to find someplace more secure, Beneto," Raphael whispered in Italian, the meaning of the foreign words forming in Caitlyn's mind without effort. "We can't keep moving it around, hoping to stay ahead of the thief." The small box or chest in his hands was about six inches long and four inches wide. The sides were made of small pieces of what looked like cloudy glass, the edges held together by gold. The lid, too, was gold, set with an enormous quartz crystal cabochon—a rounded stone. It was almost as long as the box, two inches high, and polished to glassy smoothness.

Caitlyn's heart tripped. She suddenly knew that *that* was what had been lying in the depths of the locked trunk she'd opened, when she'd visited Raphael and had been driven half mad by the sound of the beating heart. That box had been what glimmered in the depths after she'd flung aside the blanket.

"Whoever is looking for it is getting desperate," Beneto said. "They took no care to hide the signs of searching my room."

"We need someplace permanent to keep it." Raphael handed the crystal chest to the old man. "You said you had one last place you could hide it, until we find the Templar's treasure."

Beneto nodded and slipped the chest into an opening in his robe.

"Be careful," Raphael said.

"I will guard it with my life."

"I know, my friend, just as you risked your life to bring it to me from out of the ashes."

Caitlyn felt a hand lightly touch her shoulder. She started, and turned to look, but no one was there. The scene around her suddenly started to flicker, and Caitlyn panicked as she felt herself rising toward consciousness.

No! Stay here. Stay here, she desperately commanded herself.

The scene quickly stabilized. Beneto put a hand on Raphael's shoulder. "She is with us still. Do not doubt it, Raphael."

"I'm starting to believe you may be right."

Again, the scene flickered, as if some outside force was trying to draw Caitlyn away.

Stay! I want to stay with Raphael!

Beneto squeezed Raphael's shoulder and departed. As the door closed behind him Raphael began to turn toward her, and then her vision went dark.

No, she cried silently, reaching through the darkness. *Stay!*

Her vision suddenly cleared, and she found herself standing exactly where Raphael had been, in front of the window. Disappointment swamped her as she realized he was nowhere to be seen: she was alone.

Moonlight glowed through the yellow sun of the painted glass *Fiat Lux* window, and Caitlyn felt a flicker of awareness that she was dreaming; this room was the library of the Fortune School.

The mixing of real and dream worlds confused her, and her thoughts seemed to slow down, as if she were hypnotized, or drugged. She looked down at the windowsill: the potted plant was gone, and the dark square of embedded metal it had sat upon was now polished to a bright silver sheen, looking like a mirror set into the stone sill. Caitlyn leaned over it to look at herself.

A black shadow passed over the square, devoid of features. A chill ran down Caitlyn's spine, and she felt the instinct to bolt, to run from something evil that was fast approaching, but she couldn't move or look away from the square. The shadowed square darkened to a depthless black, making it look as if the plate of silver had disappeared and a deep square hole had opened in the windowsill. It mesmerized her, and as she looked into it, a small smudge of pale light formed at the bottom of the hole.

The smudge began slowly to rise out of the depths, dragging with it an inexorable sense of dread. It expanded and changed shape as it came up to Caitlyn as if from a great distance, its presence seeming to poison the very air she breathed. Her mind struggled to make sense of the thing, unable to fit a meaning to the shape. Dread tightened her chest, her breath coming in shorter gasps with each passing second, her heart racing with an inexplicable certainty that the thing slowly rising toward her was not of this world. Trapped by her fear, her body refused to flee.

The pale shape was mere feet from her now, its mass almost filling the square of the mirror. Terror burst upon Caitlyn as recognition came at last.

It was the top of a woman's strawberry-blond head.

Waves of shuddering horror rolled through Caitlyn as the head continued to rise; she could see the part atop the woman's scalp, and the pins holding in place a coronet of braids. She was paralyzed with fear, unable to move as the head continued toward the top of the hole.

The woman's face suddenly tilted upward, her dark brown eyes locking on Caitlyn's own. A scream choked in Caitlyn's throat: it was Bianca de' Medici. The noblewoman's cold alabaster face showed no expression. Her hands shot up, out of the mirror, grabbing Caitlyn by the sides of her head and pulling her with sudden fury into the depths of the hole.

Caitlyn screamed as she fell into blackness, clawing at the stonelike hands clasped to her head. The pressure of the hands increased until it felt like her skull would be crushed between them. Nor could she breathe; bands of pressure were tightening around her chest, and Bianca's blank face was the only light in the abyss.

The darkness suddenly turned to the broad light of day and Bianca vanished. The pressure around Caitlyn's chest tightened, and she looked down and saw ropes wrapped around her, her arms pinned to her sides. She was fastened to a post, and she wore the cherry-rose satin dress. All around her were stacked bundles of sticks.

A voice intoned its judgment in Latin, the meaning of the words somehow clear: she would be burned, her ashes scattered, salt sown into the ground where she had died.

Panic swamped her. She tried to speak but had no air. The faggots of wood were already lit, the fire burning with greedy flames. She struggled against her bonds as smoke stung her eyes and seared her lungs.

A flaming brand fell upon her skirts, and the silk erupted in flame. Caitlyn screamed—

And then all was gray, all sensation gone.

Caitlyn found herself hovering in the air, her bodiless soul suspended over a pile of smoldering ashes and charcoal from which fragments of charred bone protruded: it was the remains of her pyre. She watched, confused, as a hunched and hooded man crept to the edge of the pile and with a stick began to poke through the cinders. His hand was spotted and wrinkled with age, and Caitlyn knew that it was Beneto.

A moment later, Beneto's search through the ashes was rewarded when he knocked aside a bit of wood: in the midst of a black, greasy smear of carbon sat a lump of deep burgundy flesh the size of a fist.

Caitlyn knew it was her heart, untouched by the flames.

His shoulders shaking, Beneto retrieved the heart with his bare hands and tenderly folded it into a cloth. He bowed his head and wept.

And then shocking cold suddenly hit Caitlyn in the face.

Wrenched from sleep, Caitlyn sat bolt upright and knocked heads with Amalia. The princess yelped and stumbled back.

Coughing and sputtering, Caitlyn heaved for breath through a nose full of water. Her mind was caught between sleep and waking, and for a long moment she couldn't make sense of what was happening. Cold water was dripping down her face and had saturated her shirt. "*Water?!*" She gaped at Amalia. "Did you throw *water* on me?"

"I thought you were dead!" Amalia said, her face pale.

"Dead?! Why the hell would I be dead?"

Amalia shook her head. "You weren't breathing."

Caitlyn's muscles went weak. She hadn't been breathing? A flush of horror ran through her as she recalled the gray lack of sensation as she floated above her ashes.

She'd died! Bianca had killed her in that dream!

But then she felt the cold of her wet shirt, and reason sharply reasserted itself. She was alive, wasn't she? She was sitting here, awake. "How could I not be breathing? Of course I was breathing!"

"I called your name and shook you, and you wouldn't wake up."

"And knowing how bad I've been sleeping, you thought that my sleeping soundly was a good reason to wake me?" Caitlyn snapped, the frightening dream having put her on edge.

Amalia bit her lower lip. "I was scared. You looked . . . unnatural. Something wasn't right."

A shiver ran down Caitlyn's spine. She crossed her arms, rubbing them as if she could chase away the horror of the dream as easily as she could a chill. She saw the worry on Amalia's face, and her anger drained away. "I'm sorry I snapped at you," she said at last. "I was startled and lashed out. I'm sorry."

"I'm sorry I dumped water on you. But you ought to get that checked by the school nurse."

"What?"

"The no breathing. I think that's called sleep apnea. Maybe it explains your nightmares. Your brain gets no oxygen and panics."

Denial was on Caitlyn's lips, but then reason intruded. "Maybe you're right," she said slowly. Could it be that simple? Her nightmares might be caused by something as commonplace as sleep apnea.

"I'll get you a dry pillow," Amalia said.

Caitlyn nodded her thanks, but her mind was lost in confused thought. She changed out of her wet clothes and into her nightgown as she mulled over the dream she'd just had.

The nightmare about Bianca had been different than a Screecher nightmare. For all the horror, it had been more like one of her usual, vivid dreams. It had a story to it, a sequence of events. Newly dry, she sat on her bed with her dream journal and sketched out the scenes from her dream: the Fiat Lux window, Raphael and Beneto standing in front of it with the crystal chest; the silver square in the windowsill that became a pit holding a rising Bianca; the pyre; and then Beneto uncovering her unburned heart in the ashes.

She quickly thumbed back through the pages until she found the drawing she'd done that past October back in Oregon, of the dream of being burned at the stake. It was almost the same dream, except that this time there had been the addition of watching Beneto sift through the ashes afterward.

The hairs prickled on the back of her neck. "*. . . just as you risked your life to bring it to me from out of the ashes,*" Raphael had told Beneto.

Was it somehow *her* heart in that crystal box?

She shivered and tried to shove away the sense of horror.

An idea tickled at the back of her mind; she turned the pages of her journal back to the dream tarot reading and looked again at her sketches of the tarot cards.

The cards representing the people coming into her life were the Queen of Swords and the Knight of Cups. The Knight of Cups she thought she understood: Raphael. But who was the Queen of Swords?

Eugenia Snowe, her unconscious answered. A coldly intelligent woman who could help her, but who could just as easily cut her down.

But couldn't the Queen of Swords also be Bianca de' Medici?

It was the next set of cards that was most critical, the three cards representing the situation she was in: the Three of Swords, with three blades piercing a heart; the Fool stepping into the abyss; and finally, Death.

She read the notes she'd scrawled under the card showing the heart: *they seek to destroy the heart, but you must not let them.* Who was trying to destroy it, and how could she possibly stop them?

Caitlyn plucked the tarot card of the Wheel of Fortune out of the pages of her journal and read again what her mother had written along its edge: *the heart in darkness.*

What darkness? And what did it have to do with Fortune's wheel?

Caitlyn exhaled in frustration and looked at the Fool, stepping into the abyss. Her note beneath said: *I must awake to what is happening. I am at the edge of the abyss.*

They were the same words Daniela had used when talking about Brigitte's brother Thierry: *Je suis au bord du gouffre.* But what could Thierry possibly have to do with anything?

And then there was the third card in the series: Death. *Not always literal*, Caitlyn had written beneath it. *Transformation to new life*. Well, she'd just died in her dream. Did that count?

The final card, of course, was the Wheel of Fortune. She'd thought it a reassurance that the Fortune School was part of her destiny, but she wondered now if she'd been too quick to take that as the whole answer. There was a Templar fortune hidden somewhere in the castle, and Raphael was looking for that fortune. Fortune meant fate, and it meant luck—either good or bad—but it also meant wealth. Raphael needed wealth to take his sisters to England, out of the reach of Catherine de' Medici.

Was Caitlyn meant to help him find the Templar fortune?

Amalia interrupted her thoughts, returning to the room with a fresh pillow. "Here you are," she said sheepishly, putting the pillow at the head of Caitlyn's bed and plumping it. "Nice and dry."

"Thanks."

Amalia tilted her head, looking at the journal in Caitlyn's lap. "I've seen you drawing in that before," she said, a cautious curiosity in her eyes.

Caitlyn bit her bottom lip and unconsciously held the journal against her chest, protecting it from prying eyes. She'd always kept the journal to herself, unwilling to let anyone see into the chaos of her mind.

"I'm sorry," Amalia apologized, and retreated with pink cheeks. "I shouldn't have mentioned it. It is obviously private."

"No, it's okay," Caitlyn said, feeling bad for Amalia's embarrassment. She forced herself to lower the journal. "It's a dream journal, is all. None of it would make sense to anyone but me."

"You draw your dreams?"

Caitlyn nodded. "And my nightmares."

"So you have drawn those things you call Screechers?"

"Yeah."

Amalia inched closer. "Could I see one?"

Caitlyn hesitated, then flipped back to the drawing she'd done of the Screecher she'd seen on her first night at the school. She held up the picture of the screaming, clawing, femalelike creature with the wet hair.

Amalia's lips parted. "*Mein Gott*," she swore. "I think I would wake screaming, too!" She shook her head. "You *must* be tested for sleep apnea, if there is a chance it could rid you of those things. How will you ever get restful sleep, with creatures like that in your head?"

Caitlyn closed the journal. "I know. It's bad."

But if she had sleep apnea and it caused her Screecher nightmares *and* her vivid dreams of Raphael, then treating the apnea might put an end to both types of dreams.

Getting rid of the Screechers at the price of losing Raphael was not a deal Caitlyn was ready to make.

CHAPTER
Seventeen

At midnight that night Caitlyn quietly slipped from her room and headed to the Grand Salon, her heart beating with renewed excitement and fear. She'd lain in bed for the last two hours and stared at the ceiling, her mind going over what she would do differently the next time she tried lucid dreaming.

She was so grateful to Brigitte for the idea. It *had* worked, as far as getting her to Raphael was concerned. She had to take it further, though; she had to retain awareness that she was dreaming while she dreamed. It would give her some control over what happened. She could keep Bianca out of her dreams, or at least she could keep from being scared half to death by her, or burned at the stake.

But she was going to take a slightly more scientific approach this next time, and for that she needed the help of someone who could sit awake beside her.

The nightly gaggle of TV-watching girls had long since left, and Naomi was the sole occupant of the Grand Salon, curled in a big chair reading a book. The floor lamp beside her cast a soft, dim light. She glanced up as Caitlyn came in. "*Hoo hoo*," she called, like an owl.

"*Hoo,*" Caitlyn replied, smiling. It was their night owl greeting to each other. Caitlyn arranged a nest of throw pillows and a blanket on the couch. "I want to try an experiment, and I need your help."

"Yes?" Naomi sat up and put her book aside.

Caitlyn explained Amalia's idea about sleep apnea. "So I have this," she said, taking a compact mirror out of her robe pocket, "and if I seem not to be breathing, I want you to hold it in front of my nose and see if it gets foggy."

"Like in *Romeo and Juliet?*"

"Yeah. But don't take poison or stab yourself if you don't see fog."

Naomi made a sad face. "You'll think I don't care."

Caitlyn chuckled and set the mirror on the end table, along with a small travel alarm clock set to ring in the morning so she wouldn't miss class. "Don't wake me up, either."

"How could I? If you're not breathing, you're dead."

"It hasn't killed me so far. If it's sleep apnea, I'll wake myself up after a minute or so as I gasp for breath." She'd done some quick research online, to find that out. "I could be breathing, though, and it's just too shallow to tell by sight. That's where the mirror will help."

"You seem to think I have nothing better to do than sit here awake half the night and watch you sleep."

"I know you'd rather be off haunting girls with small bladders."

Naomi shrugged, her eyes twinkling. "We all have our hobbies."

Caitlyn nestled into place on the couch and pulled the corner of the throw blanket over her eyes to block the lamplight. "Good night."

"I hope so."

"Me, too." That, too, had become a ritual exchange between them.

Caitlyn listened to the soft tick of the clock on the mantel and heard Naomi pick up her book, then turn a page.

She stilled the thoughts in her mind, gently shoving them away. She became vaguely aware of her breathing deepening, and she felt her face and body begin to relax.

Raphael. I want to find Raphael.

She held his face in her mind as she sank into sleep . . .

And suddenly she found herself standing by an open interior doorway in the castle. She heard male voices, laughing loudly and joking with the rambunctious energy unique to guys playing a game. A serving girl wearing a rough gray bodice with cord lacing up the front, a brown skirt with stained apron, and sleeves rolled up past her elbows brushed by Caitlyn with a tray of food and went into the room.

Caitlyn looked down at her own clothes and saw a rose satin gown. It looked familiar, but her confused, dreaming mind could not place it. She followed the serving girl into the room, irrationally certain that the guys would think she was another servant.

Four familiar young men sat at a table in front of a fireplace, playing cards and drinking. A flush of joy went through her as she spotted Raphael: he was sitting with his back to her, but his hair and the set of his shoulders were unmistakable. Not wanting to interrupt his game, she wandered around the room, hoping he'd see her and abandon the game on his own.

There was a four-poster bed at the far end of the room, its dark blue draperies embroidered with silver thread. Wood paneling covered the walls, and the ceiling was made of thick wood beams spaced only a few inches apart. One wall was composed mostly of windows. A dim sense of recognition crept through her dreaming mind, and she turned to stare at the fireplace, feeling a dizzying sense of déjà vu. She had been here before. She knew this room.

It was Madame Snowe's office.

As soon as she thought it, she knew she was dreaming. She blinked in surprise and looked down again at her clothes, astonished by the seeming reality. But as quickly as the realization came that she was dreaming, it began to slip away. She fought to hold on to it, but it dissipated like smoke in the wind, and her mind fell back to accepting the present reality as the only reality.

Neither the serving girl nor the men seemed to care about her presence, sparing her not so much as a glance. She walked to the fireplace, above which hung a strange portrait titled *Fire*, of a man whose face had been cleverly constructed out of candles, burning wood, and oil lamps, while his body was made of cannons and guns.

"You're back," Raphael whispered beside her, his sudden appearance making her jump.

"So I am," she said, glancing up at him and then away, his closeness suddenly making her shy. She was secretly pleased, though, that he had left the card game to come talk to her.

"Let's go where we can talk." He turned away and started for the door.

Caitlyn grabbed his arm, making him jump and jerk away. She clasped her hands together, embarrassed. He'd pulled away as if he couldn't bear to be touched by her. She nodded her head toward the young men at the table, who were continuing their game of cards without Raphael. "Will you introduce me to your friends?"

"That wouldn't be wise," he said tightly.

Philippe, his blue eyes bright, looked up from his cards. "To whom are you talking, Raphael?" he asked in French.

As if he cannot see me standing right here! Caitlyn thought, irritated.

"An angel, come to spirit me away before I lose any more money to you."

Philippe laughed, and Raphael took the chance to leave, apparently trusting Caitlyn to follow.

She was slightly mollified by having been called an angel, but still, that Philippe was very rude to pretend she wasn't visible. "Who is he to you?" she asked.

"His name is Philippe, le Comte d'Ormond," Raphael said as he led her down the hall. "He invites us to his room to play cards every night."

"He's French?"

"One of Catherine's spies. Supposedly, he's here to keep an eye on the Huguenots in the area and to report on any rumors that they are organizing to free the Protestant king Henry of Navarre, who is under house arrest in Paris. Navarre is, of course, just to the southwest of here. Philippe himself will tell you that is a front, though, and that his real job is to make sure I don't escape Catherine's clutches. He can be disarmingly honest in that way."

"And Ursino and Giovanni, who are they to you?"

"They are cousins of mine, of a sort, from Florence."

"Are you from Florence?" she asked, almost jogging to keep up with his quick pace.

He shook his head. "Rome."

"And Beneto? Who is he?" she asked. "He does not play cards?"

"He's likely sleeping. He has been my teacher since I was a boy."

"Oh. What are all of you doing here? Why did you come to France and put yourself within reach of Catherine de' Medici?"

"You don't know?" he asked, pausing in surprise. "How can you not know?"

She stopped, too. "Should I?" she asked, flustered.

He frowned at her, assessing, as if trying to change a fundamental understanding of who he thought she was. "How is life at the convent?" he asked carefully, taking a lit taper out of a candelabra and leading her into a small study. He closed the door behind them and used the taper to light a pair of reflective silver sconces on the wall.

"It's all right," she said, and at his invitation she sat in a straight-backed, tapestry-covered chair with wooden arms. She smoothed her skirts. "I am not as homesick as I was at first, but the schoolwork is demanding. You're changing the subject, though."

Instead of answering, he brought the candle he held to within a foot of her face, staring intently at her.

"What are you doing?" she asked, leaning away from the flame.

"Getting a good look at you." He wedged the candle in a holder on the small table beside Caitlyn's chair and sat down opposite her, his gaze still intent upon her. "Where were you born?"

"At the ends of the earth." The answer came out of her without conscious thought.

"And where's that?"

"Beyond the ocean," she said, crossing her arms over her chest as if to protect herself, "and across the land of peoples you call savages." He was treating her like a suspect, although for what crime she couldn't tell.

"How did you get here?"

"I flew."

He flinched in surprise. "On your wings?" he asked warily. "Or a broomstick?"

She laughed and unfolded her arms. "Don't be silly. I—" she started, then broke off, frowning to herself, unable to remember what she'd been about to say. She could remember seeing clouds from above, and the sun rising over their tops, but she could form no picture of exactly *how* she had flown.

"Why do you keep coming to me?" he asked.

"You're the Knight of Cups, and this is the only place I know to find you."

He sighed in frustration. "You called me the Knight of Cups before, but what does that *mean*?"

Caitlyn blushed and didn't answer. She wasn't sure why she called him the Knight of Cups; the reason was lost in another part of her consciousness. All she knew was that she was drawn to him and needed to be here with him. She needed to hear his voice, to watch the expressions move across his face like clouds across the sky; she needed to be close enough that, if she reached out, she could once again run her hands through his hair. She couldn't tell *him* that, though.

He leaned forward, his gaze intent upon hers, his hand on the arm of her chair as if confining her to its bounds. She could feel the warmth of his closeness and smell the hint of a spicy scent on his skin. His knee bumped hers, and she felt an awareness of his presence tingle over her body. She lost herself in the deep hazel of his eyes, where the flame of the candle flickered.

As if moved by a force beyond herself, Caitlyn lifted her hand and reached toward his face. A spark of surprise touched his eyes, but he didn't move away as she lightly touched his cheek.

His skin was soft as velvet. Her lips parted on a breath, and she stroked his cheek, feeling the sharp prickle of whiskers roughening his jaw. The sensation on her fingertips was sharp and real, and it stirred awake a sleeping part of her mind.

I'm dreaming. She blinked in surprise, her hand freezing in place. *He's not real. This isn't real.*

"Caitlyn," Raphael whispered, a look of wonder softening his face.

She frowned. He *felt* real. She moved her fingertips to his lower lip, and gently stroked over the full, silken curve. *Dreams don't feel like this. I can feel the moistness of his breath. How can I be dreaming?*

Raphael reached up and held her hand. "Are you the Dark One I was promised?"

"I am Caitlyn Monahan," she said, feeling her consciousness struggle to maintain lucidity against the dream. *Do I dream, or do I wake? Am I here? If not here, where?* Her mind offered a glimpse of the couch in the Grand Salon, of Naomi reading under a lamp. The image was as distant and fragile as a dream; it felt as if it belonged to another life.

"*She* sent you, didn't she?" Raphael asked.

Caitlyn shook her head, not understanding. "I came of my own free will. To find you."

He nodded, as if that made sense to him in some way. "I need you," he said.

Her breath caught in her throat. "Anything."

"The Templar treasure," he said. "We *have* to find it."

Disappointment pricked at her. She'd hoped for something more personal. "So that you can take your sisters to England?"

"That's important, but secondary. We have a more pressing need."

"Is that why you and your cousins came to Château de la Fortune?" she asked quietly, leaning back and scolding her heart for assuming too much. "You're looking for the treasure?"

He nodded.

"But the story may not even be true; there may not *be* a treasure."

"There is. Bianca told me it exists."

The name startled her. "Bianca! Who *is* she to you? How did you know her?"

For a moment his face tightened with pain, and then he clenched his jaw against it. "She was my adoptive mother."

Caitlyn's mouth dropped open. "*Bianca de' Medici?*"

"My own mother died when I was born; my father died shortly after he met Bianca, when I was three. She took me in and raised me as her own, when I had no one else. And now the lives of my adoptive sisters, and the eternal life of Bianca herself depend upon my finding the Templar treasure."

"I don't understand. Why? How?"

"There's something I need to show you before you can understand. Come," he said, rising and taking the candle.

Caitlyn followed him out of the room and then through the castle, down to the kitchens and cellars, Raphael pausing at each corner and doorway to be sure that no one was there to see his route. He took her to a small, dirty storeroom empty except for a few rotted wood boxes, dusty clay jugs, and the remnants of what had once been a rat.

Raphael set the candle on the edge of a box and moved the jugs aside, revealing a rusted iron ring set in a floor stone. He knelt and used the ring to pull up the stone, uncovering a shallow depression in which rested an object wrapped in oiled cloth. Raphael lifted it out and sat back on his heels, then unfolded the cloth.

Candlelight glimmered in a thousand refractions in the depths of the quartz cabochon atop the crystal chest. "This is what you almost found in the trunk, upstairs," he said reverently. "It holds Bianca's heart."

Bianca's. Not hers. Caitlyn felt a giddy relief and stared in fascination at the richly decorated reliquary. She heard no heartbeats in her head.

"Do you want me to open it?" he asked, his voice uncertain.

She didn't want to see it, and yet part of her *had* to. "Yes."

He released the clasp on the lid and raised it. The heart, maroon marbled with yellow, had dried to an unrecognizable, unthreatening lump.

Caitlyn was disappointed, and repulsed. "Why on earth did you keep it?"

"Bianca told Beneto and me before she died that her heart would be in the ashes and that we should retrieve it. She said that as long as the heart was preserved she would still have a link to this earth, but that the heart would soon turn to dust unless we brought it here, to Château de la Fortune, and entombed it in the Templar treasure. If I did that, she would have the power to protect her daughters even from beyond the grave."

"How would putting her heart in the treasure do that?"

His face showed his frustration. "I don't *know*. I don't think that she herself knew; she often knew things that were true, but at first glance appeared to make no sense, or have no explanation. The worst thing, though, was that she couldn't tell me *where* in the castle the treasure was hidden."

"Raphael, who was Bianca? *What* was she? How did she even know about the Templar treasure?"

He closed the chest and slipped it back into its hiding place. "She called herself a daughter of the natural world. Not a witch, or a heretic. She didn't worship Satan or cast spells. She didn't poison people. She was something that existed outside of the Church and the laws of men."

He rearranged the jugs on top of the stone and stood, picking up the candle. "Let's go to my chamber to finish the story; we'll have privacy there."

She nodded, and they hurried silently back through the castle and up the spiral stairs. Once in his room he bolted the door and then stirred the fire to life. He pulled two chairs close to it and sat in one.

Caitlyn sat in the other, then surreptitiously kicked off her shoes and pulled her feet up underneath her skirts, settling in. The firelight caught in Raphael's bronze hair and caressed his face. She felt like she could sit there all night, if it meant looking at him.

"Bianca's story truly starts in the twelfth century, with Simon de Gagéac," Raphael said.

"The Knight Templar who once owned this castle."

He nodded. "The Templars were monastic warriors, sworn members of a religious brotherhood. Simon came from a noble family and was a devout Christian who believed that he fought in service to God. He had the rank of commander in Jerusalem, and some thought he would someday rise to become grand master of the entire order."

"So he took it seriously."

"Yes. But that all changed when he met a young woman from a small community outside of Jerusalem, a woman named Eshael. She was not Christian, Jew, or Muslim. She and her female kin instead worshipped a goddess in rites that had begun in the mists of time. To Simon, she was a heathen. But that did not stop him from falling madly, hopelessly in love with her."

Caitlyn smiled. "It sounds very romantic."

"But how often do such romantic tales end in happiness? Simon's passion for Eshael was so all-consuming that he abandoned the Templar brotherhood and his vows of celibacy and poverty. He swore devotion to Eshael and promised to take her to France and treat her as a queen. Her female kin gave her a dowry of so much gold and treasure that eight wagons were needed to carry it.

"Simon's family later said that it had been the plan of Eshael's kin from the beginning to send her and the dowry to France, where both would be safe from the wars of the Crusades. They said that Eshael and her kin used the ancient magic of their goddess to enchant Simon."

"Some people say that love itself is the most powerful magic," Caitlyn said.

"But would true love make a man go against every principle that had guided his life, and make him break vows he had made to God?" Raphael shook his head. "Simon brought Eshael here, to the château, but she would not give up her goddess and so he could not marry her. The local men were frightened of Eshael and her strange ways. There were stories of firelight in the caves that pierce the cliffs beneath the château, and the dancing shadows of local women that Eshael had converted to worship of her goddess.

"Simon's love for Eshael began to fade; he started to see evil in all she did and all she was. The final straw came after Eshael bore him their first child, a daughter. When Simon discovered Eshael consecrating their child to her goddess, the last vestiges of his love turned to hatred. In his rage, he killed her."

"Oh my God," Caitlyn whispered, horrified. "What happened to the child?"

"Simon couldn't love the girl, nor could he kill his own flesh. He sent her to distant relatives to the east and forgot about her. Simon went on to marry and have legal sons and daughters, but after Eshael's death he was never the same. He became as obsessed with his sins as he had once been with Eshael, and he was convinced that her dowry was cursed.

"Eshael's child eventually married and bore only daughters; that daughter, in turn, married and bore only daughters; and so on through the centuries, each daughter passing down this story as their legacy. The daughters of Eshael had a talent for midwifery, and they passed down that skill as well. Eventually, one of these daughters married a merchant from Florence, and so a descendant of Eshael was born just outside that great city. She was Ania, and she would one day become Bianca's mother.

"At fourteen, Ania was beautiful, but there was something otherworldly about her. Ania sometimes knew the future, and people thought there was more to her healing than herbs and hot compresses. It was something in her hands themselves that healed them.

"One day while she was out gathering herbs, she caught the eye of Cosimo de' Medici. It was the year 1535, and he was only sixteen."

Caitlyn nodded, remembering what she'd found in her research about Bianca.

"Like Simon, he went nearly mad with love. Ania became pregnant, and although there was never a possibility that she and Cosimo would marry, he promised to take care of her and their child.

"Ania's pregnancy was unusually difficult, and Ania's mother tried everything she knew of midwifery to save her daughter and the baby. When nothing worked, in desperation she experimented on Ania, trying cures she'd seen in dreams. But in the end, Ania died giving birth to her daughter, whom she named Bianca.

"Bianca told me that her grandmother always insisted that it was the medicines she'd given to Ania during her pregnancy that had changed Bianca from a normal child of Eshael's gifted line into something . . . different.

"Young Cosimo was devastated by Ania's death, but his family was ready for him to move into the city and take on his new role as a leader in the de' Medici family. He kept his word to care for Bianca and brought her with him to Florence, raising her alongside other de' Medici children. Even when he married Eleanor de Toledo and they had their own children, Bianca was treated as a proper member of the family. Eleanor is said to have loved her as her own. For a while, anyway."

"What happened to change that?" Caitlyn asked.

"Whatever gifts Bianca inherited from Eshael's line were magnified by the medicines Ania was given during her pregnancy. Even as a small child, when Bianca was angry she could make objects fly across the room. She knew who was going to die, and how and when, and she told them. She had visions of the future that always came true. And if she tried very hard, she could make a living creature sicken and die just by staring at it."

"Good God," Caitlyn whispered.

"Cosimo was the only person she loved enough to want to obey, at least occasionally. Everyone else was frightened of her and let her run wild. And Cosimo eventually lost control of her when she seduced the family priest when she was twelve."

"You mean *he* seduced *her*."

Raphael shook his head. "No. She told me he was a challenge she set out to conquer, just to see if she could do it. After that, she was beyond even Cosimo's control. She ran off with a painter: my father."

"Your father was an artist!"

"A student of Bronzino's."

"The portrait! Bronzino did two portraits of Bianca!"

Raphael nodded. "My father died soon after running off with Bianca, and even though she had almost nothing and was nearly a child herself, she took me under her wing. In time she became a celebrated beauty, and used her de' Medici name and connections to find herself ever more powerful lovers, until she finally became the mistress of Cardinal Rebiba, Grand Inquisitor of the Roman Inquisition."

"And signed her own death warrant," Caitlyn whispered.

Raphael nodded. "She had two daughters before she met Rebiba: Giulia and Elisabeta; each had a different father. Bianca traveled to Paris more than once to visit her distant de' Medici cousin, Catherine, Queen of France. Bianca hinted that at Catherine's request she herself had caused Henry II to have the jousting accident that killed him and left Catherine in control of the country.

"When Pope Pius V eventually found out that Bianca was the mistress of his Grand Inquisitor, he was enraged. Cardinal Rebiba was in charge of investigating heretics, and yet he was sleeping with one of international renown.

"Rebiba renounced her," Raphael said with bitterness. "He did it to save his own skin. He filled Pius's head with tales of her sorcery, but then he went a step further and said that Giulia and Elisabeta had inherited Bianca's satanic craft.

"Even Cosimo could not save Bianca from the stake after Cardinal Rebiba's testimony."

Caitlyn swore softly. She had a flashback to the nightmare Bianca had given her, of being burned.

"Cosimo might not have been able to save Bianca, but he did arrange to send Giulia and Elisabeta—and me—into the relative protection of Catherine de' Medici's care."

"Did Giulia and Elisabeta inherit Bianca's talents, like the cardinal said?"

"Yes. That's why Catherine holds them. France is in crisis, and she needs every means at her disposal to maintain power over it. Giulia and Elisabeta could prove invaluable weapons against Catherine's enemies. I didn't realize that at first, though. I was stupid. I trusted that Catherine's only wish would be to help Giulia and Elisabeta, and in my ignorance I made a terrible mistake."

"What did you do?"

"I told Catherine that there was a Templar treasure hidden at Château de la Fortune, and that Bianca had asked me to find it and place her heart at its center." Raphael put his hand to his face, half covering it in shame as he shook his head at his error. "I should *not* have been so naïve!" He dropped his hand and sighed. "Catherine kept the girls in Paris with her, 'for safekeeping,' while I came here to find the treasure."

"So Catherine is holding them hostage, guaranteeing that once you find the treasure you won't run off with it."

He nodded. "And now someone is trying to steal Bianca's heart. I assume it's someone in Catherine's employ, as having the heart might increase my sisters' powers. It might also be someone sent by Pius, though; he would see it as the last trace of Bianca that must be destroyed."

"*Does* the heart have power, like they think?"

"I think it does." He paused and met Caitlyn's eyes. "I think it brought you to me."

Caitlyn's skin went cold. *Bianca's burned heart* was the force that had drawn her to Raphael? She shook her head, unwilling to accept it.

"You saved me from the falling stone," Raphael insisted. "And you know something about the treasure. I swore to Bianca I would find it, and I *will*. With your help."

His intensity was almost frightening. She was still reeling from the story he'd told about Eshael, Ania, and Bianca, and from the idea that the Queen of France was holding his adoptive sisters hostage and possibly hoping to get her hands on Bianca's heart.

Caitlyn took a breath and gathered her wits, then she told Raphael the little she knew about Gerard, the last of Simon's family, and according to legend the last to know the location of the treasure that Simon had hidden somewhere in the castle. "Shortly before he died," Caitlyn said, "Gerard wrote a letter to a friend saying, 'Only the light of God can guide you to the true treasure,' meaning salvation, supposedly." Almost as an afterthought Caitlyn added, "And Gerard made an unusual sundial."

Raphael's eyes went wide.

"Why are you looking at me like that?" she asked.

"'The light of God.'"

"What is that, anyway? I mean, specifically."

"It can be many things. Truth. Christ. God's word. Righteousness." Raphael started to smile. "It can even mean . . . the sun."

Caitlyn's lips parted. "The sundial," she breathed.

He nodded, the firelight dancing in his eyes. "Only the *sun* can guide us to the true treasure."

Caitlyn's heart thumped, and she jumped to her feet. "There must be some trace of the sundial still here!"

He laughed. "It won't be pointing us anywhere right now: it's night."

"So? We can still look for it."

"We don't need to."

"Why not?"

He grinned. "I already know where it is."

CHAPTER
Eighteen

"Show me!" Caitlyn demanded.

"You can't wait until morning?"

"No!"

"Neither can I," he confessed with a grin. Candle in hand, he unbolted the door and led her out into the hall, checking first to see that no one else was about.

They went up one of the spiral staircases and down another corridor before reaching their destination: a large room at the end of one wing of the castle. Windows let in just enough moonlight to show the room's few features: a fireplace big enough to walk into; a few wooden chairs; an assortment of swords and axes mounted on the walls; some padding and shields on a rack; and a battered table on which Raphael set the candle.

"It's where the others practice fighting in bad weather," Raphael explained.

"Not you?"

"Me, too. Just not with the same enthusiasm."

"You don't like it?"

"It's good exercise for keeping strong, and it is a skill I need to have, but no, I don't enjoy it like the others do. I would rather spend my energies elsewhere."

Caitlyn went to a window and looked through a small pane of leaded glass at the valley far below, the Dordogne River a silver necklace laid in a velvet bed of trees and fields. Even in the moonlight she could tell that it was summer, not winter. "I love this view," she said.

He came to stand beside her at the window, so close that if she leaned slightly toward him their arms would touch. "I would like it better if there were a city in it," he said.

"You don't like the countryside?"

"I'm not fond of being alone."

She gazed up at him, hearing an echo of loneliness in his voice. "Are you alone, even with your adoptive cousins and your tutor here with you?"

"I was," he said, meeting her eyes.

Her breath caught in her throat. "You have no one special to you, in Rome? No girl?"

He shook his head. "I was too busy in Beneto's workshop to meet anyone. I was never one for drinking and carousing; I felt most at home in the quiet of the art studio."

"Do you mean that Beneto is an *art* teacher?"

"Of course. He was fortunate enough, as a very young man, to have been a student of Raffaello Sanzio—I'm named after him, by the way. Beneto was never able to make a name for himself with his art, but through his workshop he's created many young artists in Rome. Bianca was a great patroness to him, and he was devoted to her. He closed his workshop to come with me here, with her heart."

"So *you're* an artist, like your father was before you?"

He shook his head, clearly embarrassed. "I don't dare call myself one, yet; I've only had a few minor commissions. Someday, I'd like to have my own studio, though. Someday, when my sisters are safe."

"And what will you paint in your studio, someday?"

He looked partly away, then slanted his gaze back at her. "Perhaps I'll paint you."

Made self-conscious by the flattery, Caitlyn put the back of her wrist to her forehead and all her weight to one hip in a melodramatic pose.

"No, I wouldn't paint you like that," Raphael said softly. "I'd make you a spirit of the air, treading the clouds. A goddess."

Caitlyn dropped her wrist, embarrassed. "No one's ever compared me to a goddess before."

"Shouldn't all women be treated as such?"

She gave him a sideways, suspicious look. "It's a good thing you didn't get out of the workshop much. The girls of Rome would have been in trouble!"

He grinned and waggled his brows. "Do you think so?"

She pushed his shoulder. "Naughty boy."

"I could be much naughtier."

Caitlyn sucked in a breath, alarmed and thrilled by the dangerous look in his eyes. She clasped her hands primly in front of her. "So where's the sundial?" she squeaked.

Raphael gave her a knowing, mischievous look, then went to the middle of the room and gestured for her to join him. "Look around and tell me what you see."

She joined him in the middle of the room and only then, as she looked around, saw that one of the windows had an inset of a sun shining down on water. "The library!" she said.

"No," Raphael said, shaking his head in obvious puzzlement.

"Yes, it's . . . ," she trailed off, her mind flipping back and forth between dream and reality. *It's never been a library, as far as he knows,* she thought. She walked slowly toward the sun window, stopping in front of it. The familiar polished square of metal was set in the stone sill, reflecting moonlight. She shuddered.

"You found it," Raphael said.

She turned to him. "Found what?"

"The sundial."

She shook her head, not understanding.

"The sun comes through the window and hits the silver mirror," he said, pointing to the metal plate, "then the reflection hits the ceiling. There are time lines painted across the plaster above us, and the reflected light from the mirror will point to what time it is, using those lines."

Surprised, Caitlyn tilted her head back, looking up at the ceiling that, unlike most in the castle, had its beams hidden under a smooth, plastered surface. It was not white, though: its entirety was covered in painted designs that she could not make out in the candlelight. "The clue to the treasure is in those designs somewhere?"

"It must be," he said, excitement in his voice.

She felt the same eagerness and only wished she knew what to look for or where to begin. "What does *Fiat Lux* mean?" she asked, turning back to the window and pointing to where she knew the words to be. They were barely visible in the darkness.

"'Let there be light.'"

"Is that from the Bible?"

"You truly are a godless creature, aren't you? It's from Genesis. Chapter one, third verse. It's about the creation of the world."

"Oh," she said, embarrassed. She avoided his gaze and looked at the mirror. She was still leery of it, but curiosity made her gingerly lay her fingertip on its surface, ready to jerk back her hand at the least sign of a menacing shadow.

Nothing happened. The silver was cool and smooth under her touch. In fact, not only was there no shadow, but there was no reflection of her fingertip in the silver at all. Confused, Caitlyn once again leaned over the shining square, seeking her own gaze in a reflection.

There was nothing there but silver.

As a cold flush of shock ran over her skin, remembered advice surfaced in her mind: "*There are tests you can do in your dream, like looking at your face in a mirror: if your reflection is not normal, you're dreaming.*"

Caitlyn's mind suddenly sharpened, as if shaking off the last traces of sleep. She was dreaming. None of this was real. She slowly turned and looked at Raphael, and felt her heart contract in pain. Did this mean that *he* was a figment of her imagination?

She shook her head. She wanted him to be real. No, she *needed* him to be real. He was her Knight of Cups. Wasn't he?

"Jump up and down," she ordered through a tight throat. She would see if the figment obeyed her commands.

"Why?"

That's exactly what she would have expected him to say. She hated testing him, but she had to; she had to know if this was all a fantasy constructed out of her own loneliness.

Caitlyn closed her eyes and let an image come to mind from the secret depths of her heart: to have Raphael enfold her in his arms, one of his hands on the back of her head, the other around her waist. She imagined the warmth of his body, the pressure of his velvet-clad shoulder against her cheek. And then she waited, eyes closed, to see if it would happen.

"Caitlyn? What's wrong?"

She opened her eyes as he approached, her heart beating painfully fast. What would he do? Hold her, as she had so deliberately imagined? *Please don't. Please don't be a figment of my imagination, who does only what I want him to do.*

"You look scared." He lifted his hand and reached toward her, then hesitated, uncertainty in his expression. With great care he brushed a wisp of hair away from her face, his touch so light she could barely feel his fingertips. "Are you all right?"

"I don't know." He was doing what she truly wanted, acting as if he existed independently from her mind. "Are you real?" she asked hoarsely.

He let his hand rest against the side of her neck, apparently seeing nothing strange in her question. "Yes."

She closed her eyes, feeling the warmth of his touch. "You have no idea how much I want to believe you."

"Do I truly need to convince you?"

She felt him move toward her, every nerve in her skin aware of his closeness. One hand rested on her hip, then slid to the small of her back. The other moved from her neck to the back of her head, his long fingers sliding up into her hair.

He was doing exactly as she had imagined he would. She opened her eyes, her vision blurred with tears of disappointment.

"*Shh,*" he whispered. "Don't cry." With gentle lips he kissed her brow, her temple, the top of her cheek.

"I want to believe in you," she said, leaning against the hard planes of his chest and torso, her head coming up only to his chin. He felt warm and strong and *solid*. She could feel his soft breath against her face, and the beating of his heart.

"*Caitlyn,*" he said, yearning in his voice. He bent his head down, pressing his cheek to hers, his lips tenderly kissing the edge of her jaw, the lobe of her ear. His hands on her back and head tightened, pulling her more closely to him. He turned his head slightly, his mouth brushing over her skin to find her lips. "You cannot doubt me," he said, his mouth hovering above hers, "when it is you who may not be real."

His words sent a bolt of shock through her.

The next moment, Caitlyn opened her eyes to the Grand Salon. She was lying on the leather couch, her blanket twisted tightly around her like the enfolding arms of a lover, and the alarm clock sourly beeping notice that it was morning.

CHAPTER
Nineteen

That afternoon, Caitlyn watched the slow progression of a rectangle of light across the white, featureless expanse of the library ceiling. It was cast by the mirror she'd laid on top of the tarnished silver square in the windowsill, and she'd been watching it for over an hour. She had missed the first half of her French class, but her body refused to rise out of the chair. She was too tired, too wrung out, and too full of self-doubt to feel curiosity about the sundial.

She'd gone to her algebra and history classes that morning, but as soon as she was free for lunch, she'd found her way down into the lower levels of the castle, seeking the storeroom where Raphael had hidden the crystal chest. She'd searched for half an hour, but found only unfamiliar hallways, pipes, boilers, garbage, laundry, and storage rooms full of ratty furniture. Nothing looked familiar, and she quickly lost her orientation in the low-ceilinged corridors. Bianca's heart may have been three feet from her, or on the other side of the castle entirely.

Defeated, she'd come to the library, set the mirror on the sill, and collapsed into a chair to watch the reflection of light upon the ceiling. She was desperate to prove something—anything—about her dreams to have a concrete reality.

She was haunted by the words that Raphael had spoken, when his lips were about to kiss her own:

You cannot doubt me, when it is you who may not be real.

Did he think that *she* was a figment of *his* imagination?

She remembered her earlier theory, about she and Raphael being avatars in a dream world; so maybe Raphael really was a boy somewhere nearby, dreaming dreams of her just as she dreamed dreams of him.

Or maybe she was nuts, and the dreams were dreams, nothing more.

Naomi had left her a note in the Grand Salon, weighted down by the mirror:

Breathing: 5 times/min.

Pulse: 30 beats/min.

Diagnosis: hibernation. You're a bear, not a human.

So Amalia had been right: there was something physical happening that could be causing her nightmares. That should make her happy. It gave her something fixable, something a doctor could diagnose and write a prescription for, and then she'd sleep as peacefully as everyone else.

She'd be normal.

Down deep in her secret heart, though, she *liked* feeling different. And the dreams made her feel closer to her mother, with her tarot cards and predictions of the future.

Maybe the dreams were not just dreams. Something preternatural could be going on. Supernatural. Paranormal. Something not of the world as they were supposed to know it.

If so, what was the purpose?

Was there a purpose?

And Bianca—was she a ghost that still haunted Château de la Fortune as the Woman in Black? If she was, what did she want from Caitlyn?

Or—and Caitlyn shuddered to think it—might Caitlyn herself be the reincarnation of Bianca de' Medici? She had, after all, appeared in Bianca's dress in her dreams, and she had felt that she was the one who was burned at the stake.

She shook her head, not believing it. She could *not* be that cold-faced woman in the portrait.

Caitlyn's conclusion was that she'd have to wait to see what else Bianca—or whatever force was behind this—wanted to show her. The dreams were a story unfolding, and she had the sense that the tale was only half told. If the dreams served a purely psychological function, so be it. She'd wait them out and see what they told her about her screwed-up self.

And if a strange form of sleep apnea lay at the heart of things, maybe someday she'd never wake up, and she could disappear into her dreams forever.

Caitlyn looked up as someone approached her, and swore under her breath. It was the librarian. She must know Caitlyn was skipping class.

"M'mselle Monahan, Madame Snowe would like to see you in her office."

Caitlyn felt her stomach sink. A flush of panic washed over her, and she quickly gathered up her things as a cold sweat broke out over her body. She was skipping class, a clear violation of the rules, and if Madame Snowe threatened her with expulsion . . .

She couldn't let Madame Snowe send her back to Oregon. She'd do anything, *anything*, to prevent it. She belonged here; she knew it in her bones. And leaving the castle would mean leaving Raphael.

Caitlyn dashed down the hallways and staircases to Madame Snowe's office, silently bargaining with the headmistress the whole way to prevent her expulsion. She'd study harder, she'd do an extra paper for each class, she'd redo every assignment . . .

Madame Snowe's office door was ajar when Caitlyn reached it. She paused outside it to straighten her clothes and catch her breath, and as she did she heard Madame Snowe and Greta speaking French. The words flowed in a smooth river far beyond Caitlyn's ability to understand, but as she tugged up her socks and retucked her shirt, the meaning of the conversation seemed to come clear, as it did in her dreams, the meaning forming itself in her mind without effort. A dizzying sense of unreality swept over her, and she was suddenly certain they were talking about her.

"You've seen no signs yourself?" Madame Snowe asked.

"Nothing," Greta replied. "But then, we do not know exactly what we're looking for, or what she may be hiding."

Madame Snowe sighed. "We know she's part of the tree, but perhaps she's no more than a rotten side branch. Her blood may be too polluted."

"And if so?"

"We'll have to cut her off, for the good of the Sisterhood. We cannot waste our resources on one whose gifts may never develop."

There were murmurs and movement, and Caitlyn backed up. Greta opened the door and tucked in her chin in surprise when she saw her, then smiled warmly. "*Bonjour*, Caitlyn. You are well, I hope?"

"Yes, thank you," she gurgled.

"Good, good." She nodded and left.

Caitlyn watched her go, feeling light-headed. She hadn't understood their conversation; she couldn't have. She could barely conjugate *être*. Her brain must have made up its own meaning.

What would it mean that she was a rotten branch, anyway? It made no sense. "Cut her off" was clear enough, however. It must be her fear of being sent home making her hallucinate.

She took a deep breath and went to the door, rapping softly on the thick oak.

"*Entrez!*"

Caitlyn entered, keeping her eyes averted from the portrait of Bianca de' Medici. She didn't need another nightmare like that last one.

Madame Snowe's hair was down today, flat-ironed to a sheet of polished auburn. It made her even more starkly beautiful, and more intimidating. She wore a black skirt suit and spike heels, and Caitlyn thought that she could be the spokesmodel for an international witchcraft association.

Madame Snowe gestured at the chair in front of her desk, and Caitlyn sat, sneaking peeks around the room to confirm that it was the same one she'd seen in her dream, where the men had been playing cards.

"I understand I am not interrupting your French class to speak with you," Madame Snowe said, her face as unreadable as stone.

"No," Caitlyn admitted quietly.

"Are you unwell? Shall I call a doctor?"

"No, Madame."

"Then would you care to explain why you are skipping a class in which your last score on a quiz was sixty-eight percent?"

Caitlyn cringed. "I haven't been sleeping well," she said.

"You've been staying up late and falling asleep on the couch in the Grand Salon. Perhaps going to sleep at a decent hour in your own bed would be a suitable remedy to the problem."

"It wouldn't," Caitlyn said tightly.

Madame Snowe's right brow rose half a centimeter. "Oh?"

Caitlyn squeezed her hands together, silently debating how much to tell the headmistress. If she wanted to stay at the school, she might have to share more than she wished. "You know about the cryptomnesia type of dreams I have, but I didn't tell you that I also have nightmares."

Madame Snowe's dark eyes showed interest. "Do you? Tell me about them."

"They started when I was about twelve, and have been getting worse."

Madame Snowe leaned back in her chair and laid her long-fingered white hands across her abdomen. "Go on."

Caitlyn explained about the Screechers, Madame Snowe nodding throughout.

"Do you sometimes have nightmares of things other than these Screechers?"

Caitlyn could almost feel Bianca's painted eyes boring into her from behind. "Not really."

"How have your other dreams been, the cryptomnesiac ones? You have not reported any to me. Have you had any?"

"I've had some set here at the château, but I don't know that there's any truth to them," she evaded. She didn't want to talk about Raphael with Madame Snowe; it was too embarrassing to reveal that she may have made up a boyfriend for herself. "I'm keeping a dream journal, though; it helps me to remember them."

Madame Snowe nodded. "Good. What is happening in these dreams at the château?"

"Not much. I saw this room," Caitlyn offered weakly, hoping to sate Madame Snowe's curiosity. "Only it was a long time ago. There was a bed with dark blue curtains over there," she said, pointing, "and there was a weird painting over the fireplace of a man with a face made of burning wood and candles. It was called *Fire*."

"Ah." Snowe smiled. "That was an Arcimboldo."

"I beg your pardon?"

"Giuseppe Arcimboldo, court painter to the Holy Roman Emperor in the second half of the sixteenth century. He painted a series of immensely popular portraits composed of objects: a librarian made of books, a gardener made of vegetables, et cetera. *Fire* was part of a series of portraits of the elements."

Caitlyn blinked, surprised. The painting existed? "I must have seen the painting online at some point, don't you think?"

"Perhaps. Or perhaps there is something more interesting than cryptomnesia going on when you dream."

"Like what?" Caitlyn asked, wary but curious.

"You'll have to tell me a little more before I could hazard a guess. Do you have more you could tell me?" Madame Snowe coaxed.

Caitlyn had the strange sensation that Madame Snowe was reaching into her mind and gently nudging open doors that Caitlyn wanted to keep closed. "Er . . ."

"There *is* more that you'd like to tell me, isn't there?"

Again, the feeling of nudging, becoming a feeling of pressure now. Caitlyn's mouth moved before she could stop it. "I had a dream about Bianca," Caitlyn said.

Madame Snowe smiled warmly, and the sense of pressure eased. "*Did* you?"

Caitlyn smiled crookedly. "Maybe I like to dream about paintings over fireplaces."

"Tell me what you dreamed."

Caitlyn hesitated.

Madame Snowe waited, and as she did the sense of pressure in Caitlyn's mind began to grow again.

Caitlyn grimaced and shifted in her seat. Madame Snowe was an intense, threatening sort of confidante. "Bianca dragged me through darkness to a stake, and then I was tied to the stake and burned. Afterward, an old man came and dug my heart—or Bianca's heart—out of the ashes."

Madame Snowe's face went still, but her eyes were bright and hard. "Interesting. What do you think it means?"

Caitlyn shrugged. "I don't know. Seems kind of weird, doesn't it? Why didn't the heart burn?"

"It's been known to happen. The composer Chopin was cremated, but his heart remained untouched by the fire. Some people take that as a sign of divine protection. What happened to the heart in your dream, after the old man took it?"

Caitlyn's gaze shifted away. "I don't know."

"No idea at all?"

Again, the pressure. "It was put into a crystal chest."

"And where did the chest go?"

Caitlyn tightened her lips, not willing to say. Raphael hadn't wanted anyone to know where it was. What if the heart was still here, underneath that stone in the cellars? It wouldn't be right for Madame Snowe to have it.

"You must have seen the chest put somewhere. Hidden, perhaps, for safekeeping?"

The pressure increased in Caitlyn's mind, but she angrily shook it off. She would *not* betray Raphael's confidence. "I don't know where it is!"

188

Madame Snowe's eyes narrowed. "I do not think you are telling me the truth, Caitlyn."

Caitlyn set her jaw. "I don't know where it is."

It seemed once again that Madame Snowe was trying to peer into Caitlyn's mind, but Caitlyn kept her guard up. She wouldn't cave to the force of the headmistress's personality.

"So, is there a symbolic meaning to that dream about the heart?" Caitlyn asked, trying to deflect her. "In a psychological sense."

Snowe gave a facial shrug and abandoned her intense stare, apparently willing to let Caitlyn win this battle. "If you're asking if objects or events in dreams have standard meanings, the answer is no. The interpretation is dependent upon you, the dreamer. On the other hand, humanity has universal archetypes."

"Universal what?"

"Archetypes. They're patterns of thought innate to all mankind. They include images such as 'mother' or 'God.' Or in this case, 'heart.' What do you associate with the heart?"

"Emotions."

Madame Snowe nodded encouragement.

"Love. Heartbreak." Caitlyn searched her mind. "Life. Soul. I mean, if there is a soul, where else is it going to be than in your heart?"

"So one possible interpretation of this dream is that you are going through a difficult time, perhaps even a destruction of your old form—represented by being burned at the stake—but that an essential element of yourself will survive."

Caitlyn's brows rose in surprise. It was such a positive way to look at what had been a horrendous nightmare. "You think that might be what it meant?"

"It doesn't matter what *I* think. The dream's meaning to you is what counts."

"Huh."

Snowe smirked. "Indeed."

Caitlyn turned around and looked at the painting. "Is there any particular reason you have the portrait?" she asked.

"Beyond its being an exemplary work of art?"

Caitlyn nodded.

"I inherited it."

"So she's not related to the Fortune School or the château in some way."

A small smile curled Madame Snowe's lips. "I like to think of her as a patron saint."

Bianca was a scary sort of patron saint, in Caitlyn's book. She wished there was an easy way of checking the things she'd seen in her dreams, like the sundial, against reality. "Er . . . I'm curious about the history of the castle. I don't suppose you have any books on it? I can't find much online."

"What aspect of the history interests you? The previous owners? Its role in the Hundred Years' War?"

"Er, yeah. But also the building of it, and any rebuilding or adding on. Was it ever a ruin? Did you have to change a lot to make it a school?"

Snowe looked suspicious. "I didn't know you were interested in architecture."

"I've never lived anywhere that the architecture was interesting. Where I'm from, buildings from the 1920s are historic monuments."

Madame Snowe chuckled and got up from her desk, moving to the paneled wall of hidden cupboards. She pressed on a panel and a wide door swung open. She lifted out a thick leather scrapbook and carried it to Caitlyn's side of the desk, laying it down on the ebony surface.

"This holds all we know about Château de la Fortune," Madame Snowe said, tapping the cover. The leather front was embossed with three women dancing in a circle. "My great-grandmother purchased the château in the 1920s. It was my grandmother, however, who started the Fortune School, at the end of World War II. The family financial situation had changed for the worse, and she was an enterprising woman." Madame Snowe opened the album. The first page showed a black-and-white photograph of the castle taken from the valley below. "This is the castle as my great-grandmother first saw it." She turned through several more pages of photos, these showing rubble on the floors, collapsed beams, missing windows. "The interior was in poor repair, as you can see."

She turned another page, and Caitlyn caught a brief glimpse of a painted ceiling. Caitlyn leaned forward and then let out a mew of protest as Madame Snowe shut the album. "This is filled with what history my family has been able to gather, as well as with details on the renovation my great-grandmother undertook in the 1920s."

Caitlyn couldn't take her eyes off it. "May I look through it?"

Madame Snowe looked at her watch. "You are due in your next class in ten minutes. I don't believe there's time."

Caitlyn swallowed against the tightness in her throat. She wanted to push Madame Snowe aside, grab the album, and see what exactly had been on that painted ceiling. "May I take it to my room, to look at later? I would bring it back tomorrow morning, I promise."

Madame Snowe made a noncommittal sound and idly tapped the cover with her fingertips. "I am willing to make a deal with you, Caitlyn."

Caitlyn lowered her brows, wary. "Oh?"

"I want you to start keeping your dream journal on your laptop. Every morning when you wake up, I want you to write out everything you dreamed, and if you wish you may also attempt an interpretation, like we did just now with the heart and being burned at the stake. Every Sunday evening I want you to e-mail me your journal. Also take note of any unusual daydreams you might have, or anything else that seems not quite part of an average day. Can you do that?"

Caitlyn nodded. She would write down the Screecher stuff, sure, but she was going to keep the drawings of her Raphael dreams on paper, and private. Her dream journal was in the book bag at her feet at this very moment, and it took a deliberate effort to keep from guiltily looking down at it.

"Don't hold anything back."

"I won't," she lied.

Madame Snowe looked hard at her. "I can't help you unless you're completely open with me."

"I know." The nervous tick in her eyelid, gone for over a week now, made a sudden reappearance.

Madame Snowe's eyes narrowed, and for one long moment Caitlyn felt as if Bianca's hands were once again on her head, cold and hard as stone, squeezing, the pressure building until she feared her skull might burst like a grape.

And then the sensation was gone, and Madame Snowe was looking at her with a hint of question in her dark eyes. "In exchange, I'll give you the album to look through, because I trust you. You won't let me down, will you, Caitlyn?"

She *had* to see that album. "No, Madame," she said softly.

The headmistress handed her the album. "You may keep it for as long as you like, but you are responsible for it. I don't want to see it being passed around the table at dinner, do you understand?"

"Yes, Madame." The leather book was heavy and cool on her thighs. "May I ask a question on a completely different topic?"

Madame Snowe nodded.

"That DNA test you did on me, did it turn up any diseases?" She was thinking about what she'd heard Madame Snowe and Greta talking about, in French: that Caitlyn might be a rotten branch of some sort.

"You mean any genetic predisposition to disease. No, it did not."

"That's a relief!"

"The science is still in its infancy, of course, and this was only the most rudimentary of tests for the most obvious of markers. It is no guarantee of your long-term health."

Caitlyn scowled. "Then why do it?"

"Because some information is better than no information. Life does not give you big, simple answers, Caitlyn. It demands patience, focus, and an open, intelligent mind to gather the pieces of a puzzle and fit them together into a coherent whole. Nothing worth knowing is ever easily learned. I hope that is a sentiment you will take to heart in regards to your French lessons."

"*Oui*, Madame."

"I don't believe I need to remind you of the consequences if you fail any of your courses."

Caitlyn shook her head.

"Very well." Madame Snowe smiled, the look of it more threat than comfort. "You may go."

Caitlyn gathered her things and headed for the door. She glanced up at Bianca, smiling from her frame as knowingly as ever. Caitlyn gave *La Perla* a scowl.

"And Caitlyn?" Madame Snowe called out, making her start.

Caitlyn looked over her shoulder. "Yes?"

"Do not forget to send me your weekly journal. I can only help you if you let me see into your mind. Keeping secrets would not be in your best interest."

"No, Madame. I know."

But since when did she ever do what was good for her?

CHAPTER

That night, Caitlyn sat with the leather album at her usual desk in the Grand Salon. She was all alone, there being no sign yet of Naomi. Naomi usually spent the early part of the night trying to sleep, getting up only when she knew it was hopeless.

Caitlyn once again cursed her poor foreign language skills as she went through the album. There was an old photo of the library that showed a ceiling splotched with a few remnants of paint, some of which seemed to show lines radiating from a point close to the stained-glass window. In a close-up photo of one section of the ceiling, she could barely make out the flaking image of a mason chiseling at a stone.

Under each photo was a handwritten paragraph, in French. Caitlyn had her French dictionary open and on her laptop's browser had bookmarked a half dozen translation sites. Between the two, and after several hours, she was getting a vague sense of what the paragraphs meant.

They were a catalog of damage, along with a few notes about what could or could not be saved. The final sentences seemed to say that conservation of the ceiling would be all but impossible. The frescoes were permanently damaged by water, which had been seeping in for decades, lifting the plaster from its underlying support. A work crew mistakenly scraped off the remaining fragments of fresco before further documentation could be made.

It looked possible that there had been a sundial on the ceiling. What it may have once said about the Templar's fortune, however, was lost to history and a work crew's scrapers.

The renovations had been extensive and had involved craftsmanship that Caitlyn imagined cost a mint: sculptors to repair or replace parts of the fireplaces, the gargoyles, a marble statue of the Virgin Mary in the chapel; painters for the intricate patterns on the walls and ceiling of the Great Hall as well as for the walls of several rooms with painted fabric "wallpaper"; carvers and carpenters for paneling and cabinetry; workers in stained glass, wrought iron, stone, copper; the list went on. Madame Snowe's great-grandmother had to have been one rich lady, Caitlyn concluded.

There was also a photo of a very old Antoine Fournier, presenting the painting of Fortuna to Madame Snowe's great-grandmother. Several paragraphs recounted the painting's history.

In the 1870s, Fournier was an impoverished artist seeking patronage and a place to live. A friend of a friend persuaded the owner of Château de la Fortune to install Fournier in the abandoned castle and create an art studio in its attics, in exchange for a series of romantic portraits of the castle ruins and Dordogne Valley.

Fournier had been overjoyed at his good fortune, ecstatic to have at last found a patron. He wasn't happy to be living so far from Paris, but that was a minor consideration against the promise of food, shelter, and a place to paint. He persuaded himself that the isolation of Château de la Fortune would be good for his work.

And for a short time, it was. He completed several sketches of the castle and valley, and prepared his canvases for painting. And then, *she* came. The violent ghost. The demanding spirit. She was an enraged feminine force who would give him no rest until he obeyed her wishes and painted the goddess Fortuna with her wheel. Alone in the castle, knowing no way to protect himself from the controlling spirit, he had done as she wished. He abandoned the romantic paintings for his patron and devoted every waking hour to creating Fortuna.

By the time he finished ten months later, his health had been destroyed by exhaustion, drink, and the drafty cold of the castle. The final blow came when his patron visited to see how Fournier was progressing and discovered that his pet artist had not been painting the ruins that he'd requested. Instead, he had created Fortuna.

When Fournier explained the visits by the ghost, his patron had turned white and fled the castle. Fournier himself left the castle soon after, his energies drained, his will to paint gone. He sent the portrait of Fortuna to his patron and returned to Paris. Several months later, the portrait was returned to him, along with a letter explaining that his patron had died of a heart attack soon after his visit to Château de la Fortune. The letter explained that the patron had, as a boy, fancied he saw a ghost at the château and had been convinced that the castle was cursed. The family did not wish to be reminded of his death, and so returned the painting of Fortuna to Fournier's hands.

Fournier had packed the painting away, afraid to so much as gaze upon it for fear of reviving the female spirit who had sapped his energies. It was only toward the end of his life, when he heard that the château had been purchased by a woman and refurbished, that he was able to face the portrait again and bring Fortuna home.

Fournier insisted that Fortuna be hung at the end of the Grand

Salon. "It's what she wanted," he told Snowe's great-grandmother.

Caitlyn felt a chill on the back of her neck and cast an anxious look down the Salon at the painting. The Woman in Black and Fortuna must be connected. But why would the Woman in Black insist on that painting?

Was there a message in it?

Caitlyn got up from the desk and walked down the long room toward the painting. She flipped the switch to turn on the spotlights, and Fortuna glowed to life. Saint George killed the dragon crawling from the abyss; the castle stood strong on its cliff top; Fortuna trod the clouds; and the obsidian wheel stood frozen in its turnings, bejeweled with medallions and stones, and the enormous ruby at its hub.

Caitlyn lifted her fingers to the ruby, her fingertips hovering just above the painted gem. A memory surfaced, of her mother's tarot reading:

> ". . . if you fulfill your destiny, you will journey to
> the heart of the wheel, where all is motionless and clear.
> You will journey to the heart. The heart. The heart," she
> repeated, "the heart in darkness."

She would journey to the heart of the wheel. Was it a literal wheel, jeweled like the one in the painting? Was that the form that Eshael's dowry had taken?

And was it a literal heart?

Raphael had said that he needed to entomb Bianca's heart in the Templar treasure. Maybe the ruby in the painting represented Bianca's heart, placed at the center of a jeweled wheel.

But where was the wheel?

She sighed in frustration and flipped off the spotlights. She yawned, getting sleepy, and headed upstairs to the bathroom on the second floor to brush her teeth.

The floor was quiet, no light showing beneath anyone's door. It was a quiet that Caitlyn was beginning to feel belonged to her; it was the time when the hallways were most like they were in her dreams: empty and echoing, and filled with shadows.

She pushed open the door to the large bathroom with its toilets and shower stalls, and long row of sinks in front of a mirror. She was only a few steps inside when the hairs started to rise on her arms with the sense that she was not alone.

Her ears pricked, catching the faintest sigh of air and the hint of movement. She turned slowly around, trying to locate the source of the sound.

There was silence.

A burst of rushing noise suddenly broke through, chasing a squeak of fright from Caitlyn's throat before she realized it was the flushing of a toilet. A moment later Soma emerged from the last stall, her skin looking ashen under the fluorescent lights.

Soma smiled sickly at Caitlyn and put her hands over her stomach. "I will give you a good piece of advice," Soma said. "Never try the coconut-oil diet to lose weight. Your stomach will never forgive you."

"I'll take your word for it," Caitlyn said, weak with relief and feeling like an idiot. She'd freaked herself out with all these thoughts of ghosts and unburned hearts and de' Medicis.

Soma nodded and washed her hands. "I'd rather be fat than go through this again."

"I think you have a great figure."

"That's very kind of you. My too-tight clothes know the truth, though: no more croissants or hot chocolate for Soma. *Bonne nuit.*"

"*Bonne nuit,*" Caitlyn said. Good night.

Caitlyn brushed her teeth and washed her face. As the water ran and she rinsed her skin, the sense came to her again that she was not alone. She tried to ignore it, but the hair on the back of her neck prickled, and she couldn't resist turning sideways to take a quick look up and down the bathroom.

There was no one this time. All the stall doors were ajar, all the shower stalls had their white plastic curtains pushed to one side. She was alone.

Don't be silly, she chided herself. She encountered creepy things only in her dreams, never when awake.

She shut off the water and dried her face, and then a thought struck her. The hair on her arms rose as if it had been rubbed with a balloon.

What if I'm not awake?

A chill poured down her spine.

Remembering the tests Brigitte had taught her, Caitlyn pinched her nose shut. Her breath was immediately cut off. She looked at herself in the mirror with her fingers clamped to her nose, then made a face at herself. She was being ridiculous!

But then her ears caught a noise somewhere behind her:

Shh, shh, shh . . .

Like the rustling of silken skirts.

Shh, shh, shh . . .

The lights flickered, and Caitlyn's skin went cold. She shook her head in denial. *No!*

She turned around and leaned against the sink, gaze darting in all directions, trying to find the source of the noise. It was coming closer, getting louder.

Shh, shh, shh . . .

The hairs on the nape of her neck began to stand. The noise was coming from *behind* her.

Caitlyn slowly turned toward the mirror.

In the mirror's depths a veiled figure was advancing toward her, her skirts swaying with each *shh* of sound.

Caitlyn was unable to move or think. She watched with growing horror as the thing in the mirror came closer, the rustling of its skirts growing louder and louder with each step. *SHH, SHH, SHH.*

Caitlyn sagged against the sink, its porcelain rim the only thing holding her upright.

"*Raphael . . . ,*" the figure cried in a whisper, his name a plea from a broken soul. "*Raphael . . .*"

"*No!*" Caitlyn whispered hoarsely. "You can't be real!"

The bathroom lights flickered and went out, swallowing Caitlyn in darkness. She trembled.

In the depths of the mirror, the figure's face glowed palely behind the veil.

SHH, SHH, SHH . . .

The figure stopped a foot from the other side of the glass. Hollow shadows where her eyes should have been seemed to stare through the veil and into Caitlyn's soul.

Caitlyn whimpered. Stars flickered on the edge of her vision.

On the other side of the glass, white hands grasped the edge of the veil and began to raise it.

Caitlyn's heart gave one clumsy thump and then she felt herself fainting, a rush of blackness swallowing her, delivering her from whatever horror hid behind the veil.

Twenty-one

Caitlyn came to lying on the floor in a bare stone hallway, its limestone walls lit by the orange glow of either a sunrise or a sunset coming through the windows at the end of the hall. She sat up, dazed and confused.

She looked down at herself. She was wearing her nightgown and Fortune School bathrobe, just as she had been while studying in the Grand Salon. She didn't know where in the castle she was—or when she was—but she was glad enough not to find herself on the floor of the bathroom with the Woman in Black hovering over her. A cold shudder ran through her at the memory of the pale face behind the veil.

She was getting up off the floor when Raphael's cousin Giovanni came around the corner at the other end of the hallway, laughing and tugging a serving girl along by the hand. The girl giggled and feigned reluctance, only to be swept into Giovanni's arms and soundly kissed.

Caitlyn pressed herself up against the wall and stayed motionless, the couple too engrossed in each other to look her way, and a moment later Giovanni and the girl disappeared through a doorway.

Caitlyn started to relax, then felt a bolt of fresh alarm as she realized she *was* dreaming. Her living body must be passed out on the bathroom floor.

She felt her body, patting her arms and chest. It felt real enough, but that was obviously an illusion. She pinched her nose shut.

She couldn't breathe.

Caitlyn whimpered and released her nose. No, she *had* to be dreaming! She couldn't really be here!

She would find Raphael. Everything would make sense— somehow—if she found him.

She crept silently down the hall in her slippered feet, pausing when she came to the door Giovanni and the girl had gone through. It was half open, their whispers and giggles audible. There was a moment of quiet, and Caitlyn leaned her head into the frame of the doorway to take a peek.

Giovanni and the serving girl were together, their clothes in wild disarray.

Caitlyn gasped and pulled away, her heart thudding. She dashed down the hall and away from the too-vivid sounds and images. Her feet seemed barely to touch the stones as she ran. She flew down a flight of stairs and through a series of rooms, then into a dark narrow passageway. There was light at the end of it, the door propped open. She hurried toward the light.

It was a side entrance to a small courtyard near the kitchens. Low voices stopped her before she stepped into the fading sunlight. She hunkered in the shadows.

Philippe, le Comte d'Ormond, pressed a gold coin into the dirty hand of a weather-beaten man dressed like a peasant. She saw a flash of white as Philippe handed the man a message, which was quickly tucked into the depths of his homespun clothing. The man bobbed his head and left.

Philippe watched him go, looked around as if seeking spying eyes, and turned back toward the passageway.

Caitlyn dashed ahead, back into the depths of the château. Raphael might be anywhere, but there was a chance she'd find him in the library, studying the ceiling. She wanted to see it herself before the last of the light faded.

It took only a few minutes to orient herself and find her way there, which still wasn't enough time to figure out if she was awake or dreaming.

The library—or swordplay gymnasium, as Raphael would have it—was empty. Caitlyn walked to the center of the room and looked up.

The sundial was as clear as daylight on the ceiling. Painted gold leaf rays shot out from a central point above the *Fiat Lux* window. A red dragon entwined itself around that initial point and breathed fire toward a crust of earth above his abyss. Beyond the crust, farther out the length of the rays, were the numbered hours of the days. Each ray ran through the center of a series of paintings, each one depicting scenes the significance of which Caitlyn could not decipher. Some were landscapes; some were esoteric symbols; and others were animals, objects, people, or groups of people. A fair number of angels, demons, and creatures in between filled their own hour spaces, or hopped from one picture to the next.

It was a mad jumble of imagery, and nowhere did Caitlyn see a treasure chest overflowing with gold and jewels. If there was a map up there, she couldn't see it.

Her neck was starting to hurt from craning, so she dragged a battered table to the center of the room and lay down upon it, folding her hands over her diaphragm. The twilight was quickly fading toward dusk, but the windows faced south, and she could still make out the gross shapes of most of the images. She squinted up at them, certain there was a message there if only she could read it.

"You look like you're posing for your tomb," Raphael said.

Caitlyn jerked in surprise and turned her head. Raphael was walking toward her, a candlestick in his hand.

Relief and delight ran through her at the sight of him. "I'm a long way from dead. I want to be at least ninety before I kick off."

"Do you?"

"If I'm going to have a tomb, though, even if I'm ninety I might like to look like I'm still fifteen."

He was at the side of the table now, and he set the candlestick on the corner a foot from her head. The gentle light caressed the contours of his face and caught in the bronze glints of his hair. His hazel eyes looked down at her with something like wonder. "Is that how old you are?"

"Almost sixteen," Caitlyn said, her breath catching in her throat as the image of Giovanni and the serving girl jumped to her mind. "How old are you?"

"Nineteen." He reached out, caught a lock of her black hair where it spread across the table, and wound it around his finger. She could feel each gentle twist and tug telegraphed down the strands of hair like electricity.

"My mother wouldn't approve," Caitlyn said, her heart thumping. "She'd say you were too old for me."

"Too old for me to do what?" He brushed his finger, wrapped in her hair, against her cheek, then let the black lock uncoil itself and fall to the side. His hand remained, and she watched his face as he brought his fingertips to her lips and slowly traced their shape.

"You're warm," he said. His fingers brushed over her lips again, more slowly, the slight pressure making them part, one fingertip catching for a moment in the damp moistness inside her lips. His eyes shut and she saw a muscle flex in his jaw, and then he pulled away. He looked out the windows at the gathering darkness.

Caitlyn sat up, pulling her knees up to her chest and wrapping her arms around them, feeling strangely rejected. "Of course, she's not my real mother," Caitlyn said. "Like yours, mine died when I was small, and I was raised by someone else. Joy is just a normal, average woman, though; she's not like Bianca."

Raphael turned back to look at her. "Was she kind to you?"

Caitlyn thought of the open arms Joy had always had for her, the hugs, the reassurance, the love offered even when Caitlyn gave little back. She felt a stab of loss, and tears stung her eyes. "Yes, she was kind. Always. And more loving than I deserved."

"You miss her," he said, coming closer.

Caitlyn nodded, recognizing that truth for the first time. "I didn't think I would, but I do."

"Did the two of you not get along?"

"We're very different. She wants to understand me, but she can't." Caitlyn sniffled. "I can't understand myself, half the time."

"But that is what makes the love of a mother: whether she understands you or not, she loves you. A mother is the only person in your life who will ever love you that way."

"You're making me cry!"

"Then I will cry with you," Raphael said. "If you cannot weep for your mother, for whom *can* you weep?"

She reached for his hand and held it.

"I was afraid I wouldn't see you this time," she said after a moment, releasing his hand.

"You've come other times and not seen me?" he asked, a question in his expression.

"No. But usually I see you right away. This time I just saw—" she stopped, coloring at the memory.

"Saw what?"

She shook her head.

He leaned against the edge of the table, the tops of his thighs almost touching the ends of her slippers. He put his hands on the tabletop to either side of her, leaning so close that she would have to raise her face only a few inches to kiss him. "What did you see?"

"Giovanni . . . and a girl."

His eyes widened, and then he was standing straight again, laughing. "Giovanni thinks pleasure is the only point of living."

"What do you think the point is?"

"God knows I've wondered," he said, his voice strained. He met her eyes. "The only answer I can find is that it's to take care of those we love."

"I think that's a better answer than most," she said softly.

He gave her a wry smile. "Giovanni's is easier to live up to."

"Oh, I almost forgot: After seeing Giovanni, I saw Philippe, at a side door by the kitchens. He looked like he was secretly paying a peasant to carry a letter for him."

"A peasant?"

"A rough-looking man, dressed poorly. Maybe a laborer of some sort. You said Philippe spied on you for Catherine, right?"

Raphael frowned. "He spies openly and sends his missives in plain sight of us all. This is different. I wonder what he's up to?"

"Do you know that his room has secret cabinets built into the panels?"

Raphael's frown disappeared in astonishment. "It does?"

"Maybe he's the one who has been trying to kill you. Maybe that peasant was a worker on the scaffolding, and he placed the stone so it could fall on you."

Raphael started to shake his head, then stopped. "Catherine may have ordered Philippe to steal the heart. But no," he said, thinking aloud, "someone was trying to steal it even as we came north from Rome." He started to pace. "Could Catherine's reach extend as far as Rome? Yes. Or Philippe may not be working for her at all, on that score. Perhaps it's Pius he serves." He turned to her, his gaze suddenly intense. "Do *you* know who it is?"

"The would-be thief, or the would-be murderer?"

"They're surely one and the same. Who is it?"

"*I* don't know. How could I know?" she asked, taken aback.

He stared at her. "You still don't know what you are, do you?" He shook his head. "Sorry. Ignore me. I'm just trying to figure this out."

"You and me both," she muttered.

A hint of a smile played on his lips, his eyes meeting hers for a moment. He touched the emblem embroidered on her robe. "*Fortuna Imperatrix Mundi*. Fortune Rules the World. The motto of your family?"

"Of the . . . convent where I go to school." The Fortune School was clear in her mind, and her existence there. She felt able to think, without the usual fogginess of dream thought, but somehow that just made everything more confusing. *How can this be so real?*

"Strange motto for a convent," Raphael said.

"It's a strange convent."

He traced the emblem of the wheel with his fingertip, his touch caressing her skin through the layers of fabric. "What message does this hold for me?" he asked, as if to himself.

"Maybe that things are going to get better," she said, his touch stealing her breath and concentration.

"They will if we find the treasure." He flattened his palm over the emblem, then slid his hand up to the side of her neck.

Her lips parted. "I . . . I saw the sundial before it got dark, but I didn't see anything pointing to the treasure."

Raphael grinned and dropped his hand. "I did."

"You did?" she said in mild disappointment as his hand fell away.

He leaned behind her and grabbed the candlestick, then vaulted up onto the table and stood. He reached down a hand to help her up. "Look," he said, holding the candle up above his head. It illuminated one painted scene, of an ocean with a star shining above.

"A star over the ocean. What does that have to do with the treasure?"

"Look more closely at the star."

She squinted into the candlelight. "There's something in the center of it. It looks like a crown with a cross stuck through it."

"Yes!"

"So?"

"It's a symbol of the Knights Templar. A symbol of Constantine, originally, but they used it as one of their insignia, with the words *In Hoc Signo Vinces.* 'In this sign thou shall conquer.'"

"But what does it mean, here?"

"I think it's to tell us that we're on the right track." Raphael lowered his arm and pointed toward the window. "*Fiat Lux*, remember?"

She nodded.

"You asked me where it was from. That got me thinking. It's from

Genesis, which is the beginning not only of the Old Testament, but of existence. I think that means that this sundial is the beginning of a map."

"You mean this is the first clue?"

He nodded. "*Fiat Lux* is in chapter one, verse three. One o'clock," he said, pointing to the gold ray that ran through the ocean, "third picture."

Caitlyn caught her breath and smiled. "You might be right!"

"But I haven't figured out where that gets us. A star above the sea."

"Is there a star anywhere in the château?"

"I spent all day looking. There are several on copper spires on top of the roofs, but I can't get up there. There are some carved into fireplace surrounds. One room has a tile floor in a pattern of stars. Three windows have stars or suns in them. There's a—"

"I get the picture," she interrupted. "Stars everywhere."

"We need to figure out which star."

"They rise in the east, don't they?" Caitlyn offered tentatively.

"I thought of that. Half the stars in the castle are no more clearly east than others, though."

Caitlyn chewed her lip and looked up again at the painting. She shifted her glance to the other pictures, no more than shadows now. "What *are* all these things?" she asked, pointing to the ceiling in general. "What do they mean?"

"Most of them, I'm not sure. I saw a few biblical scenes, though, and a couple symbols of saints. The severed breasts on a platter, that's Saint Agatha," he said, pointing into the darkness.

"Good God," Caitlyn muttered, revolted. "Maybe the star isn't a literal star, but is representative of something else. Could this star represent a saint?"

"The only one I can think of with a star is Dominic, but it's usually on his forehead. There's no water associated with him."

Caitlyn looked again at the *Fiat Lux* window, which in its own way depicted a star over water. "What's the Latin for star and sea, or water?"

"*Stella, astrum,* or *sidus* for star. *Vesper* for evening star. *Mare maris* for sea. *Aqua* for water."

"*Stella aqua. Aqua stella. Astrum mare maris,*" Caitlyn mumbled, trying out the combinations, searching for she didn't know what. "*Mare maris stella. Stella mare maris.*"

Raphael grabbed her arm. "Stop. Say that again!"

"*Stella mare maris.*"

"*Stella Maris!*"

"Huh?"

"'Star of the sea.' It's another name for Mary!"

Caitlyn had a sudden vision of the photo of the marble statue of Mary, being repaired by workmen. "The chapel!"

Raphael leaped down from the table, reached up, and, with his grin flashing in the candlelight, wrapped an arm around Caitlyn's hips, lifting her off the tabletop as if she were made of feathers. She held on to his shoulders and laughed as he let her slide down the length of his body, her robe and nightgown riding up to her thighs, until at last her toes barely touched the floor. He held her there against him.

"You're a genius," he said, smiling down at her. She grinned back as he stared at her. Suddenly, she felt a shift in his mood, and she heard him clank the candlestick onto the table. His other arm came around her, pulling her against him. And then he lowered his mouth and kissed her.

His lips skimmed the surface of hers once, twice, and then on the third pass caught her lower lip between his. Her knees lost strength, and she clung to him as the kiss deepened, the movements of his lips coaxing an answer from hers. She felt like she was floating, awash in sensation.

He backed her up against the table and lowered her to it. He laid his torso atop hers, his feet still on the ground and one arm taking the worst of his weight. The other dug into her hair and cupped her head, holding her captive while he kissed her passionately. She could feel his physical strength everywhere his body touched hers.

His hand moved down her neck, and then slipped inside the top of her nightgown to caress the skin at the base of her neck.

Caitlyn gasped, alarmed at the direction he was moving. "Raphael, wait!"

His lips left hers and trailed down her throat, pausing to kiss the space where her neck met her shoulder.

He started to pull down the top of her nightgown, but she grasped his head, her hands sinking into the soft silk of his hair. "Raphael," she pleaded, aching for more even as she said it. "Stop."

His mouth lifted from her neck, and he looked at her. "What's wrong?"

"I'm not ready . . . it's just a lot all at once."

He bowed his head, his forehead resting on her chest. Caitlyn smoothed the hair on his head.

Raphael suddenly slid his arms under her back and embraced her, nuzzling a kiss into her neck. Then he was off her, pulling her upright. "I've known women who were married at age fourteen," he said lightly.

"Is that a proposal?" she asked, with an equally deliberate lightness.

"Would you take a poor artist with no land and no fortune?"

"*Fortune rota volvitur*. You don't know what tomorrow holds. It may hold the wealth of the Templars."

"If it does, I just might ask you—"

But she didn't get to hear what he said next, as his words were cut off by the shriek of sirens, and she found herself falling away from him and through a vast abyss of darkness.

CHAPTER

Twenty-two

Caitlyn opened her eyes to the European *BWOO-woo, BWOO-woo* siren sound and the concerned face of a female paramedic. She was lying down, strapped in place on a gurney that rocked with the movements of the ambulance, flashing lights from outside the vehicle reflecting on the cheek of the paramedic.

"*Qu'est-ce qui se passe?*" Caitlyn asked blearily. What's happening?

"You hit your head," the woman said in French. "You may have a concussion."

"Am I going to be all right?" Caitlyn continued in fluent French.

"Of course! But you will need stitches, and an X-ray."

"Oh," she said, and faded to black.

Caitlyn woke the second time—or was it the third time?—in a clean, uncomfortable hospital bed, in a private room similar to ones she'd seen in the States, only somehow sparser, with a vague hint of Ikea. Madame Snowe was talking to a short, dark-haired female doctor in the doorway. Seeing her awake, the doctor came over and shined a light in her eyes as she asked her questions in French.

Caitlyn scowled at her. "I'm sorry," she said in English, "but my French is terrible. Do you speak English?"

The doctor exchanged a look with Madame Snowe, then said in English, "Yes. I asked you if you knew what day it was."

Caitlyn bit her lip and thought for a moment. "If it's morning, I'm going to guess that it's Saturday. Which means I'm missing my riding lesson."

The doctor smiled and patted her on the knee. "You're going to be fine." She took Madame Snowe out into the hallway.

Caitlyn felt a dull throb on the side of her head and reached up to touch it. The spiky threads of stitches met her fingertips. She shuddered and quickly dropped her hand.

Madame Snowe returned to the room and sat down in the chair beside the bed. "*Alors!* You have given us all quite a scare. It is good that Naomi found you so quickly."

"Naomi did?"

"*Oui.* She saw your things in the Grand Salon, and when you didn't appear she went looking for you."

"I didn't mean to leave the album out," Caitlyn apologized.

Madame waved the concern away. "More important is discovering what happened. Did you slip and fall? Do you remember?"

Caitlyn closed her eyes, casting her mind back. She heard the *Shh, shh, shh* of silk skirts. Her eyes flew open. "I saw the Woman in Black."

Madame Snowe's lips parted in surprise. "*Vraiment?*" Truly?

"I heard the sound of rustling skirts, and then the Woman in Black was in the mirror, looking out at me."

"What did she look like?" Madame Snowe asked breathlessly, leaning forward.

Caitlyn shook her head. "She started to lift her veil, but I fainted. And I must have hit my head on the sink or the floor." She reached again for the stitches on her head.

"*Ne touche pas.*" Don't touch.

Caitlyn dropped her hand again.

"Do you remember anything else?"

Caitlyn's guard went up. "Not until the ambulance."

Madame Snowe sat back with a soft grunt of disappointment. "You were speaking fluent French in the ambulance the first few times you woke, although with a strangely . . . archaic accent."

"Really?" Caitlyn asked in surprise.

"It is strange that you can speak it when half conscious, but forget it in the classroom, *non?*"

"Very strange. And very inconvenient," she grumbled.

"So. The doctor says that you will be fine, that there is no swelling in your brain and your skull is intact." Madame opened her purse and took out her cell phone. "Your parents, however, will need to be reassured. They know what happened, and I promised that you would call them as soon as you woke." She dialed the number, handed the phone to Caitlyn, and stepped out into the hallway to give her some privacy.

There were several moments of hissing silence as the call was connected, and then the *brrrr brrrr* of the phone ringing. After three rings the phone was picked up.

"Hello?" It was Joy's voice, and Caitlyn sucked in a breath. She never realized how good it would feel to hear her voice.

"Mom?" Caitlyn said, and her voice cracked. Something about being sick in the hospital, five thousand miles from her family, was throwing her back into a childlike state. She suddenly wanted to be hugged and told that everything was going to be okay.

"Caitlyn! Oh honey, we've been so worried about you! Are you all right?"

"Yeah, I'm fine." Caitlyn rubbed her runny nose on the back of her hand and tried to keep from crying. "I slipped and fell in the bathroom, is all. Whacked my head."

"Do they have good doctors over there? Are they taking good care of you?"

"They seem to know what they're doing. I'm fine, just . . ."

"Scared?"

Caitlyn swallowed a sob, then hiccuped. "Not really." She was starting to feel embarrassed by her tears. "I'm fine, and Madame Snowe is right here with me."

"Sometimes you just need a hug."

Caitlyn sniffled. "I guess."

"I wish I could give it to you, honey."

Caitlyn wanted to feel comforted—yearned to feel comforted—but somehow wasn't. Instead, Joy's babying prickled at Caitlyn like an itchy wool sweater.

"Your father wants to talk to you."

"Okay."

There were whispers, and the phone being fumbled between hands, and then Caitlyn's father came on the line. "We hear you conked your noggin pretty good."

"Yeah, and I've got the stitches to prove it."

"But you're doing okay?" he asked.

"Yeah."

"Good. Good."

An uncomfortable silence descended. Caitlyn waited to hear

something more tender from her father, but as the seconds passed, she realized it wasn't going to happen. She could feel his unease through the phone line, as if he knew he was supposed to say something more but didn't know what.

Caitlyn felt a familiar hurt inside, but this time, unexpectedly, compassion came with it. Her dad couldn't help being the way he was, any more than she could help being herself. He couldn't help not understanding her, and being, she now recognized, a little afraid of her.

She showed him mercy and asked, "So how are the boys doing? Are they winning their games?"

She could feel his relief. He talked happily about her brothers' sporting events for several minutes while Caitlyn stared at the wall, making "uh-huh" noises, and then Joy came back on the line. "Are you sure you're doing all right, honey? If you need me to, I'll come be there with you. I'll get on a plane tomorrow if that's what you need."

"No, don't do that. I'm okay. I just needed to hear your voice, I guess." She remembered the conversation she'd had with Raphael, about the unconditional love of a mother, and for the first time she gave Joy some of the credit she was due. Joy didn't understand her, but no matter what she did, Joy continued loving her. That was more of a gift than Caitlyn had ever offered her in return. She didn't know if she *could* fully offer it, but for Joy's sake she could pretend. "I miss you, Mom. And I love you."

There was a suspicious sniffling sound at the other end, and then Joy said, "I love you, too, honey. You know I do. Always have, always will."

"I know. Me, too." It wasn't the whole truth, but she knew it was the right thing to say. Sometimes, it wasn't *her* feelings that mattered.

The call ended, and Caitlyn leaned back against her pillows; a moment later she reached back and pulled a pillow out and hugged it to her chest.

It offered cold comfort and smelled of bleach. She tossed it aside.

She couldn't be a child anymore, hoping for parents to kiss her forehead and make everything better, and raging when they could not. They had given her what they could, but her place was no longer with them. She had moved on.

It was now up to her to turn Fortune's wheel and make her own destiny.

CHAPTER
Twenty-three

"Caitlyn! You're back!" Naomi cried, poking her head into Caitlyn's dorm room.

"Yes, thank God," Caitlyn said. She'd spent thirty-six hours in the hospital under observation, coming back to the school only this Sunday morning. "They wouldn't even let me go to the bathroom without a nurse there to hold my hand."

Naomi came in and sat on the end of her bed. "I'm so sorry. I had to call for help, though. There was so much blood."

"No, I'm glad you did. I would have lain there until morning if you hadn't." Caitlyn lifted a hank of her hair and turned her head so Naomi could see the wound. "Five stitches."

"Brilliant!" Naomi said with gruesome delight. "I wish I'd taken a picture of the bathroom. It looked like a pig had been slaughtered, and there you were lying in the middle of it. What happened? Do you remember?"

"The short story is I fainted and hit my head on the sink. Then, when the paramedics got here, they took my pulse."

Naomi looked meaningfully at Caitlyn.

"Yeah. They did not like what they found. The doctors eventually shrugged it off, though, since I'm fine."

"Very Gallic of them. 'Eh, so zhe seemed dead, vhat of it?'" Naomi said in a mock French accent. "So what's the long story? *Did* you faint?"

Caitlyn chewed her lower lip. She'd decided in the hospital that she wanted to tell Naomi *everything* that was going on. Naomi was the only girl she could trust not to gossip, as well as being the only girl she thought might understand.

"Will you close the door?" Caitlyn asked. "I have something I want to tell you."

Naomi closed the door and came back to the bed, sitting on the end. Her face was concerned. "What is it?"

Caitlyn took a deep breath. "I hope you don't think I'm crazy after you hear this." And then she told her everything, from Raphael to the Woman in Black to Bianca to the Templar treasure.

"*Mon Dieu*," Naomi said when Caitlyn finally finished. Her eyes were wide. "That is one heck of a story."

"Do you think I'm crazy?"

"Crazy? No!"

Caitlyn slumped in relief. "Good."

"You're not crazy; you're a witch!"

Caitlyn sat back up. "What!"

"I don't mean it as an insult," Naomi assured her. "I think you have some sort of special power. Don't you see?"

"See what?"

"You're a magnet for ghosts. You're like a medium; you talk to spirits. Only in your case, you don't do it during a séance; you do it while you dream."

221

Caitlyn had never looked at it like that before, and she wasn't sure how she felt about the possibility of being a medium. "It's the one consistent element, isn't it?" she asked. "The Screechers, the Woman in Black, Bianca, maybe even Raphael: they could all be ghosts."

"What else could they be?"

"Beats me."

"If they are all ghosts," Naomi went on eagerly, "it seems clear that some of them—or at least one of them—has a purpose for visiting you."

"Which is?" Caitlyn asked, faintly bewildered. She almost couldn't believe Naomi was taking her theory and running with it. She wasn't even questioning that Caitlyn was telling the truth!

"They obviously want you to find the Templar treasure."

"But I doubt it's still here. The castle has been renovated from roof to cellars; they would have found it."

"But why else would you be going on this treasure hunt with Raphael, in your dreams? It must still be here." Naomi hopped off the bed. "Are you allowed to walk around?"

"Yeah."

"Then let's go see her!"

"Who?"

"Mary, of course!"

Caitlyn laughed and reached for her shoes, careful not to bend over too quickly. "I've never seen you so excited."

"Caitlyn, until you came along, there was nothing at this school that was worth my excitement."

They went together to the chapel, a small, airy structure slightly apart from the château proper, rooted on its own outcropping of rock. It was used only for the a cappella choir's practice and the occasional lecture by a visiting expert. A van shuttle provided transportation to the village of Cazenac for any girls who wanted to attend religious services, or who wanted a change of scenery.

On this March day, the sky was bright blue, the sun's rays giving cold illumination to the late-winter landscape of grays, browns, and muted greens. A blustery wind stole the heat from their bodies as they crossed the short distance from château to chapel.

Once inside, the light took on a different quality. It was softened by the colored glass of the windows, as if tamed to serenity. Caitlyn stood for a moment soaking it in, enjoying the old-church smell that she thought must, like "mother" and "God," be an archetype of human existence.

"Here she is," Naomi said.

Caitlyn joined her in an alcove. Carved of white marble, the life-size Mary stood with her hands pressed together in prayer, her eyes cast heavenward. She wore a long robe and a crown with twelve stars upon a head of long wavy hair. The statue was set in an arched niche in a marble wall carved with myriad designs, the complexity of which rivaled the sundial ceiling.

"Now what?" Naomi asked.

"Start looking for anything that might be a symbol of the Knights Templar. Anything with a cross in it."

Naomi gave her a look. "Caitlyn. This is a church. There are going to be crosses."

"Unusual crosses, then."

Naomi muttered but went to work searching the details of the statue and its surroundings. Caitlyn started to do the same but then remembered the sundial, and stood back, looking at Mary and trying to think.

The sundial had told them where to look for the clue. There was no writing on the statue, though.

Caitlyn's gaze roamed over Mary, then settled on her hands, pointing upward. Her eyes, as well, were cast up. Caitlyn followed to where they pointed.

A scallop shell was carved into the peak of the arch above Mary.

Caitlyn took a chair off the end of a row and started to carry it over to the statue.

"Caitlyn, let me do that," Naomi said, taking it from her. "Did you forget you had your head split open?"

"Put it by the statue."

Naomi did, then put a steadying hand on Caitlyn's hip as she climbed onto the chair to look at the shell.

It was the size of Caitlyn's hand and for all the world looked like the symbol on a Shell gasoline sign.

Except for one detail.

At the base of the shell, where all the radiating lines met at the hinge, was a smooth spot on which was carved a cross with arms of equal lengths. Inside each quadrant formed by the cross, another small identical cross was carved.

Caitlyn had seen the symbol before, on a Web site about the Templars. It had been one of their seals.

"What do you see?" Naomi asked. "Is it the next clue?"

Caitlyn smiled down at her, elation bubbling in her chest. "What can you tell me about the symbolism of a scallop shell?"

"Either we're taking a trip to the beach, or we're having *coquilles Saint Jacques* for dinner." At Caitlyn's look of puzzlement she said, "Scallops with mushrooms, cream, and parmesan."

Caitlyn laughed and climbed down from the chair so that Naomi could take her place and look at the carving. "I don't think either of those hold the answer."

"You never know."

"Anything?" Naomi asked a week and a half later, as they hiked down a trail through the woods with their ten other geology classmates. They were on an afternoon field trip to study the local karst landscape, karst being the formations formed by eroded limestone, Caitlyn learned. Their first stop was to be the *gouffre* into which Brigitte's brother Thierry had tried to commit suicide.

"Nothing!"

Naomi cursed under her breath.

"Tell me about it," Caitlyn agreed.

It was a sunny, chilly late March day, but blessedly free of wind. Caitlyn's ears ached from the cold, but it felt good to be outdoors, tramping through a forest of pine, evergreen oak, and bare deciduous trees. The rough path was a mix of dirt and pale limestone, its edges softened by a lining of moss, ferns, and shrubs, many of which could have been found in the woods near her house back in Oregon.

"I haven't remembered a single dream since the night I hit my head," Caitlyn said. They were at the back of the group, a half dozen feet behind Amalia. "Even my attempts at lucid dreaming don't help. I'm starting to get scared that my dreams are gone for good."

"Scared" didn't begin to describe the increasing panic she felt at not being able to return to Raphael. Every free moment she had, she closed her eyes and tried for a lucid dream. Brain static was all she got. Nights were no better.

Her written dream journals sent to Madame Snowe were bare, and she feared the headmistress thought she was hiding something. She'd considered making up dreams, only rejecting the idea in the end for fear that Madame Snowe, with her PhD in psychology, might read unintended meanings into the fake dreams, and think Caitlyn more nutty than she already was.

Naomi was shaking her head. "There's a purpose to your dreams. They can't stop yet: they're not finished. We haven't found the treasure!"

Ahead of them, Amalia glanced back over her shoulder, a question in her eyes. Caitlyn nudged Naomi's arm in warning. "Shh!"

"Sorry," she whispered. "It's frustrating, is all."

"I know. Believe me, I know."

Caitlyn had thought the answer to the puzzle was only steps away once they found the scallop shell. It had taken only half a minute on the Internet to discover that it had three main symbolic meanings.

The first was fertility and love; it was the symbol of Venus. Botticelli had put Venus on a scallop shell in his famous painting of her birth.

The second meaning was the Celtic death journey. The lines on the scallop shell converging to one point looked like the rays of the sun, setting to the west at the end of the world. More specifically, setting at Finisterre, literally "the end of the earth," on the Atlantic coast of Galicia, in Spain. Coincidentally, the Latin name for the Atlantic had been *Mare Tenebrosum*, which translated to either "Sea of Darkness" or "Abyss of Death."

Caitlyn couldn't help noticing how often "darkness" and "abyss" had come up in her dreams. There was something there.

The third symbolic meaning of the scallop shell could also have a connection to a treasure map: the shell was the symbol of Saint James, who was one of Christ's apostles.

King Herod Agrippa beheaded James in 44 A.D., in Jerusalem, and legend had it that his body was sent on an unmanned ship to Spain for burial. The ship was wrecked on the coast, however, and the body lost. It washed ashore some time later, undamaged, and covered with scallops.

It seemed an odd sort of miracle to Caitlyn. The scallops were native to Galicia, however, and had long been a symbol of the region.

James's final resting place became Santiago de Compostela, one of the most popular pilgrimage destinations in the Middle Ages. A scallop shell from the shores of Galicia became a souvenir of the pilgrimage, and proof of completion of the arduous journey. Eventually, the scallop shell became a universal symbol of pilgrimage.

Caitlyn was surprised to find that one of the pilgrimage routes to Santiago de Compostela had passed right through the Perigord Noir region. The map she'd seen online had had too large a scale to tell how close the route had come to Château de la Fortune, though.

Assuming the scallop shell above the statue of Mary to be a reference to Saint James, Caitlyn had made a list of identifying traits for the saint, including a floppy hat and mantle as well as the Cross of the Knights of Santiago. Armed with this list, Caitlyn and Naomi had roamed the castle looking for Saint James.

He was nowhere to be found.

Caitlyn feared that, like the sundial, his image had been destroyed by time. If that were so, she would never find the next clue unless she got back to Raphael's world. Even if she was wrong and the shell did not represent St. James, she doubted she'd figure out what it *did* mean without Raphael. She needed him.

And not just for the treasure.

The group came to a stop, halted by Madame Brouwer, their tall Dutch geology teacher who looked like she should be playing professional beach volleyball, not teaching girls about rocks. "If you are ever lost in the woods, look for these markings on trees or stones," Madame Brouwer said in her hearty voice, pointing her walking stick to a painted short white horizontal line above a red one, on the trunk of a tree. "They are markings of the Grande Randonnée trail system that covers France and extends throughout Europe, and the markings will eventually lead you to a village. This portion of the Grande Randonnée we are on now has been trodden by pilgrims to Santiago de Compostela for over a thousand years."

Caitlyn caught her breath and looked at Naomi, who appeared just as surprised. The very trail they stood upon was the pilgrimage route!

As Madame Brouwer continued to talk, Caitlyn's mind wandered down the path to a new idea. Maybe she was wrong to look for an image of Saint James. Maybe it was the pilgrimage route itself that mattered. The path was part of the pilgrimage route, and the pilgrimage route led past the *gouffre*. The abyss. Maybe the treasure was in the *gouffre*!

Her heart thumped in excitement. Could it be that simple?

The trail came out of the woods to a clearing, in the center of which was the *gouffre*, an enormous hole in the pale rocky ground, at least thirty feet across. Scrubby-looking bushes and tufts of grass surrounded its rim. The girls at the front of the group inched toward a clear spot at the rocky edge, one by one leaning cautiously over to peer into its depths. Caitlyn waited impatiently for her turn.

Madame Brouwer picked up a stone and tossed it into the *gouffre*.

After a couple seconds, a distant, plunking splash burped up out of the depths. "Fifty meters deep," she said, sounding pleased.

There was water at the bottom.

Caitlyn's eyes widened. Of course! All the pieces were fitting together. Didn't all the clues so far have to do with water? *Stella Maris*, the Star of the Sea. The scallop shell that also meant the end of the earth at the edge of the Atlantic, the Sea of Darkness, also known as the Abyss of Death.

And abyss and *gouffre* meant the same thing!

And the dragon: on the sundial there had been a dragon at the base of the rays—rays that resembled the lines on the scallop shell. The dragon had also crawled out of a chasm in the painting of Fortuna. The dragon was a sign of the devil, and according to local legend, the devil used the *gouffre* as his doorway to Hell.

Feeling almost faint with anticipation, Caitlyn leaned over and whispered to Naomi, "I think the treasure is down *there*. Everything points to it! It all fits!" Caitlyn quickly went through her reasoning.

Naomi thought for a moment and then nodded, her eyes sparkling. "If it is, how will we get to it?"

"I've seen people on TV rappelling down rock faces. It can't be that hard to learn. I wonder if there's anywhere nearby we could take a lesson?"

Madame Brouwer, who had been saying something about limestone, stopped and gave them a look. "Caitlyn! Since you're so interested in talking, please tell the class how this *gouffre* was formed."

Caitlyn's face burned as her classmates turned to stare at her, their expressions a mix of pity and gleeful expectation. Caitlyn's already-racing heart beat double time, almost sounding like there were two in her chest. Her vision swam at the edges.

Fortunately, Caitlyn had paid attention in class when Madame Brouwer lectured about the *gouffre*. "Rainwater has carbon dioxide dissolved in it, making it acid. This water seeps through cracks in the limestone, dissolving it. As the cracks get bigger, the water flows faster, and water erosion starts speeding up the process. Eventually, big holes form in the rock, making caves, and if the roof of the cave gets too close to the surface, it collapses. So this is really the open roof of a cave."

Madame Brouwer grunted in approval and addressed the whole class. "The *gouffre* is not an isolated cave. The water that flowed into this space also had to flow out. Speleologists have mapped an extensive system of caves in this area, including passages that lead off of the *gouffre*."

Caitlyn's stomach sank. If there had been treasure at the bottom of the *gouffre*, someone would have found it ages ago.

"Many passages, however, are unexplored due to rock falls, flooding, and the technical difficulties and dangers of exploration," Madame Brouwer went on, reviving Caitlyn's hopes.

The thumping of her heart was neither slowing nor quieting; instead, it seemed to be growing louder, filling her head. Pinpricks of light dotted her vision.

Madame Brouwer's voice seemed far away, barely reaching Caitlyn through the sound of her own blood rushing in her head. "Let me warn you that caves in their natural state are not full of paved, level pathways, mesdemoiselles, so I advise against exploring any caves you may come upon. They are instead excellent places to break a bone and die, hundreds of meters from the light and air. And if it's not a broken bone that gets you, then a flash flood will be your end. Or a rock fall. Or getting wedged into a crack from which you have not the strength to remove yourself.

"Even those deaths," Madame Brouwer went on, "horrible as they might be, would not match the one of getting hopelessly lost, your torch battery burning down until it casts nothing but a dim yellow glow, and then that, too, fading until all is darkness such as you have never experienced. In the cold darkness of the caves, your eyes will never adjust. The temperature will be a constant thirteen degrees Celsius, bringing on hypothermia. Even if you find water uncontaminated by bat guano, and have enough clothes to stay warm, you will die of starvation. Alone. In blackness." Madame Brouwer looked at them one by one. "So do not venture into caves without a guide, *d'accord?*"

"*Oui!*" the class chorused, horrified by the grim description.

The girls ahead of Caitlyn moved away from the viewpoint, and it was finally her turn to look over the edge of the abyss. She stumbled forward, the beating of her heart seeming to knock her off balance with every thump. "*Je suis au bord du gouffre,*" she whispered, and leaned forward. *I am at the edge of the abyss.*

The rock walls of the pit were streaked with gray from long exposure, and small scrubby bushes and clumps of grass had taken root in crevices inside the throat. About fifteen feet down, the *gouffre* widened into a cavern, its walls stretching away into darkness. A slanting shaft of sunlight illuminated an aqua-blue pool at the bottom.

Her heart gave one last, loud thump, and then stopped. Time froze, the world caught in utter silence as Caitlyn stared into the abyss. She had a sudden vision of a heart being lifted from the ashes, its chambers still contracting with life, pumping air where once blood had flowed. And then the moment was shattered by a burst of sound like the beating heart of the earth itself, crashing inside her skull. Caitlyn lost her balance and yelped, falling forward, her arms flailing the air. She heard a shriek of voices from behind her, and from the corner of her eye saw Naomi reaching for her.

From the depths of the abyss came a roar like the breath of a dragon. A blast of air rose up from the earth and lifted Caitlyn, throwing her back from the edge, tossing her like a paper doll back across the path. She had a glimpse of the flying hair and lifted clothing of her classmates, and then she fell to the ground, wrapping her arms over her head. The burst of wind disappeared as quickly as it had come.

Madame Brouwer crouched down beside her, her hands running over Caitlyn as she asked quick questions to assess the damage. The other girls stood in a gaping circle around them, bug-eyed. Amalia was so pale she looked like she'd lost a gallon of blood. Naomi was holding herself as if the temperature had dropped thirty degrees.

As the shock faded away, Caitlyn began to breathe again. "I think I'm okay," she told Madame Brouwer. Okay, except for the vision of Bianca's still-beating heart.

"What happened?" Naomi asked in a quavering voice, her question directed at Caitlyn but answered by their geology teacher.

Madame Brouwer looked back toward the *gouffre*, her face betraying unease. "I've never seen a cave wind of such force. It makes no sense for it to be so strong coming out of such a wide opening, unless something cataclysmic has happened beneath the earth." She turned back to Caitlyn. "The moment before it started, it looked as if you were about to fall. Was there a downdraft pulling you in?"

"I . . . I thought I heard a loud noise, and it knocked me off balance," she said.

Madame Brouwer frowned. "I didn't hear anything. Class?"

The girls shook their heads.

Madame Brouwer helped Caitlyn to her feet and did another

quick assessment on her condition. Satisfied that Caitlyn was shaken, not broken, Madame Brouwer went back to the abyss and looked over the edge. "Nothing is different. But perhaps from where you were standing, you could hear something that we could not. Or perhaps there was a microburst of air from a thunderhead." She looked up at the clear sky, shrugged, and then turned away from the abyss. "I think you should visit the nurse, as a precaution." And to the class, "Could I have two volunteers to accompany Caitlyn back to the château?"

Every hand in the class shot up. Caitlyn was surprised and flattered for a moment, but then saw the frightened looks on her classmates' faces. No one wanted to hang around the *gouffre* anymore. Madame Brouwer seemed to be the only one who thought there was a purely scientific explanation for what had happened.

"Amalia, Naomi, thank you," Madame Brouwer said.

The three of them trudged back down the trail, shoulders hunched and silent until they were well out of earshot of their classmates, and then as if at a silent signal they stopped. Naomi spoke first. "Caitlyn, what happened back there?"

"That wasn't just wind," Amalia said. "It meant to do what it did; it meant to push you away from the *gouffre*."

Naomi shivered. "And it was cold. Really cold."

"I don't know what happened."

"What was the noise you thought you heard?" Naomi asked.

Caitlyn glanced at Amalia.

"I know something strange has been going on with you beyond your Screechers," Amalia said. "You don't have to tell me what it is if you don't want to."

Caitlyn met Naomi's gaze, a silent question passing between them. Naomi shrugged.

"It's like this . . . ," Caitlyn began, and gave Amalia a rundown of Raphael and the treasure stories. "What I thought I heard at the edge of the *gouffre* was a very loud heartbeat," she finished.

Amalia swore softly. "Bianca tried to lure you into the abyss, but something else pushed you away and saved you."

Caitlyn chewed her lip. "Maybe."

"You wouldn't be the first person she's lured into the *gouffre*," Amalia argued.

"Thierry," Naomi said softly.

"I've always thought that some higher power made him do it," Amalia said. "The guy was too big of a jerk to want to kill himself."

Caitlyn blinked in surprise at Amalia.

Amalia crossed her arms protectively over her chest. "He cheated on me."

"But I thought you just went out with him a couple times, to be a rebel?"

Amalia's cheeks turned pink. "It was a little more serious than that. But then I found out he was seeing two other girls—*two!*"

"Bastard!" Naomi said.

Amalia shrugged, obviously uncomfortable. "It was for the best. He started selling drugs, too, and I didn't want to be around that."

"Wow," Caitlyn said. "So being rich really *doesn't* buy you any class."

Naomi shook her head. "Major wanker."

"I never told anyone about his cheating on me," Amalia said. "Especially not Brigitte. She idolizes him. Or she used to, anyway. And there's no point in saying anything now."

"No," Caitlyn agreed.

"So what do we do now?" Naomi asked. "I don't think it's a good idea to go back to the *gouffre*."

"I agree," Caitlyn said. "I need to get back there, but in a dream, not in real life. I can be scared in a dream, but nothing can truly hurt me."

"I wish waking life was like that," Amalia said. "Wouldn't you stay in that dream world forever, if you could?"

"But if I was there forever, it wouldn't be a dream anymore," Caitlyn said, as they resumed the hike back to the château. "It would be real. *This* would be the dream."

"But you'd have your Raphael," Naomi said.

It made Caitlyn wonder. Would she do it, if by some miracle such a thing were possible? Would she give up her present life to live in that world?

Was love worth that?

"I don't know if I would want to live there, even with him, even if it were possible," Caitlyn finally answered. "But I don't think I can live here, without him."

Naomi gave her a knowing look. "Then we'd better find a way to get you dreaming again."

CHAPTER
Twenty-four

MARCH 31

More than a week had gone by since the incident at the *gouffre*, and there was still no sign of a dream. No sign of the Screechers, either. No strange, hypnagogic images as Caitlyn dropped off to sleep. No half-remembered odd stories swimming in her brain when she awoke. Nothing.

After years of dreading the things that might visit her in her sleep, Caitlyn now wished that they'd come screaming into her brain in full horrific glory. Even having the wits scared out of her was better than this blankness that descended with sleep, offering her nothing but lost time between night and morning.

Even Madame Snowe had something to say on the matter. She called Caitlyn in for a conference, concerned about the blank dream journals.

"I can't just stop dreaming forever, can I?" Caitlyn had asked, her voice hinging on hysteria. "That's not possible, right?"

"Unfortunately, it is." Caitlyn detected an undercurrent of anger in Madame Snowe's voice, as if Caitlyn had deliberately done something to annoy her. "It's very rare, but Charcot-Wilbrand syndrome has been studied since the 1880s. Brain injury can result in a total loss of dreams. Your brain didn't seem to have swelling, but perhaps the doctors missed something."

"But the dreams will come back, right?"

"They can, yes, but if they do they are often weaker and less frequent. Less vivid. A shadow of their former selves, if you will." Madame Snowe's nostrils flared, as if something about Caitlyn's lack of dreams was somehow contemptible.

"That can't be me! They have to come back," Caitlyn said, desperate for reassurance.

"Perhaps you will be lucky," Madame Snowe said grimly. "*Fortune rota volvitur.*"

Caitlyn had shaken her head, bewildered by the headmistress's harsh tone and at the possibility of losing her dreams, and Raphael, forever.

"Screw Fortune," Caitlyn muttered now, remembering.

"What was that?" Amalia said, looking up from the heavy tome she was reading.

"I was cursing the whimsies of Fortune."

"Curse the typesetter who did this book, while you're at it. The print is nearly impossible to read."

Caitlyn, Naomi, and Amalia were seated around a library table they'd taken over for the past week. Using the excuse of Caitlyn's history paper, they'd enlisted the librarian's aid in unearthing every book in the Fortune School's library that touched on Catherine de' Medici's era in France and Italy. It turned out to be a lot of books, the de' Medici family having been an interest of Madame Snowe's family, undoubtedly because of the portrait they owned of Bianca de' Medici.

Another, much smaller stack of books contained one volume on the Knights Templar, three geology texts, a slim guide to cave exploration, and two books on hypnotism.

Whenever they had free time, Naomi and Amalia skimmed the books in French and Italian, while Caitlyn plodded through the ones in English. They were looking for any mention of the people Caitlyn had seen or heard about in her dream, but as the days went by without success, Caitlyn began to feel the weight of doubt. With the doubt came guilt at the efforts Naomi and Amalia were expending on her behalf.

The guilt had been chewing at her with increasingly sharp teeth, and she finally couldn't stand it anymore. "Maybe this is pointless," Caitlyn said. "Maybe there's nothing to find. They were just dreams, after all. They seemed real, but—"

"But nothing," Naomi said. She turned a page and kept reading.

"We don't have any proof that anything I saw in my dreams was real. If anything, it's looking like I imagined it all. I'm probably losing my mind."

Naomi looked up from her reading. "Caitlyn, we felt that wind at the *gouffre*."

"Madame Brouwer says now she's sure it was some sort of microburst, a sort of reverse tornado from a storm cloud. They can be strong enough to flatten trees."

"Then why didn't it so much as snap a twig? Why did it only mess our hair?"

"Face it. You're stuck with us," Amalia said. "Stop whining and go back to reading."

Caitlyn bent her head over an open book, but she didn't see

the words on the page. Instead, she saw herself sitting at a table with two girls who were willing to give all their time and energy to help her. It reminded her of her old friends back at home— Jacqui and Sarah.

"Caitlyn," Amalia suddenly said in a quiet, strained voice, "tell me again the name of Raphael's teacher."

Caitlyn sat up straight. Naomi put down her book. "Beneto."

Amalia shoved her book into the center of the table so they all could see. "This is the diary of Marguerite de Valois, Catherine de' Medici's daughter." Amalia ran her finger under the French sentences as she translated aloud. "I was left to console the wards Giulia and Elisabeta, as they had learned that their brother was dead. His teacher, an insane old man named Beneto, was put to death this morning for the crime."

"What! No!" Caitlyn pulled the book toward her, scanning the French passage for herself. She saw the words for *brother* and *dead*, and Beneto's name. "It can't be. It can't!"

"Caitlyn," Amalia said hesitantly, "maybe the reason you can't dream about Raphael anymore is that he was murdered right after your last dream."

"No," Naomi said, shaking her head. "What would be the point of that? I think Caitlyn hasn't dreamed because she had to learn about Beneto before she went back to Raphael. She has to warn him."

Amalia pointed to the book. "But she doesn't. Otherwise this book wouldn't say Beneto was put to death for his murder."

They looked at one another. Caitlyn pressed her fingertips against her temples, trying to think, trying to push aside the flushing panic that she was too late, that Raphael was going to die because she'd hit her head and lost her dreams. "This sounds like one of those paradoxes that keep showing up in science-fiction stories. If I warn

Raphael and Beneto doesn't kill him, then does the book change? Will any of us remember seeing it written the way it is now?"

Caitlyn shook her head, struggling through the warped logic. "Maybe we're thinking about this the wrong way. We're acting as if I'm going back in time, but I'm not. I'm dreaming. If anything, Raphael may be a ghost who is visiting my sleep and creating a dream world around me that he uses to tell his story. Maybe this isn't about my stopping something that happened in the past. It could be about learning something that matters right here, right now. For some reason, I need to know his story."

"Or maybe he needs to know his own story," Naomi said.

Caitlyn dropped her hands. "What do you mean?"

"Maybe he doesn't know what happened to him. He needs you to help him figure it out."

"Four hundred years after his death?" Caitlyn asked. "Why now? Why me?"

Amalia answered. "Because you're the first person who could hear him. You're a medium."

Caitlyn dismissed the idea with a shake of her head. "No other spirits ever talk to me."

"Those Screecher things are ghosts, aren't they?" Naomi asked.

"I don't know *what* they are. If they're ghosts, they're crappy, insane ghosts who spend all their time screaming."

"Maybe that's the type you attract."

"Great."

"Who knows what real ghosts are like?" Amalia asked. "Maybe a coherent one like Raphael is a rare exception."

"That brings us back to the first point, doesn't it?" Caitlyn said. "If he's a rare exception, then there may be a purpose behind these dreams, beyond helping Raphael to the 'other side' or whatever it is that's supposed to happen when we die. There may be something important about his story that will matter to us here, now."

"Or matter to *you*," Naomi said. "We're peripheral."

Caitlyn remembered the things Madame Snowe had told her about dream interpretation. Raphael—whether he had an external reality or was just a part of her imagination—might be trying to give her a message about herself. But what? And if she found out what, would Raphael stop visiting her, his work done?

She pulled Marguerite de Valois's diary in front of her, looking again at the lines with Beneto's name. "Something about all this is real, but I'm never going to figure out what unless I dream again." She looked up at her friends. "Anyone have a magic potion to make that happen?"

"I don't," Amalia said, and hesitated. "But Brigitte does."

CHAPTER
Twenty-five

"Zolpidem tartrate," Amalia read off the label, and handed the prescription bottle to Caitlyn. "The magic dreaming potion, as promised."

Caitlyn took the bottle and looked at it doubtfully. It was later that same evening, and she was sitting on her bed in her nightgown with Amalia and Naomi.

"It's also known as Ambien," Amalia said. "It's a sleeping pill. I told Brigitte I was having trouble falling asleep, and she gave me the whole bottle. She hasn't used any for months; she says it gives her weird, vivid dreams that she has a hard time shaking off in the morning. Apparently, it has a reputation for doing that."

"Which means," Naomi said, "that it has a good chance of giving *you* some dreams, as well. It might be the kick start your brain needs."

"A *kick start* doesn't sound like something you want to do to your brain," Caitlyn said nervously. "Are you sure this stuff won't hurt me?"

"Positive," Amalia said. "And just in case, Naomi and I will take turns watching over you all night."

"You're going to be fine," Naomi reassured her.

Amalia took the bottle back and shook out a pill into her palm. She considered it for a moment, then shook out one more. "Here."

Caitlyn hesitated; taking sleeping pills worried her. Her brain was messed up enough as it was.

"You want to see Raphael, don't you?" Naomi said. "You have to tell him about Beneto. You have to save his life."

Her quibbles were washed away under a wave of renewed urgency. Raphael needed her. She wouldn't—*couldn't*—let him die! Caitlyn scooped up the pills, dropped them on her tongue, and took a gulp of water. Amalia and Naomi moved off her bed and she got under her covers. "How long until I feel it?"

"Fifteen or twenty minutes, if you don't fight it," Amalia said.

Naomi shut off Caitlyn's bedside lamp. "*Fais des beaux rêves.*" Sweet dreams.

Caitlyn shut her eyes. They would be sweet only if she could save Raphael.

She floated bodiless in darkness, surrounded by silence. She lingered there for an unknown stretch of time, directionless, emotionless, until a faint spark of light formed in the distance. Her consciousness flashed her the image of Raphael.

"Raphael," she whispered into the void, and from her heart she felt a surge of emotion. She was drawn toward the light that was he as if they were tied together by a golden cord. "Raphael, Raphael . . ."

The light expanded, blinding her for a split second, then the void was gone, and a sense of her body settled around her and gave her weight. Beneath her bare feet she felt the coldness of stone. The darkness had given way to the gray landscape of Raphael's bedroom, the moonlight that came through the window so bright she could almost see color. She stood beside his bed, wearing her long white nightgown.

She saw him, and tears of mingled relief and joy stung her eyes. Her chest tightened, her heart feeling ready to burst. *He's still alive! And I'm here! I'm finally here with him!*

Raphael slept, one arm flung above his head, his hair spilling across the pillow, the sheet pushed down to his waist. His bare torso showed muscled strength even in sleep. He was gloriously alive and beautiful. She was almost afraid to believe that she had found her way back to him, and reached out to trace her fingertips over the planes of his chest and prove he was real.

Suddenly, Raphael grabbed her hand in a hard grip, and his eyes flew open. She gasped. For a long moment he stared at her in confusion, and then the veil of sleep cleared from his face. "I knew you'd come back to me," he said, his voice hoarse with emotion. He tugged her down onto the bed and into his arms, and held her as if he would never let her go. She felt him shaking, and he put his hand on the back of her head, holding her close as he nuzzled his face into the corner of her neck, his breath warm against her skin. She felt his lips moving against her as he spoke. "I'm not going to let you disappear on me again," he said into her hair. "I'll find a way to keep you here with me."

She closed her eyes, lost in the joy of being once again in his arms. She never wanted to part from him again. "How?" she asked, and wanted the answer with every fiber of her being.

"By never letting go."

Caitlyn entwined her fingers in his hair. Being enclosed within his embrace felt *right*, as if she had been there a thousand times before and would be there a thousand times again. He kissed her neck.

"I want to stay here forever," Caitlyn said.

"Can you? Do you know how?"

The question stirred the sediment in Caitlyn's mind, and her waking life began drifting up into her consciousness, breaking through the surface of the dream. She shook her head and leaned back from him so she could see his face. "This isn't real."

He smiled and touched her lips with his fingertips. "Not in the sense that anyone else would understand. But you're real to me. The Church would see this as the worst sort of sin, but I lost respect for it long ago. They can send me to Hell if they want, better there with you than in Heaven without."

Caitlyn frowned, confused. "But—wait a minute. *I'm* real to *you*? Don't you mean that you're real to me?"

He smiled indulgently. "I'm not the ghost."

Caitlyn's lips parted. "Raphael. Neither am I."

He stroked the side of her face. "I know you don't realize it."

"No, I'm alive, just not in this place." She struggled to sit up, and he sat up along with her. "I only see you when I sleep; you appear only in my dreams. I'm dreaming right now."

He took her hand, his voice soothing. "No. If that were so, I would not exist when you were not here. But I do. I am not a figment of your imagination."

"No! You're a ghost, haunting my dreams. You may have lived once, but you died. Beneto murdered you."

He frowned. "Beneto? No, that's impossible."

"I read it in the diary of Marguerite de Valois. She comforted Giulia and Elisabeta when they heard of your death. Those are your sisters, aren't they?"

"Yes. But Beneto would give his life for me, and we're both very much alive. He obviously has not killed me."

"He will!" Caitlyn exclaimed. She paused and took a breath.

245

"Raphael, this is not real. I am a student in a girls' school at Château de la Fortune in the year 2011. You died over *four hundred* years ago."

His gaze locked with hers, powerful even in the moonlight. "Caitlyn. I do not know when you lived or where you came from, but I know that I am alive and you are a spirit. I've known you were something not of this world since the day you saved me from the falling stone. You were with me in a locked room, and then you vanished. That's why I acted so strangely when next I saw you. You're the only ghost I've ever seen, and I didn't know what to make of you."

Caitlyn shook her head. "I'm *not* a ghost. I vanished from that room because I woke up."

"Stay here with me until morning, and I will show you."

"Show me what?"

"That light passes through you."

"*What?*" She couldn't believe this. Nothing made sense.

"I don't know how it is that I can touch you and see you. But light—sunlight, candlelight, firelight—passes through you. The brighter the light, the more transparent you become. And no one can see you but me."

"That only proves what *you* think and experience. I'm alive. I'm sure of it," she insisted, even as doubt crept into her voice. "At least, I'm pretty sure. I'm a student at the Fortune School, in the year 2011."

"*Two thousand eleven?*" he asked, the date only now seeming to sink in.

She nodded.

"Two thousand eleven. You can tell me the future of the world?"

"I can tell you *your* future. Beneto is executed for your murder!"

He shook off her words dismissively. "So you were a student at the Fortune School. Caitlyn, can you remember what might have killed you, or why you became a wandering spirit? Were you ill? Was there an accident?"

She shook her head. "Nothing happened, except I fainted and hit my head. But I already knew you by then."

"The first time you saw me, I was riding in the valley, right?"

She nodded.

"You think you dreamed that."

She nodded again.

"Caitlyn, what happened to you right before you had that dream?"

"I had it on the trip from the Bordeaux airport to the school. It was just a car ride. Nothing happ—" She suddenly saw the bright headlights of the semitruck coming straight for her through the rain. She heard the blare of the horn, felt the violent jerk of the Mercedes as the driver tried to evade impact. "Oh my God," she whispered. "We could have crashed." Panicked disbelief rose in her chest and she squeezed his hands. "I'm dead?" She shook her head in disbelief. "I never made it to the Fortune School? I imagined everything? Amalia, Naomi . . . But why?"

"Maybe you weren't ready to die."

Her breath came in quick gasps. "I'm *not* ready! I have a whole life to live!"

"Then live it here, with me."

She looked at him as if she were seeing him for the first time. "But if I died, why did I come here to you?"

"Because I needed you."

"Ghosts don't go back in time! I should be haunting people in the twenty-first century, not the sixteenth!"

"What rules are there for what happens after death?"

"Oh my God." She got up off the bed and began to pace. "*Ohmigod ohmigod.* My mom, she must be devastated. My brothers. My father. My friends. They must all know." She stopped in front of him. "Why did I come here to you, instead of going to them to say good-bye?"

He shook his head, having no answer.

Her heart ached with the sudden panic of loss. Tears spilled down her cheeks. "Will they miss me?"

He reached up and gently brushed the hair back from her face and tucked it behind her ear. "Yes."

"I was going to go to college. What am I going to do now?" she cried.

"Stay here with me."

"*Can* I? Or am I going to vanish?"

He pulled her across his lap and into his arms, cradling her against his chest. He pressed his lips to the top of her head. "We'll find a way to keep you here. There's a purpose to your presence. You were sent to me."

"I don't understand how I could have imagined everything at the Fortune School. It seemed so real. Madame Snowe, Brigitte, and that story about Thierry and the *gouffre.* The painting of Bianca de' Medici. I thought Bianca was haunting me. Why did I think that?"

His hands that had been stroking her hair stopped. "Bianca was haunting you?"

"She showed me her death, and Beneto taking the heart from the ashes of her pyre. I don't know why she showed me that, or why I sometimes hear it beating. Is she trying to scare me away from you?"

His fingers tightened in her hair. "No."

"What does she want of me?" Caitlyn asked.

"I think she wants your understanding. And I think she brought you here for me."

"To help you?"

"Yes. But that's not all."

"What else?"

"I think she meant for you to be my bride."

CHAPTER
Twenty-six

Caitlyn stuttered, astonished, "You, you think . . . You think Bianca was playing matchmaker with us?"

"She used to tease me that she knew who my soul mate was, but that I wouldn't believe her if she told me. She said I'd love this woman so strongly that even death could not keep us apart. The only hint Bianca would give to this mystery woman's identity was that she would have skin pale as the moon and hair black as midnight. She called you my Dark One." He touched Caitlyn's cheek. "It's you."

Caitlyn's breath caught in her throat. Hope, fear, and disbelief all fought within her. She couldn't take it all in, or find an answer that made sense. She didn't know what was real. Was she alive or dead? Dreaming or awake? Had she ever been to the Fortune School, or was all that no more than the dreams of a restless spirit?

A cold wash of shock flowed down her body as an image came to mind: a skeleton in black armor, riding a white horse. Death.

Her mother had predicted this. Her words during the tarot reading came back to Caitlyn. *Death is the force that will create your new life. It is the mechanism of transformation. Welcome it.*

Oh God. It *was* true: she was dead. She had died in a car crash, just like her mother. Everything that happened at the Fortune School had been a dream. When she had seen Château de la Fortune in person for the first time, and felt the sense of belonging, of coming home, it was because she had seen the place her spirit would haunt for eternity. She hadn't left the castle since that day.

She was dead.

Dead.

She looked at Raphael and felt her heart ache with the strength of her bond to him. He was her only reality, now. She had no existence beyond him. "If I'm a ghost, how is it that we are together?" she whispered, seeking reassurance.

"I don't know, but here you are. I understand now why Bianca said I wouldn't believe it."

Caitlyn shook her head. "Why would she choose a dead girl for you?"

"She only saw the future, Caitlyn. She didn't control it."

Caitlyn struggled to think through her shock, to find a meaning for everything she thought had happened at the Fortune School. "If Bianca brought me here to you, then maybe she was also part of everything I thought I learned at the Fortune School." She looked at him with fresh urgency. "Raphael, your mother may have meant for me to tell you that Beneto would kill you."

He shook his head in sharp denial. "I can't accept that. Beneto was devoted to my mother and has been like a second father to me. He thought Bianca's existence upon this earth was a miracle, not an evil."

"Marguerite's diary—"

"You said he was executed for my murder, right?"

She nodded.

251

"That doesn't mean he was guilty. It means he was a scapegoat. Someone else is responsible for trying to kill me."

Caitlyn didn't believe it, but she didn't know what to believe about anything, at that moment. "Then maybe it's Philippe," she said. "Did you ever check the hidden cabinets in his room?"

"Beneto did. He discovered that Philippe is a bit more than a spy for Catherine." Raphael grinned, his teeth shining in the moonlight. "His true loyalty is to Henry of Navarre, the very man whose Huguenot supporters Catherine sent him here to keep tabs on."

"So you don't think he's the one trying to kill you, either?"

Raphael shook his head.

"Even if it's not Beneto," Caitlyn said, her throat tight, "whoever is trying to kill you will succeed."

Raphael stood, clearly agitated, and stirred the fire to life with a poker. Caitlyn waited, watching the emotions run like water over his features. He threw a piece of wood on the fire and turned to her. "My mother said that even death would not keep you and me apart. If I'm murdered, we'll still be together."

"Where? I have seen no afterlife."

He shrugged. "We'll cross that bridge when we come to it. Together." He held out his hand to her. She took it, and he gently pulled her to her feet. He bent her hand over his, raised the back of it to his lips, and kissed it. He looked up at her from under his brows, his head still bent over her hand. "Tell me you'll be mine, Caitlyn. Forever."

She met his eyes and felt the fear and shock give way under the love in his gaze. There was no other world but the one she shared with him. Her heart had belonged to him since long before she saw him riding in the Dordogne Valley and recognized him as her Knight of Cups. All her life she had known he was somewhere, waiting for her, just as she waited for him.

Yes, she would gladly give up her life to be with him. "I'll be yours, Raphael. Until the end of time."

He gathered her close in his arms and held her. Caitlyn closed her eyes and rested her head against his chest. It still felt like she was in a dream, but now that she knew she had Raphael's heart, she didn't ever need to wake. They would face whatever came, together.

"There's something we need to do before whoever is out to kill me succeeds," he said, releasing her.

"What's that?"

"Find the Templar treasure and entomb Bianca's heart within it, as she requested before she died. It's more important than ever: we may need Bianca's power to stay together, beyond the limits of death. If the heart is destroyed and, along with it, the last remnants of her power . . . ," he trailed off, obviously unwilling to complete the thought.

"Death might have the strength to separate us, after all," Caitlyn finished for him. The threat lit a fire under her determination to find the Templar treasure. It was her own future that now depended upon it. "The scallop shell. It's the next clue."

"You found the shell, too?"

"With my friend Naomi." She frowned. "Imaginary friend Naomi? Anyway, we found it above the statue of Mary. It's the symbol of Saint James, isn't it?"

He nodded. "And where did that send you?"

"Along Saint James's way, to the *gouffre* in the woods."

His eyes widened. "The *gouffre*?" He laughed. "No, you were right about Saint James's way, but not about the path in the woods. Come, I'll show you."

He dressed and led her out of his room and down through the castle to a large empty room that had windows looking directly out over the valley of the Dordogne. A fireplace dominated one wall, and dark wooden beams spanned the ceiling ten feet above their heads. Caitlyn turned around in the middle of the room and imagined it filled with leather couches, Oriental carpets, desks, and a painting of Fortuna.

"It's the Grand Salon," she said in wonder. "I stayed up late here to study most nights, and to talk with Naomi. Or at least I thought I did."

"Did you ever take note of this?" He lowered a candle so that it illuminated the painted tile floor upon which they stood.

It took her a moment to make sense of the design. "It's a map!" she said in surprise. "I only ever saw this room with its floor covered in carpets."

He moved the candle for her as she searched out the contours of Europe and the Middle East. "The lines," he said, pointing to dark red routes that looked like they belonged in a road atlas. "They are pilgrimage routes." He followed along with her as she traced Saint James's way to the scallop shell marking Santiago de Compostela.

"Do you think the treasure is under this tile with the shell?" she asked excitedly.

"I thought it might be at first, but there's no Templar symbol by it."

"Have you found one anywhere on the map?"

He nodded, and led her across Europe. "This is the most popular route between Paris and Jerusalem," he said, pointing out a line. "The Templars began their existence as armed protection for pilgrims heading to the Holy Land. There," he said, pointing to a picture halfway along the route. "Two men on one horse."

Caitlyn nodded. She'd seen the image online. It was supposed to represent the initial poverty of the Templars, who began so poor that they had only one horse for two knights.

A feeling of disquiet went through her. How did she learn that, if none of her time at the Fortune School had been real? Could that piece of information have come from Bianca, as well as everything else new she thought she'd experienced?

"So where's the next clue?" she asked.

"I was hoping you could tell me."

She gnawed a fingernail, looking at the two men on the horse, riding toward Jerusalem. Her glance flicked to Jerusalem itself. It was at the very edge of the map, beneath the wall on which Fortuna had hung.

She remembered Madame Snowe's album about Château de la Fortune, and the picture of Antoine Fournier. The caption had said he'd chosen where to hang the painting. Caitlyn closed her eyes and summoned an image of the painting.

Fortuna treaded the clouds, one hand on the jeweled wheel, one hand pointing downward. One foot rested on a wisp of vapor, while the other pointed down in the same direction as her hand.

Caitlyn opened her eyes. If Fortuna were hanging on the wall right now, she'd be pointing at Jerusalem. "Where do all the pilgrims go, exactly?" Caitlyn asked carefully. "What's there to see in Jerusalem?"

He gave her an incredulous look. "Are there many people in two thousand and eleven who do not know these basic things?"

"I never went to church. And hey, I might not know where pilgrims go in Jerusalem, but I'll bet I know more than you do about biology, geology, and dinosaurs."

"Assuredly, you do. I have never encountered a dinosaur, and do not even know what one is. But to answer your question, there are several holy sites in Jerusalem, but the main one is this," he said, pointing to a picture of a blocky building with two domed roofs. "The Church of the Holy Sepulchre. It's where Christ was crucified and buried."

Part of the building reminded her of something . . . recognition sent a bolt of excitement through her. "That smaller dome," she said, pointing, "the one on the short round tower! It looks like the well in the château's courtyard, doesn't it? The stone base of the well is exactly like the base of that building, and the ironwork that holds the bucket looks like the dome."

Raphael dropped the candle in surprise. He scrambled to pick it up again, its flame still burning. "The well! I always thought there was something peculiar about its design. That has to be the next step."

"I solved the scallop clue?"

"It all fits! Water. *Stella Maris*, the scallop shell, the water under the sun on the window; they all refer to water, like in a well!"

Caitlyn grinned, pleased with herself. "I thought it was the *gouffre* for the same reasons, and some reasons to do with death, too." She quickly ran through her reasoning about Finisterre and the Abyss of Death. "But that painted tile definitely looks like the well."

"We'll find out either way, won't we?" He scooped her up in a bear hug.

"Find out what?" a voice asked from the doorway.

Caitlyn turned her head.

It was Beneto.

CHAPTER
Twenty-seven

The flaming scrap of oil-soaked cloth fell deep into the narrow darkness of the well until it was no more than a faint point of light, and then it suddenly went out.

"That's a long way down," Caitlyn said.

"You didn't see it?" Raphael said.

"See what?" Caitlyn and Beneto said in unison. Caitlyn realized with vague surprise that they were all speaking Italian. Were the dead natural linguists? Too bad she hadn't had that gift while still alive.

"My eyes are not as strong as they once were," Beneto said.

Caitlyn cast a dark look at the old man who formed the third point of their triangle of people bent over the edge of the well, staring into its depths. As Raphael had warned her, she was invisible to Beneto, and he could not sense her presence. At Raphael's insistence she'd tried to touch Beneto, to give him some sense that she was real, but her hand had slid away from him as if repelled. It had felt like trying to press together the positive sides of two magnets.

It was the hour before dawn, a faint hint of purple touching the horizon to the east. They were hoping to complete their exploration of the well before anyone else in the château stirred.

"There was a dark spot in the shaft wall about a quarter of the way down, between me and you, Caitlyn," Raphael said.

Beneto's gaze flicked to the space where Raphael had told him she was standing. She could see the hesitant disbelief in his eyes, the old man unable to either fully accept or refute Raphael's claims that a ghost was helping him find the Templar treasure. Caitlyn was surprised he was going along with the idea of her without protest. Surely even a man who had spent years around the psychic Bianca de' Medici would have had a few more questions for Raphael than Beneto had, about his fantastical claims. Anyone rational would assume Raphael was insane.

"I don't trust him," Caitlyn complained, staring at the art teacher.

"Then trust me and my judgment."

Caitlyn scowled. What else could she do? She had voiced her concerns. She couldn't force Raphael to take her point of view.

Raphael tied a lantern to the end of a rope and started lowering it down the well, its flame casting an orange glow onto the stones. About twenty feet down, a jagged fissure opened in the wall, looking like a black slash in the orange lantern light. It was big enough for a man to crawl through.

"There," Raphael said, and tied off the rope on one of the iron posts piercing the rim of the well.

"It looks like the entrance to Hell," Caitlyn said.

"Only if it kills me," Raphael said with a grin, and started tying a thicker rope to two of the iron posts, anchoring it firmly. The ropes attached to the bucket and winch were too old for even Caitlyn to be willing to risk her ghostly weight to.

"Bianca will protect you," Beneto said to Raphael.

Caitlyn looked in surprise at Beneto. That was a lot of faith to have in a dead woman. One might as well build a temple in her honor and worship her as a goddess who could interfere in the lives of mortal men.

"Let me go first," Caitlyn said, as Raphael tossed the free end of the rope into the well. He had knotted it every few feet to make climbing easier.

"What type of man would send a woman first into danger?" Raphael asked incredulously.

"How could I possibly be hurt? I'm dead, remember?"

He shook his head. "I don't know what laws of nature are at work here. I have yet to see you walk through a wall or fly. Nor are you dressed appropriately."

Caitlyn reached down and tied up the hem of her nightgown between her legs, making a rough sort of romper out of it. Her feet were still bare.

"She wants to go first?" Beneto asked, eyes searching the space where Caitlyn stood.

"She thinks she's invulnerable."

"She will be less vulnerable than you."

"Thank you, Beneto," Caitlyn said.

"She says thanks," Raphael passed along.

Beneto grunted in acknowledgment. "Let her go first. Don't let your eagerness blind you to what is practical."

"It was chivalry, not eagerness."

"That's sweet of you," Caitlyn said, and climbed up onto the edge of the well, swinging her legs to the inside.

"Caitlyn, no!"

Her stomach flipped as she got a good look at the distance

259

between her dangling feet and the lantern glowing down below. It seemed much farther than it had a moment ago. She didn't want to think about the even farther distance between the lantern and the water. "It's the best way, Raphael. You know it is."

He started to come around the well, and she knew he was going to try to stop her. There was no time for hesitation or second thoughts. She grabbed the rope and swung to the center of the shaft, her bare feet finding balance on a knot. "Whoa," she said, feeling the strain of her weight on her arms. For a ghost, she seemed awfully heavy. The last time she'd climbed a rope had been when she was in gym class, in fourth grade. It had been a lot easier then, when she was still a scrawny monkey of a child.

"Careful!" Raphael cried.

She grinned at him. He looked half out of his mind with worry, and afraid to interfere lest he knock her from her precarious perch. "Fear not! The girls of the future are a resourceful lot."

He put his hand to his forehead, eyes wide with worry.

His fear made her feel daring. She began to lower herself down the rope, glad for her bare feet that let her feel for the next knot. It took only a minute to reach the level of the lantern and fissure. The orange light reached a few feet into the limestone opening, and Caitlyn peered into the shadowed depths, half expecting to see the glint of gold.

All she saw was rock and shadow.

"Anything?" Raphael called from above.

"No treasure. But I think it might be the entrance to a tunnel or cave system. I can't see the back."

"Come back up."

She looked up at him, his face framed by a faintly lightening sky. The only time she'd seen him in full daylight had been on that first day, when he was riding near the Dordogne River.

The cleft in the rock was a foot away from where she clung to the rope. She reached out, feeling for handholds.

"Caitlyn! What are you doing?"

She found a grip in the edge of the rock and pulled herself toward it, her heart thumping. How to make the transfer? She didn't see how she could get enough of her upper body into the opening to keep from falling down the well once she released the rope.

"Caitlyn!"

She let go of the stone and swung back to the center of the well. With a firm grip on the rope, she released her foothold on a knot and dangled for a moment, one foot cautiously kicking at air until it met the stone lip of the fissure. She dug in her heel, pulling her body closer and then sliding both legs onto the cold stone. There came a precarious moment when she was half in the cave, half out, and she had to lower her grip on the rope to move any deeper. Her arm muscles were beginning to quiver. She took a brief look downward at the black depths. "Not a good place to be, Caitlyn," she whispered to herself.

She shifted her grip. Her hands slipped, her body tilting forward for an endless moment before she caught herself.

She heard a keening groan from above.

She used her feet and buttocks to inch herself deeper into the opening until at last she felt her center of gravity shift to inside the mouth of the cave. She let go of the rope and grabbed solid rock.

Her breath released in a heavy sigh of relief, and she realized she was shaking.

"Caitlyn! Are you all right?"

She poked her head out the opening and looked up. "There'd better be another opening to this cave somewhere, because I am not doing that again on the way out."

He chuckled and repeated her words to Beneto.

"What do you see?" Beneto called down, a note of embarrassed self-consciousness in his voice. Caitlyn suspected he thought he might be talking to air.

"Let me look." Caitlyn crawled deeper into the cave. It was only as she moved that she remembered what Madame Brouwer had said about natural cave floors not being paved and flat.

But this one was. She was inching her way over a surface built of square blocks of stone.

A few feet in, the roof above her head rose out of her reach, and the stone floor began to slant downward. It was too dark to see what lay beyond. She returned to the opening.

"It's man-made!" she called up. "It goes somewhere."

"Take the rope down behind us," Raphael said to Beneto. "We don't want anyone to guess where we are and follow."

Beneto handed him a leather bag, and Raphael slung its strap across his chest. It held the chest with Bianca's heart, Caitlyn knew. They'd decided to bring it with them in hopes that they could at last entomb it as Bianca had requested.

Beneto put his hand on Raphael's shoulder. "Be careful."

Raphael nodded. "I will." He swung his legs over the edge of the well and started working his way down the rope. He made short work of it, swooping into the fissure with an ease that put Caitlyn's efforts to shame. He untied the lantern and brought it in with him. A moment later Beneto raised the rope.

They quickly moved deeper in the cave to where they could stand. The brighter light showed Caitlyn how dirty she'd already gotten. Her nightgown was smeared with mud and lichen, and was wet through.

She gestured at herself and smiled. "When you look good, you feel good."

He wrapped an arm around her neck and pulled her close for a hard kiss on the lips. "I like you dirty." Then he scowled and gave her a gentle shake. "Don't ever scare me like that again, swinging on the rope."

"I won't. I'll find a new way," she teased.

He gently touched her hair, his expression somber. "I've already lost one person I cared for deeply. I won't lose another."

She stood on tiptoe and kissed his cheek. "You'll never be rid of me. Remember, even death holds no boundaries for us."

He nodded. "Let's go find some treasure."

There was no mystery to which way they should go, the stone path a veritable Yellow Brick Road through the earth. The passage remained narrow for several hundred feet, sloping downward, its walls smoothed by the rushing of waters long gone. Someone had taken advantage of a natural route through the stone; there were only a few tight spots where the builders of the passage had clearly taken a chisel to the stone. The air smelled of rock and dampness, and felt cold and thick in Caitlyn's lungs. She was quickly chilled; she wished she'd taken heed of Madame Brouwer's warnings about the temperature inside caves and borrowed something warmer.

The fissure they'd been following ended in a low-roofed chamber decorated with cave formations. Several stalactites slowly dripped water into a shallow pool. The path wound through the maze of columns. They followed it, hunched double, both holding a hand above their head to protect against bumps.

"It's beautiful," Caitlyn said, as they passed lacelike crystals that covered an outcropping of rock.

Raphael made a noise of acknowledgment, but moved forward without slowing. Caitlyn followed. There would be time enough to gawk at stones on the way out.

The path led into a rabbit-hole tunnel that forced them to crawl. Caitlyn's appreciation for the wonders of the cave quickly faded under the pressure of the stones on her knees and palms. Claustrophobia began to tighten around her as her vision shrank to nothing more than Raphael's feet and rear in front of her and the shifting shadows of the lantern. She breathed through her mouth and tried to stay calm, tried not to think about how hard it would be to turn around in the narrow confines.

They both let out a breath of relief when at last the tunnel ended and they came out into a fair-size cavern. The path was carved into its edge, the center of the cavern falling away into darkness. They could hear a stream gurgling in its depths, the sound echoing off the stones.

"How far do you think we've come?"

"A quarter mile at most."

"That's all?"

He chuckled. "I know. It feels longer."

"Will the lantern burn long enough for us to find our way out again?"

"Maybe. Even if not, we could feel our way."

Caitlyn made an unhappy sound in her throat, remembering what Madame Brouwer had said about caves.

He took her hand. "We'll be fine. Courage, my sweet."

Onward they went, the constant movement warming Caitlyn. Or was she imagining that? How could a dead person be warmed by exercise?

A faint sound touched upon her hearing and she stopped, jerking Raphael to a stop with her. The hairs rose on the back of her neck. "Did you hear that?" she whispered.

He shook his head. "What was it?"

She held up her hand for silence and turned to face back the way they'd come. Her ears strained for a hint of sound or a change in air pressure.

Nothing.

She shook her head and shrugged. "I thought I heard movement behind us."

Raphael looked back into the darkness. "Air?"

"Maybe." They'd felt occasional breezes as they moved, hinting at openings to the world above.

They continued, Caitlyn keeping her ears perked for a repeat of whatever had caught her attention before. Soon, though, the rushing of another underground stream drowned out any hopes of hearing if anyone—or anything—might be following them.

Raphael suddenly stopped and handed her the lantern. "Put this behind you."

She fumbled with it and did as bid. They were in yet another narrow passageway, and she could barely see around him. "What is it?" she whispered.

He was staring intently ahead of them. "Do you see light?"

Caitlyn set the lantern on the path behind her and cupped her hands around her eyes to cut out any glare. She caught a faint lightening of the darkness from the corner of her eye. It disappeared if she looked straight at it. "Yes!"

She gave him back the lantern, and they hurried forward. Caitlyn sensed a change in the air: it was fresher, hinting more of vegetation now than of stone.

"This doesn't just lead outside, does it?" she asked, suddenly worried that all they'd found was a secret route out of the castle.

He didn't answer. The path led them toward the light and it grew brighter with every step. Just when Caitlyn was about to resign herself to the disappointment of trees and fresh air, they came out of the passage into a room of dimly sparkling crystal frost, illuminated by a pool of aqua-blue water that came in under translucent limestone drapery formations that made up one wall of the room. Sunlight both filtered through the stone curtains and refracted through the water.

"Oh my," Caitlyn whispered.

In the center of the room sat a round, obsidian altar two feet high and wide, capped with gold. Around the altar stood a circle twenty feet across, made up of twelve obsidian obelisks, each one four feet high and a foot in diameter, the tops capped in gold. Each gold cap was studded with a different color of jewels.

"It's Fortuna's wheel," Caitlyn said in stunned comprehension. "The painting I told you about, that hung in the Grand Salon; in it, Fortuna's wheel was black, with gem-studded gold medallions. It was depicting *this*."

"This must have been Eshael's dowry," Raphael said. "They didn't need five carts to carry it home from the Holy Land because it was so rich; they needed five carts because it was *stone!*"

"It must have been part of Eshael's religion. This must be where she worshipped her goddess."

Raphael raised the lantern, the added light refracting off the jewels and the crystal-encrusted walls. "It's no wonder that Simon de Gagéac thought the dowry was cursed and was afraid to spend it. I wouldn't have the nerve to pry the gold off those stones."

Caitlyn shook her head. "Neither would I."

Raphael went to the edge of the pool. "I think it's your *gouffre* on the other side. So we were both right—" He broke off suddenly, his eyes focusing on something behind her. "What are *you* doing here?"

Caitlyn quickly spun around.

Ursino and Giovanni stood at the opening to the passageway, their daggers drawn.

CHAPTER
Twenty-eight

Ursino and Giovanni ignored the question, their attention focused on the circle of stones and gold.

"Holy mother of God," Giovanni said. "It's enough to buy ourselves a kingdom!"

"I told you God would reward us for destroying the heart of the witch," Ursino said.

Raphael slowly drew his own dagger, his eyes wary, his knees bending to prepare him to move quickly in any direction.

Giovanni ran his fingertips over the emeralds on the post nearest him, then pried at one with a fingernail. "I didn't think you meant it so literally."

"So *you* two are the ones who have been trying to steal the heart, and to kill me," Raphael said.

"Without success, alas," Ursino said, coming into the circle of stones. "Every carefully planned accident came to naught. I was beginning to doubt God's favor for our purpose, until I realized how strongly the witch's power still beat in her heart. Obviously, we had to gain control of that, before we could be rid of you."

"You won't find it," Raphael said, keeping distance between himself and Ursino.

"Beneto told us where it was," Giovanni said.

Caitlyn gasped, her eyes going to Raphael.

Raphael was shaking his head. "I don't believe you. Beneto would never betray me."

"The old man did not mean to betray you, and certainly not so quickly," Ursino said. "It's just that I'm very good at delivering pain. Every man will break, if you know how to hurt him."

Raphael's face darkened. "Is he dead?"

Ursino shrugged. "That's in God's hands."

"Just as you are in ours," Giovanni said.

"Who's paying you?" Raphael demanded. "Who wants me dead so badly that they could tempt you to murder?"

Ursino laughed. "Raphael, have you never understood the de' Medicis? No one has to pay us for cleansing the family of a witch like Bianca, and her Satan-spawn daughters! Murderers and tyrants we will tolerate and even flourish through; power-hungry schemers will elevate our status; liars and thieves enrich us; but witches are beyond the pale even for the de' Medici family. A dynasty that has spawned popes will not tolerate a witch and her offspring. When we have destroyed both you and the heart, we will deal with Giulia and Elisabeta."

"Bianca was no witch. Better you go and cleanse the family of Catherine; there's the truest witch the de' Medici's have birthed!"

The men laughed. "Those are lies told by the desperate against a de' Medici they fear," Ursino said, and gave a quick nod to Giovanni.

Giovanni rushed Raphael, Ursino moving in at the same time.

"No!" Caitlyn screamed, and tried to grab Ursino. Her hands were repelled as they had been with Beneto.

Giovanni and Raphael grappled, Giovanni knocking the dagger from Raphael's hand as Ursino grabbed the leather bag and jerked it off of Raphael. Giovanni held Raphael's arms pinned from behind as Ursino opened the bag and took out the crystal chest. He tossed the bag aside and put his hand on the lid.

"You had better beg for God's protection if you think you're going to open that and live," Raphael threatened.

Ursino shot him a look tinged with fear, then crossed himself and said a prayer. He lifted the lid of the reliquary and looked within.

"What does it look like?" Giovanni asked warily, as the seconds ticked by.

Ursino shook his head, then chuckled in relief. "Like a withered piece of bad meat." He laughed aloud and nodded at Raphael. "I want you to watch me destroy it." He grinned, and lifted his dagger over the heart in the chest.

"No!" Caitlyn shouted, and threw herself at him again, reaching for his arm.

"Caitlyn, no!" Raphael cried.

She hit Ursino, for a brief moment feeling that strange repulsion she'd felt before, but then her body went cold and her vision turned gray. A moment later she was on the other side of him, stumbling to a stop. She'd gone through him.

Ursino was looking around wildly, arm still poised above the chest. "What was that?" he cried. "A cold wind, moving through me!"

"Spirits!" Giovanni shouted. "Destroy the heart, Ursino, quickly!"

Caitlyn lunged again for Ursino, and as she did Raphael spun in Giovanni's grip and grabbed his wrist, jerking it hard. Giovanni cried out, his dagger dropping to the ground with a clatter.

Caitlyn flung herself again against Ursino and the chest. *Bianca, help me!* she silently begged, as Ursino swayed under her assault, the

270

lid of the reliquary falling closed as he stumbled. Caitlyn once again passed through him.

Giovanni and Raphael were fighting hand to hand, their fists making thick sounds on flesh, their bodies grunting with pain and effort. Blood smeared both their faces, and they fell to the ground tangled together. They rolled together toward Ursino, and he stepped out of their way, toward the altar.

Caitlyn saw their only hope. She threw herself again and again through Ursino, keeping him off balance as he struggled to open the crystal chest. With each stumble he came closer to the altar, until he was right up against it. In desperation he thunked the chest down atop the altar for stability and opened its lid.

Caitlyn, struck with a sudden knowing, threw her body over the chest on the altar. The crystal reliquary sank into her rib cage, lodging where her own heart was beating. Caitlyn heard the sound of it, suddenly amplified, ring throughout the stone chamber: *thu-THUMP, thu-THUMP!*

She slowly looked up at Ursino, expecting to see the dagger coming down on the heart.

Instead, terror filled Ursino's face, and his eyes met her own. Caitlyn realized he could suddenly see her.

She pushed off the altar and slowly stood, and as she did so she saw that she was clothed in cherry-rose satin. Her hands were long-fingered and white; they were Bianca's hands. Of their own volition they lifted and grasped Ursino on either side of his face.

"You dare to touch my heart?" a voice not Caitlyn's own said from her throat.

Ursino screamed.

Bianca's hands pressed inward on Ursino's head, and after a moment of that magnetic-opposite resistance Caitlyn felt them break through, vanishing into Ursino's skull. His scream of terror turned to one of agony as blood began to well from his eyes.

A cry of pain from behind her made Caitlyn spin around, her hands tearing out of Ursino's head, leaving him to collapse on the ground.

Raphael and Giovanni were on their knees, Raphael with an arm around Giovanni as if holding him in an embrace, but his other hand pressed against the base of Giovanni's jaw, turned now unnaturally far to the left. As Caitlyn watched, Giovanni crumpled to the ground, his head flopping on a broken neck. Horror mixed with a primal joy: Raphael had won.

Raphael turned toward her on his knees, but the effort was too much and he braced himself on the ground with an outstretched arm. It was then that Caitlyn saw the dagger embedded in his chest and the blood saturating his doublet. Her breath froze in her chest.

Raphael looked up at her, his face ashen and bewildered. "Mother?"

Caitlyn stepped away from the heart on the altar, and the rose satin gown vanished, leaving her in her dirty nightgown. She dropped down beside Raphael, her whole body shaking with the sudden terror of losing him. "It's me, Caitlyn. Don't try to move."

He dropped onto his hip. Around the dagger, blood bubbled with escaping air. Raphael coughed, and a trickle of red spilled out the side of his mouth. He raised one hand to the dagger, trying to grab the handle.

"No!" Caitlyn cried, even though she knew it was too late for either of them to do anything to change what was happening. She knew his lung was collapsing. "I'll go get help."

His eyes met hers, and in them she read his knowledge of his fate. He started to collapse backward. She caught his shoulders and eased him to the ground, and then brushed the blood from his lips with her fingertips. "Don't go, please," she whispered, begging. Tears roughened her voice. She felt her heart breaking into a thousand pieces. "You can't go. Please don't go."

"I come," he said hoarsely, the sound barely audible on his weak breath, "to you."

She took his hand in hers and felt it already turning cold. "Even death will not keep us apart," she said through her tears, and prayed that she spoke the truth.

A whisper of a smile touched his lips, and then the last of the tension left his body. Caitlyn's breath caught on a sob.

He was dead.

CHAPTER
Twenty-nine

Before the first tear could spill down Caitlyn's cheek, a faint, glowing form began to rise out of Raphael's entire body, and with it rose Caitlyn's heart. He was coming to her!

A long-fingered white hand suddenly pressed over Raphael's chest, pinning the rising glow atop the body. Caitlyn cried out, then looked up into Bianca's pale face, her coronet of red-blond hair in perfect order, her carved features betraying no hint of grief or sympathy. "What are you doing?" Caitlyn cried.

The glow began to thrash under Bianca's hold, struggling to come free.

"Let him go!" Caitlyn screamed, and grabbed for Bianca's arm.

A thunderclap of sound went through Caitlyn, and the world went black.

Caitlyn fell through darkness, her soul sinking powerless into a vast abyss. There was no sound, no sight, nothing but the endless sinking and her silent screams as the pain of loss ripped through her. She felt the essence of her being disintegrate; without Raphael, she was nothing. She had no anchor, no being.

"Raphael!" she cried, and tried to picture his face. It would draw her to him; it would help her find him. "Raphael!"

Points of light began to flash all around her, like distant stars. She focused on the nearest one and flew toward it, the point of light expanding as she approached, growing wider. It went from a few inches to a foot, to a yard, then all at once it stretched beyond the edges of her vision and she was standing in the grass of the prehistoric Périgord Noir, watching a herd of aurochs amble by with their enormous horns shaped like lyres.

"No!" Caitlyn protested aloud, her voice small in the quiet landscape. This was not where she wanted to be! She shut her eyes tight and pictured Raphael's face. "Raphael! Find Raphael!"

She felt herself falling, and when she opened her eyes she was once again in the void, the darkness around her pricked with light. She recognized the abyss now: it was the space between her waking and her dreams. It was a nonplace, between one existence and another. She had been here just after taking the Ambien.

In one of the lights she would find Raphael. A flicker of hope gave her energy, and she dove at a light.

A bloody sword sliced through the space where she stood. It was twilight, and she stood in the midst of a battle being fought by armored men. The stench of blood, guts, and feces filled her head. She locked eyes with a warrior, and his eyes widened as he seemed to perceive her, but then the tip of a pike burst through his chest. Caitlyn screamed and covered her face.

"Raphael!" she cried, and this time pictured Château de la Fortune as she fell through the abyss and toward another light.

She felt solid ground beneath her feet and opened her eyes. She was in a dark corridor. "Raphael?" she called softly, and started down the hallway. Silk skirts swished around her legs, and when she looked down she saw that the skirts were the black of mourning, their color a mirror of the ache in her soul. "Raphael? Where are you?" she called.

Shh, shh, shh . . . her skirts went.

She descended stairs and started down another corridor. A figure stood halfway down it. "Raphael?" she called, hurrying her steps.

Shh, shh, shh . . .

She came close to the figure, but realized a black veil of mourning covered her head, blurring her vision. She grasped the veil's hem and started to lift it.

The figure before her turned into a smear of gray, a shrieking Screecher with dark pits for eyes and mouth. The sound pierced Caitlyn's skull and she fell back in terror, once more into the abyss.

"Raphael, where are you?" she cried into the darkness, loss and frustration consuming her. "You are dead; I am dead! We were supposed to be together forever! Raphael! Raphael!"

The next light she dove into dropped her into the art studio, where the last hints of sunlight filtered through the skylights. Antoine Fournier slouched on a stool, staring at a blank canvas in the dimness.

"*You!*" Caitlyn cried, and pointed at him.

Fournier looked up at her voice, and then fell off his stool, his eyes wide.

Caitlyn looked at his blank canvas and laughed hysterically. "*I* know what you have to paint! You'll paint Fortuna and her wheel, and hang it at the end of the Grand Salon. You'll paint that, or nothing, Antoine Fournier!"

She threw herself back into the abyss and tried again to find Raphael, calling his name as she dived into each light and found herself over and over in the corridors and rooms of Château de la Fortune. Each figure she approached, thinking it was Raphael, turned instead into a Screecher, screaming and clawing and running mad.

Panic began to consume her. She could not find him. She had lost him; Bianca had stolen him from her, forever.

Her spirit began to weaken, a growing grief killing her hope. She made one last attempt to find Raphael, diving with the last of her will toward a light. She opened her eyes and found herself standing in a vast space, black except for a wide rectangle of light ahead of her. "Raphael? Raphael?" she called weakly. She walked toward the light, the susurrus of her skirts her only answer.

Shh, shh, shh.

The rectangle turned into a window of sorts, and someone with dark hair and pale skin was standing on the other side, staring in at her. Caitlyn approached cautiously, the face of the person coming clearer with every step.

She knew that face. Even through the black veil that blurred her vision, she knew. She had seen it every day of her life.

Caitlyn stopped a foot from the window and stared into her own pale face, staring back at her with a look of horror, her sea-green eyes wide with shock.

Of course, I'm frightening myself with this dark veil, Caitlyn thought. She grasped its hem and started to raise it.

On the other side of the window, she saw her other self's eyes roll up into her head, and then the other self collapsed. Caitlyn rushed to the edge of the window, reaching through in a too-late attempt to catch her. There was a sick *thunk* of skull against a hard object, and then the *whump* of a body hitting the floor. Caitlyn leaned through the window and looked down at a row of sinks, and at her other self in her nightgown, blood pooling around her on the bathroom floor.

It took a moment for what it meant to sink in, and then she shook her head violently in denial. "No! *No, no, no!*" she cried.

She remembered the Screechers she'd encountered in the corridors: Screechers who, in the split second before they'd turned to gray smears of shrieking terror, had looked human.

One had been Mathilde.

"No! It can't be!" She screamed, "Raphael! I need you! Raphael . . . !"

But there was no one to answer, and there never would be. She would haunt these halls forever, seeking him.

For *she* was the Woman in Black.

CHAPTER
Thirty

Caitlyn woke to the gray light of dawn coming in the windows of her dorm room. For a moment she hung in a space between sleep and waking, not knowing who or what she was. A deep part of her clung to the moment of confusion and warned her that she did not want to remember the answers to those questions.

She heard the soft sound of a turning page, and turned her head. Amalia dozed in her bed, while Naomi sat at the foot, her back against the paneled wall, reading a book.

I'm back, Caitlyn thought.

But where is "back"?

She stared at Naomi, and tried to decide: Was this nothing but the dream of a wandering spirit with nowhere else to go?

As if she felt her gaze, Naomi looked up from her book. Her face brightened. "You're awake!" She shook Amalia's foot.

Amalia jerked awake and popped up onto her elbows, her face still bleared with sleep. "I'm awake, I'm awake! What happened?"

"Did you find Raphael?" Naomi asked. "Did you warn him?"

The images of the fight in the cavern flooded in upon Caitlyn. She saw the knife in Raphael's chest, the blood upon his lips. "It wasn't Beneto," she said, her voice cracking. "It was Ursino and Giovanni. They . . . they . . ." She tried to say it, but the words wouldn't come.

The pain that been held at bay for a few sweet moments came rushing back and pressed upon her chest like a thousand pounds, crushing her. Her face twisted with grief, and a sob tore from deep in her gut.

She rolled away from her friends to face the wall, curled into a ball, and wept.

She sleepwalked through her English class and French conversation lab, barely aware of the people around her. Grief consumed all lesser emotions, and wrung from her all ability to think or care about anything else. She sat stunned and silent through her classes.

It was only when she got to her art class that something stirred to life within her.

"Self-portraits today!" Monsieur Girard declared, handing out mirrors. "Every great artist has used him- or herself as a model."

Caitlyn set up her easel and mirror next to Naomi. "You okay?" Naomi asked, looking worried.

Caitlyn shrugged one shoulder, the corners of her mouth turning down. Words were beyond her.

Caitlyn picked up her charcoal and looked in the mirror. She saw a pale, haunted face with shadows beneath reddened eyes, and black hair that hung lank against her cheeks. She turned to her paper and began to cover its surface in black charcoal. Her arm moved with steady deliberation, and slowly turned the pristine white to a void of darkness. When her charcoal was down to a stub she set it aside and picked up her kneaded eraser. Bit by bit she lifted out pinpricks of light in the darkness, and then in the center of it all she created a pale face behind a veil, the eyes empty hollows, the mouth a slash of grief. She worked without care for accuracy or her own physical likeness. She cared only for the reflection of her soul, not her face.

She felt someone standing behind her, and turned.

Monsieur Girard stood considering her picture. He had one arm crossed over his chest, that hand grasping his other elbow, and his index finger tapped his bottom lip. His eyes were narrowed, his head tilted.

"An interesting departure from your usual style," he said at last. "The proportion of nose to chin is not quite right, but the image holds emotional power. Good work."

Caitlyn stared at him in astonishment.

He ignored her surprise and moved on.

Caitlyn met Naomi's eyes, needing confirmation that she'd just been complimented for her black smear of a picture.

Naomi's lips quirked. "Teacher's pet," she teased.

Caitlyn felt a dart of amusement and surprised herself with a chuckle, and for the first time since she'd woken that morning felt a connection to the world.

She looked around her as if waking from a dream.

This was the world she returned to every morning, with the regularity of clockwork. There had been no skipped days, no missing time, no gaps in the story of her life here. She did not vanish from rooms, as she did in Raphael's world. She did not step in and out of time. She wore no unexpected cherry-rose satin dresses. She lived here. She was *real* here.

She was alive, not a ghost. She was not dead in any physical sense.

She looked back at her drawing and recognized herself. She *was* the Woman in Black, but she was also Caitlyn Monahan.

It took her several more days to figure it out. When she did, she didn't know whether to laugh or to cry. When she explained it to Naomi and Amalia, they were as dazed as her. There was no arguing with the logic, though.

Caitlyn was not, as Raphael had concluded, dead. The Fortune School was not a dream of a lost spirit. She had not perished in a car crash on the way here from the Bordeaux airport. Her soul might have withered and died when Raphael breathed his last, but she could not mistake her present reality for a dream or an afterworld.

She was a ghost, but not dead. It was an idea that made no sense until she remembered what Amalia had said: no one knew what ghosts were truly like. Who was to say that a ghost could not be of a living person?

When she was asleep there were no Screechers visiting her, no evil spirits coming to torture her. Rather, she was the one suddenly appearing in the darkness and terrifying people who lived in the past. Her so-called Screechers were the people who caught a glimpse of a dark shape in the night, a shadow moving where all should be still.

Her spirit walked through time while she slept. She saw it now: every dream she'd ever had had taken place in the past of the locality where she lived. In Oregon she had dreamed of the pioneer girl Emily, and as a ghost she had ridden behind Emily on her horse; *she* had been the Umpqua Maiden, spoken of in legends that went back centuries.

Her mother had not come to visit her on the night before she left Oregon for France. *She* had been the one to travel back in time to visit her mother. *She* had been the one who told her own mother that she would die when Caitlyn was four. Her mother had said she was no good at predicting her own future.

She hadn't had to be. Caitlyn had done it for her.

Caitlyn hadn't just dreamed the past. She'd visited it. And as the Woman in Black, she'd haunted it.

A spiritual fly on the wall, she'd been invisible to most of the people she'd encountered. Most who had seen her or sensed her had turned into Screechers, their frightened screams sending her tumbling back through time to her own bed, where she woke drenched in sweat, her own screams of terror ripping at her throat. They'd scared each other half to death.

A few had been different. Emily, the horse-riding pioneer girl, had known that Caitlyn rode with her and enjoyed the secret.

Raphael had been real. Her dreaming soul had traveled through time and found him, when he had lived at Château de la Fortune over four centuries earlier.

She didn't know what purpose might have been served by their meeting. If Bianca had brought her to Raphael, it must have been so that she could help him find the treasure and preserve Bianca's heart. But maybe Caitlyn had been meant to save Raphael's life, as well.

She'd failed Bianca there, though.

Caitlyn understood, now. Bianca had not wanted Raphael's spirit to be with Caitlyn for one simple reason: she didn't deserve him. Bianca had chosen the cruelest punishment of all.

Caitlyn would live out her life without ever seeing Raphael again.

CHAPTER
Thirty-one

"Geology, incomplete. Western civilization, fail," Madame Snowe read in disgust, walking back and forth beside Caitlyn like an angry policeman. "Algebra, fail. French, fail. Madame Tatou says you cannot even say 'My name is Caitlyn' in French. The only class in which you have done well is art. But then, Monsieur Girard has always been impressed by black moods. He mistakes them for signs of an artistic soul."

Caitlyn stared at her hands in her lap, barely hearing Madame Snowe through the empty darkness of her grief. She didn't care that she was yet again in the headmistress's office, and yet again in trouble.

Madame Snowe slapped the report onto her desk and crossed her arms, staring hard at Caitlyn. "You have lost weight. Your friends say you barely talk. Your teachers say that you go through the motions of being a student, but that there is no one home inside your head. And you send me a dream journal that says only, 'I am dead,' with no

284

explanation." Madame Snowe grasped Caitlyn by the chin, forcing her face up. "Tell me a brilliant story to explain why you have failed me, Caitlyn, or pack your bags. I will put you on the first flight back to Oregon."

Caitlyn had been expecting this moment from the time she woke up from her final dream of Raphael, six weeks ago. Madame Snowe's threat held no sting, however. Everything she'd thought she'd wanted had changed when she'd fallen in love with Raphael; everything that mattered to her had gone when he died. France held nothing for her, now that he was gone.

Caitlyn met Madame Snowe's eyes. "I am a ghost."

Madame Snowe released her chin and sat on the edge of her desk. She crossed her arms. "What does that mean?"

Caitlyn stared into Madame Snowe's eyes, no longer frightened of the headmistress. What was she compared to Bianca de' Medici? "'I am a ghost' means that I am nothing. I am empty. My soul has died."

"I see."

"Do you?"

"You are suffering from depression. You will need to go on antidepressants."

Caitlyn laughed. "No pill will fix this."

"You will take them, or you will go home."

"Send me home. There's nothing here I want."

"That's the depression talking."

Caitlyn narrowed her eyes at Madame Snowe. "I won't take pills."

Madame Snowe's jaw tightened. "Then you've decided, haven't you? You're going to throw away an education you could only dream of back in your provincial home. There are no second chances with me, Caitlyn. This is it."

"Good."

Madame Snowe's cheeks brightened with anger. "You are expelled! Pack your bags. You will leave tomorrow morning."

Caitlyn stood and turned, walking toward the door feeling strangely light, as if only loosely connected to her body. For a moment her eyes met those of the portrait of Bianca. *I'm sorry*, Caitlyn said silently. *I would have saved him if I could.*

The halls of the dormitory wing were filled with flitting girls, everyone relieved that final exams were finished and break was about to begin. When she got back to her room, she found Brigitte chattering excitedly to Amalia.

"He'll be here any minute! I didn't even know he could drive again! But Mama says he has been working through his rehabilitation with astonishing speed, and he wanted to surprise me by driving down alone," Brigitte said in French, and then seeing Caitlyn switched to English. "My brother Thierry is coming to visit!"

"Great." Something more seemed in order, so she added, "Your parents were okay with letting him drive alone?"

Amalia looked at her in surprise. "How did you know he was driving alone?"

Caitlyn gave her a look. "Brigitte just said."

"But your French—"

"He says he wants to see all my friends, too," Brigitte interrupted. "He wants to see if he will remember anyone. But *I* think he wants to see *you*, Amalia." Brigitte giggled. "I think his heart still remembers you even when his mind has forgotten the past, yes?"

Amalia's brows went up. "I'm sure he doesn't remember me."

"Then you can enchant him all over again," Brigitte said. "It would not be so bad if we were sisters some day, would it?"

Amalia smiled, but Caitlyn saw the strain of it.

"What time is it?" Caitlyn asked Brigitte. "You'd better go down and watch for him."

Brigitte checked the time on her phone. "You're right! But I'll call you when he arrives." She made kissing sounds to them both and scampered off.

"What did Madame Snowe say?" Amalia asked, when she had gone.

Caitlyn shrugged, affecting nonchalance, but she suddenly realized that her expulsion meant she would be leaving her new friends. Her throat tightened. "She said what I expected. I've been expelled."

"No!"

"I go home tomorrow."

"Caitlyn!" Amalia gripped her shoulders. "Caitlyn, did you tell her what happened?"

She shook her head.

"You have to! Or blame it all on the Ambien, and me: it was my fault you took it. It did something to the chemicals in your brain. You haven't been the same since."

"She wants me to take antidepressants."

Amalia hesitated, then dropped her hands from Caitlyn's shoulders. "Maybe you should."

"I'm not going to take pills. Besides, I failed all my classes."

"But—" Amalia started, and was interrupted by the ringing of her cell phone. She checked the display. "It's Brigitte. You and I will talk about this tonight, Caitlyn. There's no reason for you to go home." The phone kept ringing. Amalia swore in German and answered it.

"Thierry is here," she said, hanging up. "She wants us to come down and see him. I don't think it's because she thinks his amnesia will suddenly disappear and he'll remember any of us. I think she's nervous about being alone with him. Brigitte doesn't do well with awkward social situations. She wants her friends around her for protection."

"A buffer," Caitlyn said.

"Come with me. You don't have to meet him. You can just hang around in the background."

Caitlyn nodded. "Okay."

On the way down to the courtyard they stopped by Naomi's room and dragged her along. "I need someone to loiter with," Caitlyn told her.

The gentle warmth of May greeted them as they stepped out into the sunlight. Amalia went alone toward Brigitte and Daniela, the two of them standing by a silver sports car and a tall, blond young man. Caitlyn wandered over to the well, Naomi following.

"I still think we should get a blowtorch and cut loose the grate," Naomi said, as they leaned their forearms on the edge and peered into the shaft.

Caitlyn wrapped her fingers in the heavy, rusted screen welded over the top of the well. "Even if the ring of stones and the heart are still there, I don't want to see them. I don't want to see Raphael's bones." She shrugged. "It's too late to look now, anyway." She told Naomi about her expulsion.

Unlike Amalia, Naomi didn't try to change her mind. "You've given up, haven't you? You don't want to be here anymore."

"Maybe it's better that I live someplace like Oregon, where there is not so much history. I'll stand a better chance of controlling my dreams."

Naomi nodded, but her eyes were sad. "I'll miss you."

Caitlyn nodded, feeling tears sting her own eyes as well. Across the courtyard, the girls and Thierry started to move toward the entrance to the castle. Amalia gave them a nod.

Thierry looked over at them, then turned to Brigitte and asked her a question. Brigitte looked over at Caitlyn and Naomi and shook her head, then tugged him with her into the château.

"He must have asked if he knew us," Naomi said. "How strange that must be, not to remember your own life."

Caitlyn looked up at the blue sky, dotted with clouds. Over a wall of the castle she could see green treetops swaying in a breeze. "I'm going to walk down to the *gouffre* and say good-bye to Raphael. I won't have another chance."

"Would you like company?"

Caitlyn smiled and shook her head. She, Naomi, and Amalia had walked down to it the weekend after her final dream, but there had been no sound of a beating heart, no strange bursts of wind, and, worst of all, not even the faintest sense of Raphael's presence. Whatever had been haunting the *gouffre* seemed to be gone, and with it any danger to Caitlyn, if danger there had ever been. For all she knew it *had* been a microburst of air that threw her, like Madame Brouwer suggested. Or if it had been Bianca, her purpose might as easily have been to preserve Caitlyn from harm as to cause it. Without that blast of air, Caitlyn would surely have fallen.

They parted, and Caitlyn headed off for the *gouffre*. The woods were alive with the quiet sounds of spring: squirrels scrambling on tree bark, birds chirping and leaping from branch to branch, flies and mosquitoes buzzing, leaves rustling in the breeze on the limbs overhead. Her shoes crunched on the gravel and dirt path, the loudest sound of all. The tension she didn't know she'd been holding started to release. She felt as if the forest was a shelter from the world.

A smile pulled at the corner of her mouth. She'd had to come five thousand miles, leaving behind a home state renowned for its natural beauty, to realize she felt most at peace in nature.

Her smile faded as she came out of the woods into the clearing that held the *gouffre*. She cautiously approached the viewpoint on the edge, inching forward until she could see into the depths. A pair of swifts chased each other inside the shaft, their shrieklike calls echoing off the stone walls. The sun, almost directly overhead, illuminated a wide swath of clear blue-green water at the bottom, its surface unruffled by wind. Caitlyn could see stones and fallen tree branches beneath the surface, and dark shadows that likely led to underwater caves.

The last time she was here she'd fought her way through the underbrush to the other side of the *gouffre*, to where she could see the wall of the shaft beneath where she stood now. Down near the water's edge, sheltered by an overhang, she'd seen a glimpse of limestone drapery formations reaching down into the water. They must have formed long before the *gouffre* filled with water.

Caitlyn stretched out her arms to either side like a bird, closed her eyes, and tilted back her face to feel the warmth of the sun. *"Je suis au bord du gouffre,"* she said softly to the air, hoping for she knew not what. A heartbeat. A whisper from Raphael. A sense that she was not alone.

The shrieking swifts were her only answer.

Caitlyn dropped her arms and opened her eyes. Some small part of her had clung to a sliver of hope that Raphael was still here, waiting for her, that death had not indeed been able to part them.

"*À Dieu, mon cher*," she said, the French coming easily to her lips in a way it never did in class. "*Jamais je ne t'oublierai*." Good-bye, my dear one. I will never forget you.

She turned away from the abyss.

A tall young man stood blocking the path to the castle. Caitlyn took a startled step back.

"*Non!*" the blond man shouted, holding out his hands palms forward, as if to hold her motionless.

"You're Brigitte's brother, aren't you?" Caitlyn asked anxiously in English, recognizing him. Knowing who he was—a brain-damaged man who'd once been a suicidal drug addict—didn't calm her.

He was staring at her, hard. "*Je ne parle pas Anglais*."

"That's okay. We don't really have anything to say." All she wanted was to get out of there. She smiled and gestured with her hand, asking him to move aside from the path. "Go on, let me by."

He moved slightly to the side, still staring at her. She was going to have to pass within inches of him.

Dammit, why hadn't she taken Naomi up on her offer of company?

"You've come to see where you had your accident, haven't you? It's all yours." Caitlyn vacated the viewpoint and held her hand toward it in invitation, hoping he'd switch places with her. She'd at least get a head start running back to the château.

His gaze flicked to the *gouffre*, and he started toward the viewpoint. Caitlyn tried to give him a wide berth, alarmingly aware of his size. He was about six feet three inches, and fit. She avoided looking at his face, afraid that eye contact might somehow set him off. She watched his feet instead, coming closer, closer; a moment more, and he would be past . . .

He stopped right in front of her.

She gasped and looked up into pale blue eyes that held a look not entirely sane. She turned to run.

His hand shot out and grabbed her arm, stopping her. She screamed.

"Caitlyn!" he shouted, and gave her a shake.

The sound of her name shocked her into a moment's silence. She gaped at him, her heart pounding.

"Caitlyn," he said again, plaintively this time.

"What do you want?" she pleaded, tugging at her arm.

He sank to his knees in front of her and pressed her captured hand against his chest. "Raphael," he said.

Shocked, and then immediately angered, Caitlyn tried to jerk away. "Who told you about him?"

"Caitlyn," he said again, and then a torrent of Italian spilled from his lips.

The words flowed around her, incomprehensible for several long moments, but then her mind began to catch them, their meaning sinking into her as easily as if she had been born to the tongue.

"I have waited so long to find you," he said. "For four hundred years my soul was kept tied to this earth by my mother's promise that I would be with you again."

Caitlyn stopped her struggles, her blood feeling as if it were draining from her body. She looked down into his imploring face, each feature of it unknown to her, but the look in his eyes said that he knew her. "It can't be you," she said in Italian, confused, not able to believe it. "How can you be Brigitte's brother?"

"Thierry died in the water below, a suicide. After he abandoned his body, I took it."

Disbelief mixed with insane hope bubbled in Caitlyn's chest. "That's impossible."

"But when I came back into the world I was in the hospital, and nothing was as I knew it. I did not know this body in which I live, or the people supposed to be my family. But I knew I must come here, to find you. When I saw you headed this way, I escaped from Brigitte and her friends and followed." He grinned. "I learned to drive a car so I could come. It's much better than a horse."

Caitlyn's heart thundered in her chest, hurting her with the hope that flamed to life. She gently tugged her hand free of his grip and put her palms to either side of his face, the feel of his cheeks and jaw not what she remembered from Raphael. "Can it really be you?"

"My beloved, even death could not keep us apart."

A sob of joy tore from Caitlyn's throat. Raphael wrapped his arms around her hips and pulled her against him, burying his face against her belly. Caitlyn sank down inside his embrace, her arms around his neck, and then he was kissing her with the pain of four centuries of solitude. He lowered her to her back on the rough ground and covered her with kisses.

"Get off of her!" a girl shouted, and a leafy branch came beating down on Raphael's head. He braced himself to protect Caitlyn from the branch, and then female hands pulled him away from Caitlyn, the branch still beating at him. "Why did you follow her? Leave her alone!"

"Amalia, Naomi, no!" Caitlyn cried, and threw herself between branch and man. Her friends were panting, their hair wild, their stance that of warriors. "It's not Thierry! It's Raphael!"

Amalia and Naomi pulled in their chins. "What?"

"*Buon giorno*," he said over Caitlyn's shoulder.

"Raphael took Thierry's body after he died in the *gouffre*. Sort of, you know, recycling." Caitlyn started to laugh, feeling herself on the edge of joyful hysteria. Behind her, Raphael wrapped his arm around her waist, pulling her against him, his own body shaking with laughter, although she knew he hadn't understood her words. "It's Raphael," Caitlyn repeated, tears streaming down her cheeks. "It's Raphael."

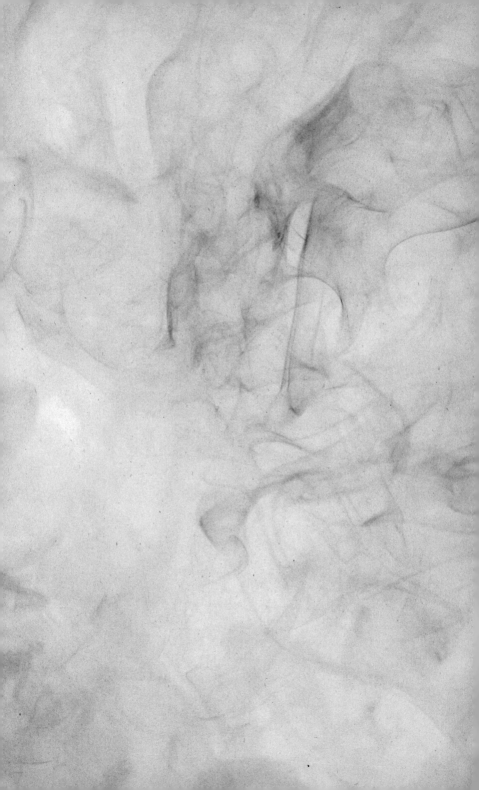

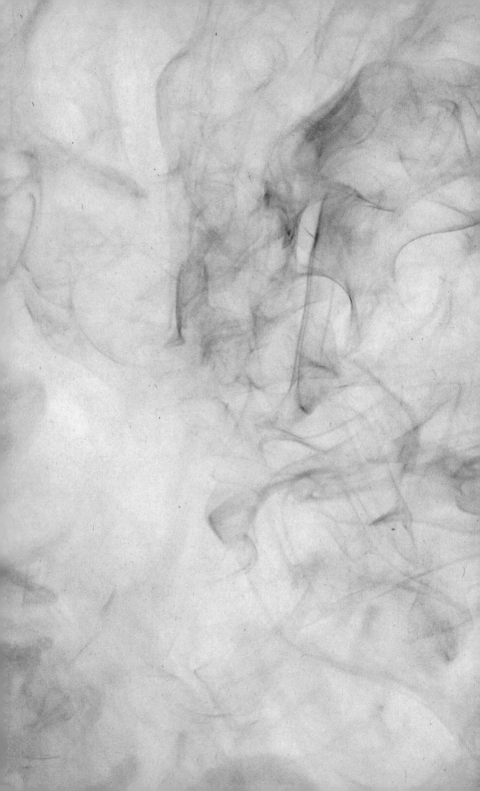

Epilogue

The water felt like ice against Caitlyn's skin, despite the short wet suit. Her fear did her no favors, either, chilling what blood in her body remained warm. Through her mask she watched the ends of Raphael's flippers disappear under the curtain of limestone at the bottom of the *gouffre* pool. She groaned. It was her turn. She took one last, ragged breath through her snorkel and dove to follow.

Caitlyn went down until her ears ached with the cold and then slid through the opening under the drapery formation, certain that at any moment she would find herself trapped against the stone. A moment later, however, she was swimming upward toward a luminous ball, like a fish drawn to the moon. She emerged gasping from the water, her pulse pounding.

Raphael reached down and pulled her out of the water so that she was sitting on the edge of the pool with him. Madame Snowe and the geology teacher, Madame Brouwer, were already there, taking off their flippers and snorkels. A waterproof diving light sat on the stone beside Madame Brouwer.

"You're okay?" Raphael asked in Italian, having adopted the Americanism "okay" with the same enthusiasm he'd brought to cars, ice cream, MP3s of classical music, and the Internet.

"Yeah. The anticipation was worse than the reality."

Madame Snowe chuckled as she got to her feet, dripping water from her lithe frame. "I am still surprised and delighted with your language skills, Caitlyn," she said in French.

Caitlyn grinned. Telling Madame Snowe the whole story had been a decision that she, Raphael, Amalia, and Naomi had come to together. It had been a gamble, but it was Caitlyn's only hope of staying in France and completing her schooling after Madame Snowe had made it so clear that there were to be no second chances.

The four of them had gone together to Madame Snowe's office, which had not amused the headmistress, suspecting as she had that they were going to plead for clemency. Madame Snowe's first surprise had been the reverence with which Brigitte's brother had stood in front of the portrait of Bianca de' Medici, tears filling his eyes. Her second surprise came when Caitlyn introduced him as Raphael, Bianca's adoptive son.

After that, she'd been quiet and listened.

Caitlyn was still astonished that they'd been believed, her inexplicable foreign language skills notwithstanding. Her expulsion had been repealed on the sole condition that she and Raphael lead Madame Snowe to the chamber where Raphael had died. Other than that, the headmistress had said very little about their tale.

Brigitte and Daniela had been surprised that "Thierry" had fallen in love at first sight with Caitlyn, but Caitlyn seemed to have gained Daniela's respect as a result. It made Caitlyn think even less of the Spanish girl, to judge Caitlyn better just because a guy liked her. Caitlyn followed Madame Snowe's advice, however, not to say a word to Brigitte or Daniela about Thierry not really being Thierry. Even if Brigitte believed such a tale, it could give her only pain.

The fissure in the well, they soon discovered, had been bricked shut. Rather than go to the work of breaking through it, they'd decided to try to approach the chamber from the *gouffre*. Now here they were, a week later, after some intensive lessons on rappelling and ropes.

Caitlyn and Raphael got to their feet, and Madame Brouwer raised her diving light and shone it about the room.

The walls sparkled with the crystal formations Caitlyn so clearly remembered, and within their shelter stood the circle of obsidian and gold stones, with the altar at the center. They seemed unaltered by time, the gold undimmed. The light passed over the walls and then to the dark maw of the passage, where Ursino and Giovanni had appeared with their daggers drawn. There was no sign they had ever been there: no bag of rotting bones and cloth on the ground, no ancient stain of blood on the stone. The only thing in the room was a dark mass on the altar in the center of the circle.

They all approached slowly. Caitlyn shivered, the cave's air cold on her wet body. Raphael reached it first and drew off the rotted cloth, the fabric falling apart under his touch. Madame Brouwer aimed her light at the object.

A thousand refractions of light gleamed within the quartz cabochon atop the reliquary holding Bianca's heart.

Raphael drew in a surprised breath, then carefully opened the lid. "It's still here," he said in awe.

"The heart in darkness," Caitlyn said, suddenly understanding the words her mother had written on the tarot card. *This* was the heart, lost in darkness for four centuries until Caitlyn came to Château de la Fortune. Caitlyn was struck by a sudden realization. "The heart *is* the ruby at the hub of Fortuna's wheel, in Fournier's painting," she said.

"Of course . . . ," Madame Snowe murmured.

Raphael seemed not to have heard; he was still gazing upon the heart for which he had lost his life, four centuries earlier. He looked up at Caitlyn, his eyes wide. "I remember now. Philippe came and took away the bodies, but he left this here, untouched. Beneto must have survived the attack by Ursino and Giovanni, and told him to follow us down here."

"And then Beneto was blamed for your murder," Caitlyn said. "Philippe must have framed him."

"No," Madame Snowe said.

They both turned to look at her.

Madame Snowe knelt beside Raphael and gazed upon the heart, her expression rapt. She looked like she'd found the Holy Grail. "Philippe, le Comte d'Ormond, accompanied Beneto when Beneto went to Catherine de' Medici and asked to become the guardian of Giulia and Elisabeta. Catherine was angry that he didn't have either the heart or the treasure with him, and she thought he was trying to grab the power of the sisters for himself. She accused Beneto of killing Raphael and had him executed.

"Philippe's true loyalties lay with Henry of Navarre, however. In a move meant to hurt Catherine and wreak revenge for what she'd done to innocent Beneto, he stole the girls from under Catherine's nose and took them to Navarre."

"Giulia and Elisabeta survived?" Raphael asked.

"Of course," Madame Snowe said. "They both married. They had children. They lived to be old women."

"How do you know this?" he asked.

Madame Snowe smiled. "Raphael, do you not recognize Bianca's kin?"

He shook his head, as puzzled as Caitlyn.

"I am a descendant of Elisabeta."

Caitlyn's jaw dropped. "No way!"

Madame Snowe got to her feet and came over to Caitlyn. She touched the underside of Caitlyn's chin with her fingertips, tilting up her face as if to see it better. "And Caitlyn, have you not recognized your kin in me, either?"

"Wh-what do you mean?"

"Your great-great-grandmother, many times removed, was Giulia. You and I, Madame Brouwer and Greta, Madame Pelletier and all the rest of the Sisterhood of Fortuna, are the lost daughters of Bianca de' Medici. It is why you were chosen by the Sisterhood to come to the Fortune School. Two more lost daughters will join us next term."

"B-but why?" Caitlyn stuttered.

"Isn't it obvious?"

Caitlyn shook her head.

"Caitlyn, you have inherited Bianca's psychic gifts. We all have, in one form or another. In you, though, we hoped that they might take a special form. We hoped that you might be the Dark One."

Caitlyn's eyes widened, and she exchanged a meaningful look with Raphael.

"What is it?" Madame Snowe said, catching their silent communication.

"Bianca called my future love my 'Dark One,'" Raphael answered.

Madame Snowe's lips parted in surprise, and she looked at Caitlyn with a renewed wonder. She smiled as if in disbelief and shook her head.

"But what did *you* mean by it?" Caitlyn asked her.

"My great-grandmother had visions, and often made predictions; unfortunately, they usually came in obscure rhyming form. She made one about the Dark One." Madame recited in English, and then translated for Raphael:

> *"From the New World's western shore*
> *Comes a Dark One, young and poor,*
> *Black of hair and pale of face,*
> *Without bidding she will chase*
> *The source of Sisters' power real*
> *In the heart of Fortune's wheel.*
> *Only when this Dark One's found*
> *Can our powers be unbound."*

They all turned to look again at the heart in its reliquary, at the center of the black and gold wheel of stones. "You expected me to find this, all along," Caitlyn said, feeling strangely betrayed. "Why didn't you tell me?"

"Because we weren't sure you were the Dark One. When you first came to us, you seemed to show nascent signs of a gift trying to emerge through your dreams, but then they never seemed to amount to anything. Then you hit your head, and the dreams stopped altogether. For obvious reasons, the Sisterhood cannot have rumors spread about that we are a group of psychically gifted women. If you were not one of us in talent as well as bloodline, you could not be told our secrets."

"So if I hadn't found the wheel, and Bianca's heart . . ."

"You already know the answer," Madame Snowe said. "You would have been sent home. The Sisterhood is not a charity, Caitlyn, and you had failed all your classes. What more could you expect?"

Caitlyn shook her head, chilled by Snowe's harsh practicality. As her mother had warned her, the Queen of Swords could help her with one hand, and as easily cut her down with the other. Expedience ruled. "The cheek swab you made me do for the DNA test; that was to see if I was a descendant of Bianca's?"

Snowe nodded. "And while the test did confirm that you are of Bianca's lineage, we have unfortunately not yet isolated the genetic markers that tell whether or not a lost daughter has psychic powers. We have found some descendants in whom abilities are weak, undeveloped, or, in some cases, all but nonexistent."

"But not in me."

"No. But even without the DNA test, I would now know you were one of the Sisters. You have brought us not only Bianca's heart, but the stone circle of worship from whence the line of Eshael originally sprang!"

Madame Snowe gestured around her at the stones, her face glowing with a possessive awe. She turned back to Caitlyn. "We of the Sisterhood use our powers to make the world a better place, but many of us have discovered our powers too late in life to fully develop them. We now see bringing the young daughters of Bianca to the school, and training them to properly harness their potential, as crucial to our mission. And now that we have our mother's heart," she said, turning back to the reliquary and lifting it reverently in her hands, "there is no limit to what we can achieve."

Raphael came to Caitlyn and put his arm around her shivering shoulders, and she leaned into his warmth. His strength and solidity comforted her and felt like a shield against the chill of Madame Snowe's ambition.

"Is this what Bianca wanted? A coven of her descendants, worshipping her heart?" Caitlyn softly asked Raphael.

Raphael tightened his hold on her. "She wanted power, she wanted freedom, and she wanted her children to survive. Beyond that I could not say."

Caitlyn watched the light sparkling in the cabochon atop the reliquary, still held high in Madame Snowe's hands. Bianca de' Medici, burned at the stake in 1572, had risen.

Author's Note

The roots of *Wake Unto Me* stretch more than a decade into the past, to when I first saw the portrait of Lucrezia Panciatichi by Bronzino, at the Uffizi Gallery in Florence, Italy. I came around a corner and saw her, sitting cold and still with her knowing eyes. This portrait, and one other by Bronzino, were the inspiration for Bianca de' Medici. The novelist Henry James describes the Lucrezia portrait in *The Wings of the Dove*:

> *"The lady… (with) her eyes of other days,*
> *her full lips, her long neck, her recorded jewels,*
> *her brocaded and wasted reds, was a very great*
> *personage—only unaccompanied by a joy.*
> *And she was dead, dead, dead."*

The second Bronzino portrait that served as inspiration was a death portrait of the real Bia de' Medici. The real Bia (possibly short for Bianca) was the illegitimate daughter of Cosimo de' Medici, Grand Duke of Tuscany. Cosimo fathered her when he was sixteen; the identity of her mother was a secret, never revealed. Bia died of a fever at age six, and Bronzino most likely painted her after that, at the request of her heartbroken father. In the painting, Bia is pale and dressed in white, denoting death. This whiteness gave me the idea to nickname the fictional Bianca *La Perla*, The Pearl.

The de' Medici name, and the dates of the portraits, brought me to the idea of incorporating Catherine de' Medici, queen of France, into the plot. Her husband Henry's affair with Diane de Poitiers is the stuff of legend: it was Diane de Poitiers who built the arched bridge addition to Chenonceau, the famously beautiful castle that spans the river Cher in the Loire Valley. Henry died in a gruesome jousting accident, his eye socket and brain pierced by splinters from a shattered lance. After his death, Catherine de' Medici evicted Diane from spectacular Chenonceau and took it for herself; in trade she gave Diane the inferior Château de Chaumont, a few miles away. Catherine's royal residence was at Château de Blois, however, where she was kept busy fighting to keep her sons on the throne of France.

As for Château de la Fortune, it does not exist. It is instead a compilation of all the castles I visited in France a couple of summers ago. The location and the exterior are from Château de Beynac, on the Dordogne. The interior spaces share much with both Chaumont and Blois, however, which are a couple of hundred miles north, on the Loire. The secret cupboards in Madame Snowe's office are taken from Catherine de' Medici's secret cupboards at Blois, and the dining hall description also comes from there. The *Fiat Lux* window was inspired by similar painted glass windows at Chaumont; Madame Snowe's office and Philippe's bedroom and blue drapery—hung bed are